Prais
Nick

"*The Troop* scared the hell out of me, and I couldn't put it down. This is old-school horror at its best. Not for the faint-hearted, but for the rest of us sick puppies, it's a perfect gift for a winter night."

—Stephen King

"Lean and crisp and delightfully over-the-top. Think *Tales From the Crypt*, think early Crichton, think King on coke. . . . Disquieting, disturbing, and it's also great fun to read."

—Scott Smith, author of *The Ruins*

"Utterly terrifying."

—Clive Barker, creator of *Hellraiser*

"A grim microcosm of terror and desperation . . . haunting."

—Christopher Golden, *New York Times* bestselling author

"Fans of unflinching bleakness and all-out horror will love this novel. . . . Disturbing."

—*Publishers Weekly* (starred review)

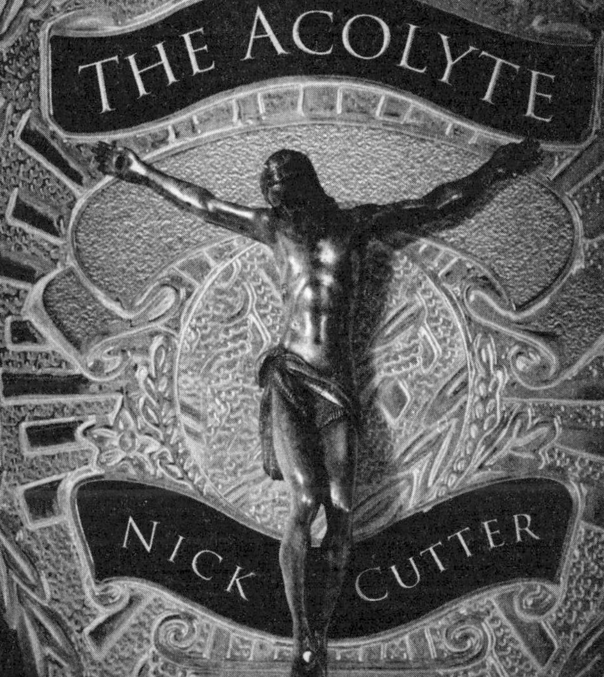

CZP

ChiZine Publications

FIRST EDITION

Distributed in Canada by
PGC Raincoast Books
300-76 Stafford Street
Toronto, ON M6J 2S1
Phone: (416) 934-9900
e-mail: info@pgcbooks.ca

Distributed in the U.S. by
Diamond Comic Distributors, Inc.
10150 York Road, Suite 300
Hunt Valley, MD 21030
Phone: (443) 318-8500
e-mail: books@diamondbookdistributors.com

Library and Archives Cataloguing Data Available Upon Request

Cutter, Nick, author

The Acolyte / Nick Cutter.

Issued in print and electronic formats.

ISBN 978-1-77148-328-5 (pbk.).--ISBN 978-1-77148-329-2 (pdf)

I. Title.

PS8607.A79A26 2015 C813'.6 C2015-901093-4
C2015-901094-2

CHIZINE PUBLICATIONS
Toronto, Canada
www.chizinepub.com
info@chizinepub.com

Edited by Brett Savory
Proofread by Sandra Kasturi

Canada Council for the Arts Conseil des arts du Canada

We acknowledge the support of the Canada Council for the Arts which last year invested $20.1 million in writing and publishing throughout Canada.

Published with the generous assistance of the Ontario Arts Council.

Printed in Canada

THE ACOLYTE

"Writing for a penny a word is ridiculous. If a man really wants to make a million dollars, the best way would be to start his own religion."

—L. Ron Hubbard, founder of Scientology

"Tired of lukewarm Christianity?"

—Evangelical Tract Distributors

This is the story of Jonah Murtag.
Jonah was a righteous man, the one blameless man of his time.
He walked with God.

I dreamed of a time as a child when I saw a Muslim lit on fire.

This was back during the Great Purge. Jews and Sikhs and Hindus and the rest booted out of their homes, made to live behind high barbed wire fences. Christian Citizen's Brigades came together: packs of men with Bibles and baseball bats.

It was one such pack that descended on the Muslim, who was riding his bicycle outside the newly erected Little Baghdad perimeter. I was six or seven; we were on an elementary school field trip. Our bus driver stopped to root the Brigade members on.

The Muslim was mentally handicapped. It was difficult to tell at first—mainly it was his sunny smile that persisted while the white men shouted at him. He kept smiling even as a rock pinged off his bike fender.

The pack circled him. The Muslim's smile persisted, which seemed to incense them all the more. Someone kicked him off his bike.

They lashed the man to the frame of his bicycle with old clothesline or something. He moaned and said stuff everyone assumed was Arabic but may well have been gibberish. They dumped a jug of liquid over him: gasoline would seem most logical but I recall the resiny smell and the purple sheen as the sun fell through it, and later realized it was likely turpentine.

"Not in front of the kids," one of the men said.

"Let them watch," said another. "The same as what's being done to us by the other side. They need to understand how it is."

Someone produced a book of matches. They were lit then tossed at the Muslim's face. The flames *whuffed* out before hitting him. The air shimmered above the Muslim's shoulders: turpentine fumes, everything gone swimmy.

"This is how they do it, anyway," one man said to nobody in particular. I remember his hands: the look of bones wrapped in pig leather. "Light themselves up. Part of their religion."

As an adult I would understand what he was talking about: the ritual of sati, where an Indian widow immolated herself on her husband's funeral pyre. But that was a Hindu tradition and this was a Muslim man. Not that I could have said anything then, or that it would have made any difference at all.

The final match in the book ignited the airborne turpentine particles: a low *whuph* as a purplish cowl licked to life around the Muslim's body; in that moment he was beatific.

The flames robed his arms and legs but the pain hadn't registered yet—in fact, the man seemed giddy as this weird light blossomed all around him—his hair catching fire. Some of the men looked away as they might from a very sick man. There was no sound at all: not screaming or even the crackle of flames. I remember wondering: *Have I gone deaf?*

The Muslim man tried to stand but couldn't with the ungainly weight of the bicycle lashed to his back. His shoes scuffled the pavement as fine threads of flame licked from the toes, and finally the pain threw him up like a marionette in the hands of a spastic puppeteer—he spun raggedly, confusedly, fire clawing down his throat to ignite the last vestiges of oxygen in his lungs. Teeth of flame spat off the rubber bike tires as they spun on lazy trajectories, two fiery pinwheels. The Muslim man shuffled across the street and ran blindly into the ghetto fence, pedals snagging in the chain links to pin him there, erect, while he burned.

Article I:
He Carries His Cross

**"Church and State.
No Longer Shall the Devout Draw Any Such Distinction
Henceforth and Forevermore, Be It Known:
The Church IS the State."**

—*The New Republican Testament*, 5th Ed., Preface

Most Beloved Followers,

You hold in your hands the doctrine of the Republic in which you live and serve. Its holdings are sacrosanct and immutable.

These are your laws. The laws God has set down through the Divine Fathers and administered by The Prophet of your city-state. These laws are unbreakable. Whosoever may challenge these laws must be put down and cast aside by all devout and obedient Followers.

Heathens are encouraged to abandon their retrograde faiths and embrace the healing light and the divine sanctity of this, the perfect and only—

One True Faith.

REVISED STATUTES

Chapter 86
Police Department of New Bethlehem
Section 86.420

Faith Crimes Unit—Duties and Responsibilities.

1. Acting on orders from the Divine Council at New Kingdom, each Republic city [New Jericho, New Halah, New Bethlehem, New Nazareth, New Beersheba] shall form a Faith Crimes tactical unit, culled from the most skilled or otherwise apt members of the rank and file. Officers of this unit [hereinafter known as Acolytes] are tasked with:

(1) Enforcing moral law pursuant with the Biblical doctrines of Judeo-Christianity as revised through *The New Republican Testament*;

(2) Searching out and eradicating all non-conforming faiths, their artifacts, sites of worship, and practitioners.

2. Should the agenda of the rank and file contravene those of the Faith Crimes Unit, or should jurisdictional lines be crossed, the objectives of the Faith Crimes Unit shall take predominance in every circumstance.

1 INITIATION

"Tell us, cadet Murtag."

Naked. Laid out on a marble slab. Where? A meatpacking plant? Condemned factory? The marble was ice-cold up the knobs of my spine.

The initiation happened years ago. I am speaking from memory now.

Men in crimson robes clustered around me. Their faces stared from lush, reddened hoods: my instructors, chiefs, and captains. Though it was pure blasphemy to think it, their faces looked to be poking from the folds of impossibly large and terribly loose vaginas . . . though of course I'd never seen a real vagina. An anatomical diagram, once, in a library book that survived the Great Purge, but never in the flesh, as it were.

"What is your secret, cadet Murtag? So we can trust you."

Hollis, my future chief, was asking the questions. Beyond the ring of hoods stood my fellow top-ranking cadets: Garvey and Cruikshank and Applewhite. All stripped buck naked, hopping foot-to-foot on the stone floor.

"You will see the banned texts," Hollis went on. "You will come to know the heathen gospels, the tracts and treatises of their backward faiths. We must trust you'll not be corrupted, and so—we must trust *you*."

They already knew everything about me. What schools I'd attended, how many shekels in my bank account at First Divinity, what I tithed last year, that I had scarlet fever as a teenager, the high school essay I'd written called "A Mighty Fortress is Our God."

The point was to *make* me say it. Confession being good for the soul. Confession *is* good for the soul. God is good. The Prophet is good. The Republic is good.

Our way of life—*good*.

I said, "My mother was given The Cure."

"She was an insurrectionist?" said Hollis. "She wished to see the downfall of the Republic?"

"She said things she shouldn't have. This was back near the beginning of it all. I repeated those things in school—"

"Ratted her out?" Hollis grinned. "Your own mother?"

"No," I said. "It was accidental. My teacher told someone. She . . . said some foolish things. Had sinful thoughts. One day they came and took her away."

Hollis said, "Do you still see her?"

"Occasionally. Birthdays, Mother's Day. She doesn't even recognize me half the time."

"Do you hold any lingering animosity toward the Republic for what was done?"

"No." And I meant it. "She deserved it."

A golden sheet was wrapped round me. All those scarlet-ridged faces stared at me with newfound solidarity. All those grinning vagina-entombed heads.

I had done it. I was one of them.

An Acolyte.

2 Routine Roundups

The house is a gabled two-storey with ivy creeping up one side. Near the Stadium SuperChurch but not within the exclusive ring set aside for Ministers and dignitaries. A house you'd peg a Deputy Minister to live in: a hard-charger and his photogenic three-and-a-half kids.

But this particular gabled two-storey was packed full of homosexuals. We'd known about their cell for a while. They were a harmless passel of nancies. But it was a slow night.

Angela Doe, Garvey, and I were hunkered in a van idling streetside. Upon the van's exterior was painted a garish mural featuring *Buckles the Birthday Clown*. BUCKLES IS A FULLY LICENCED AND REPUBLIC-VETTED ENTERTAINMENT SUBSIDIARY read the small print looping over the wheel wells.

The house was bugged. The three of us wore headphones. Scratchy voices fed into them:

Voice 1: "Now look—*look*. This is about impulse control, okay? Look but don't touch. Or look but don't give the impression you *want* to touch."

Voice 2: "But then that's not impulse control, is it? It's a mask."

[INAUDIBLE CROSSTALK]

Voice 1: ". . . and in time, that mask can become permanent. Take every impulse, put it behind the mask—the mask becomes you."

Garvey's face pinkened. Especially intolerant of gays, was Garvey.

"Let's get in there," he said darkly.

"Would you be so upset," Doe asked, "if it were a bunch of queer women?"

Garvey stared at her. "What do you think? Don't even talk to me about it—don't put the image in my *head*."

We exited the van. Riot shields and tactical shotguns—check. We crept up to the porch. The door was unlocked. Garvey booted it in anyhow. Pure cowboy.

"Faith Crimes Officers! On your knees!"

The homosexuals—I counted eight—were seated in the front room. They were dressed conservatively, button-down shirts and tan slacks: the drab look of husbands and fathers, as I'm sure a few were. For some reason I'd been expecting decadence and debauchery: guys swanning about in pink feather boas while a naked midget tinkled away on a grand piano.

"Face down," I said. "You are in direct violation of Republican law."

Their leader held up a bunch of silverfish-eaten pamphlets from Exodus International.

"We're trying to change," he pleaded. "We want to cure ourselves."

Doe and Garvey started slamming them to the floor and cuffing them with zip-strips.

I repeated the Republic mandate: "Any Follower who harbours impious thoughts is to report to the nearest conditioning facility to undergo faith counselling—"

"And then what?" their leader shrieked. "They cut your head open and burn the sin out! They turn you into a vegetable!"

I headed into the dining room: mattresses butted end-to-end on the hardwood floor. Throw pillows tossed about. Pornographic magazines . . . upon closer inspection, they were just yellowed Sears and Roebuck advertising supplements. The "Summer Fling" editions: chiselled men in swimwear and jockey shorts. One pic showed a shirtless guy fly-fishing in his underwear. Garvey joined me. He picked up a catalogue, and gave the half-naked fly-fisherman a good long gander before flinging it away.

"Sickos, these guys."

I left him to bag up the catalogues. I headed to the van and radioed the meat wagon. When it showed up, we loaded the criminals in. They'd be cooling their heels at the nearest Reconditioning Centre within the week. Or they'd have a Come-To-God moment.

Night.

West end of the city now, down along the river: storage barns and flophouses with whitened angles, everyplace looking like a black cardboard cutout. Wind scored the rusted docks and filled my head with the smell of steel.

"Ten to one we don't need these suits of armour," said Garvey, buckling his Kevlar leggings.

Doe cinched into a bulletproof vest. "What if you hadn't been armoured up for that Mormon shakedown?"

A month ago we'd busted a cell of Latter-Day Saints worshiping in an abandoned warehouse. Their sentry had shot Garvey point-blank with 20-gauge wadcut buckshot.

"Mormons are kooks." Garvey said, jacking shells into the

breech of a Mossberg. "We're talking about a religion founded by a guy who stuck a glowing pebble in his hat and followed it to some golden plates buried under a tree. Polygamous psychos."

I scoped a lit window at the northeast corner. "These guys are kooks, too."

"These guys are docile." Garvey said, wiping down the face-shield of his riot helmet. "Harmless nutbars."

Once we were buckled and strapped, I knelt in the alleyway. I led the prayer.

"Lord, we seek your blessing in this enterprise undertaken in your name. For the safety of your vessels, that we possess the courage to complete your good work, we pray to you, O Lord."

"Lord, hear our prayer."

"For the Divine Fathers at Kingdom City and their humble emissaries here in New Bethlehem, the power to enforce the glory and purity of the One True Faith. We pray to you, O Lord."

"Lord, hear our prayer."

"Amen."

Doe flicked my face-shield down. "The Lord be with you, Acolyte Murtag."

"And with you, Acolyte Doe."

Garvey said, "What am I, the heathen scourge?"

Doe sighed. "And also with you, Acolyte Garvey."

We stood in the hallway outside the third-floor suite. Voices seeped through the cheap pressboard door:

"Let's find another incident you feel you can comfortably face . . . okay, I got a blip there. Backtrack it with me."

Garvey mouthed the words: *Auditing session*. Adrenaline throbbed my veins, a high hat tempo picking the underside of my neck.

I mouthed *Go*.

Garvey trained his shotgun on the doorknob. Blistered metal and wood splinters. I booted the door, snapping the security chain, and we steamrolled in.

"Faith Crimes! On your knees!"

A well-lit room. Four folding tables. Eight collapsible chairs.

Eight fugitives: six men, two women. Tacked to the wall: a silk-screened portrait of their messiah.

Milky pale. Toad-faced and onion-eyed. A silk cravat twisted round his neck.

L. Ron Hubbard.

Garvey kicked over a table and sent an E-meter flying. A willowy Scientologist stood up. Garvey tagged him with the butt of his shotgun. The Scientologist's specs snapped over the bridge of his nose and he went down.

"Everyone on the floor!" he bellowed. "Suck shag!"

The Scientologists were half-deaf from the shotgun blast and half-hypnotized from their auditing sessions. Doe brought her boot down on an E-meter, which splintered under her foot like a cheap calculator.

"Know what it is?" she said to the whimpering zealots. "A gizmo that reacts to the sweat on your palms. Plastic and wires; costs eleven shekels to make. You're all heading to Reconditioning Centres—for what? Playing with a *toy*."

"Don't listen to her."

That willowy Scientologist staggered up. Blood flowed down the sides of his nose. His busted spectacles hung from one ear.

"What we do here, we do for the good of the human race."

Garvey grabbed the fugitive by his lapels and jammed a forearm under his chin.

"Hate to break the news, but your whole faith is a cash grab. That guy"—a disgusted nod at L. Ron—"lived in the middle of the ocean on a yacht staffed by young boys, a pedophile perv, his crimes funded by morons like you."

The Scientologist gagged but his eyes were bright and pure, filled with the zealous mania you tend to see a lot in my line of work.

"Do you actually believe," Garvey went on, "that there are aliens living inside you?"

Garvey and Doe were simply executing directive 46.23 of the Faith Crimes charter: *Expose the gross inadequacies and inconsistencies of all false prophets and/or faiths.*

"Do you know how utterly *moronic* your religion is?" said Garvey.

"No more moronic than a saviour who dies on a cross and rises three days later," the Scientologist said.

Garvey brought his shotgun's stock down into the guy's mouth. Teeth pelted the wall. The Scientologist went down twitching.

None of us paid attention to the lone Scientologist near the door. Tubby and pimpled in a purple angora sweater, displaying signs of life equal to your average houseplant. Nobody caught her hand moving under a table for the pistol duct-taped there.

The first slug drove into the wall behind Doe's head. Purple Angora shot again: the slug shattered a ceiling tile. Then she was out the door. My head snapped to Doe—wide-eyed but unhurt—before I turned to trail her.

Purple Angora streaked down the hallway. She spun and fired. Plaster and wood chips flew. I hipped my shotgun and pulled the trigger. *Boom*. The centre of her body turned into red mashed potato. Tatters of purple fabric blew out in a starfish pattern.

I backtracked to the room. Doe hadn't moved. I clocked the slug's trajectory: it had missed her skull by an inch.

I touched her shoulder. "You alright? Hey. *Hey*."

Doe's short-clipped hair reeked of cordite. The ends were frizzed as if they had come close to an open flame. I leaned close. Knowing I shouldn't—not now, not in front of the fugitives, not at all, not *ever*. My lips brushed her forehead.

"Angela, I'm sorry. She was my cover."

Doe gave me a forearm shiver. I rocked back on my heels. She jammed her knee into a Scientologist's spine and cuffed him.

In the hallway, I radioed in a Fire Team. Pie-eyed tenants occurred in doorways. One of them asked what was the rumpus.

"Gather whatever's precious to you and clear out," I told all of them.

Doe's shotgun barked. I poked my head back into the room. Doe had blown a hole in L. Ron's face.

THE ACOLYTE

The landlord wore a gigantic crucifix on a chain round his neck.

"This isn't Christian," he said. "My livelihood. All I've got."

"Same as cockroaches," I told him. "Harbour them, you pay the extermination fee."

"How could I know they were philistines?" Jesus Christ dangled and swayed from the landlord's neck. The guy was sweating like a hog; that cheap metal crucifix would oxidize. Our Saviour would turn green before long.

I shrugged. "Conducive environment. Screen your renters more closely."

The Fire Team arrived. They donned flame retardant suits, shouldered their flame-throwers and double-timed it up the stairs.

"I go to high mass three times a week!" the landlord shrieked. "When the collection plate passes, I give more than my share—I support The Prophet with my entire soul!"

Fire ripped through the suite. The window trembled, warped, blew outwards. There was a sound like fine linen tearing as air vacuumed through the breach. The Fire Team's tanks were filled with a jellied gasoline/holy water mix: scourging and sacramental. We all watched. The fire mesmerized. Perpetual motion, twisting and ravenous. There are some shapes that live only in flame. Oily black smoke poured from the window. The landlord was on his knees on the sidewalk, howling, beating his breast. We cleared out.

3 OLD BLACK MAGIC

Station house.

Incident report. I'm team leader—i.e.: head paper pusher. Doe will never make team leader; as a woman, she'd already hit her mandated ceiling. Our pay scale was based on Leviticus 27: *And thy estimation shall be of the male from twenty years old even unto sixty years old, thy estimation shall be fifty shekels of silver. And if it be a female, thy estimation shall be thirty shekels.*

I typed up the incident report and dropped the carbons in Deacon Hollis's mail slot. I crossed the bullpen and scanned the Ongoing Investigations corkboard:

Unlawful Worship/Animal Sacrifice. Wiccans operating in East Seraphim Park and environs. 20 to 25 fugitives, Caucasian M/F 16–50 yrs. Threat: low. Priority: low. Investigating Acolytes: Henchel/Brewster.

Unlawful Worship/Conspiracy/Danger to Public Peace. Muslim cell loosely centred in Hollis Heights/Kiketown adjacent. 6 known fugitives, Islamic M 15–35 yrs. Possible Hasidic sympathizers at Demsky's Kosher Meat Mart. Threat: high. Priority: high. Investigating Acolytes: Applewhite/Mathers/Palmer.

I tuned in the local feed of Republic Public Radio. The news was out over the wire:

". . . A daring police sting netted seven faith criminals this evening. The fugitive Scientologists were practising in a condominium complex in the Underdocks neighbourhood. Though heavily armed, they quickly surrendered and were taken into custody without incident. Blessed are those who walk with the Lord. Blessed are those who follow His Prophet. At the tone, RPR news time eleven o'clock."

The shop front was tall and narrow, wedged between a soup kitchen and a blood bank. A large wooden ram's head hung on two chains above the door. The windows were darkened but a neon sign blinked *24HRS*.

A single aisle split the shop. Animals were penned in chicken-wire enclosures on either side: lambs, goats, hares. Caged birds hung on the walls.

"Officer Murtag. So good to see you again."

The shopkeeper: tall and narrow, like his shop. He smelled of alfalfa.

I said, "I need an offering."

"Whole offering or blood offering?" Then, in answer to his

own question: "I suppose that depends on the nature of the offence, does it not?"

I thought about Purple Angora. Her stomach blown out. Tatters of purple wool. I pointed to the nearest goat. "How about that one?"

"That's a good goat," the proprietor said without much conviction. "Yes, that one would make a fine whole offering. But—"

He grabbed a wooden pole and slid its hooked tip through the eyelet of a wicker birdcage.

"Luzon Bleeding Heart doves," he said, bringing the cage down to eye-level. "Beautiful creatures. Your soul will leave without a smirch upon it."

"It wasn't really a *dove* offence."

"Understood." The proprietor rubbed his jaw, considering. "Well, if you're dead set on a goat, may I suggest this younger one instead?"

"How much?"

"Seven shekels, thirteen gerahs."

The proprietor clipped a collar around the goat's neck. Its horns had been sanded down to nubs.

"This way," he said, beckoning toward a curtained aperture at the back of the shop. "The priest will be waiting."

The altar was the size of a supply closet. Portraits: one of Jesus Christ, another of The Prophet. The priest was snoring behind the dais. The goat chewed on my trouser cuff.

"All apologies, my son," the priest said, waking. "Quiet night."

The priest was haggard in the way a lot of these old shrine-tenders could be. Years ago he probably had his own church, his own diocese, his own admiring flock. He donned a vulcanized rubber apron and a leather belt strung with glittering knives. He rinsed out the tossing bowl and set it beside the sluice grate.

The goat flicked its ears. The goat chewed the priest's robe.

"Your name, my son?"

"Murtag."

"What is the nature of your offence, my son?"

"Deliberate injury." A beat. "Resulting in death."

The priest nodded. "Did you attempt it in anger?"

"Yes."

"Was it out of duty?"

"Yes."

"In service to our Lord and our Prophet?"

"Yes."

The priest looped a noose around the goat's hind legs. He pushed a button on a control box, winching the animal into the air. The goat thrashed and bleated.

"Lord, behold this offering from thy humble servant."

The priest removed a long-bladed knife from its leather sheath.

"Accept this gift, O Lord, given freely and with open heart, that it may cleanse the stain of sin from his soul. We ask this in thy name, amen."

The priest set a hand upon the goat's chin, below the tufted beard. The goat's eyes were bulging black bulbs. The priest drew his knife across its neck in a practiced slice.

The animal made a breathless noise. The priest gripped its muzzle, collecting blood in the bowl. He flung blood upon the wall. He spoke the words.

The priest again filled the bowl. He flung blood upon the wall. He spoke the words. Next he unkinked a hose and began to spray down the wall.

"You may go now, my son. Your sins have been expiated."

On my way out, the proprietor asked what I'd like done with the animal.

"The priest is a licenced butcher," he told me. "Five shekels to have it drawn and quartered, wrapped in waxed paper and delivered to your door."

I told him no. My freezer was already full of goat.

The view out my apartment window was beatific.

Lit crosses topped every building, every condo complex, every factory, every house whose owners could afford the expense. Neon crosses, Plexiglas crosses, huge wooden crucifixes bound in blinking Christmas tree lights.

A blackout hit the east side. The crosses all went dead, blackness like a wave rolling across the city. My fridge motor cut off. The red numerals on my bedside clock winked out. I sat in the sweltering dark. Every night a blackout: energy must be conserved. Yet the halo of spotlights ringing the Stadium SuperChurch still burned.

I lay in bed and tried to fall asleep. No luck. How many goats over the years? How many doves, rabbits, sheep? I felt like an alcoholic who's got to the point his cells crave the sauce so bad there's no enjoyment in drinking anymore; he boozes to keep himself on an even keel.

Make an offering. Purge thyself. Eat of my body. Drink my blood.

Repeat after me: *Jesus Christ is the Son of God, who died to absolve the sins of mankind.*

As a child, one morning I'd come downstairs to find a man in a white suit talking to my mother in our kitchen. He told her that our church had been closed but there was a new church, a *better* church. The man in the white suit said he would be positively delighted if she and I would consider attending.

I remember other things, little things, but this is essentially where my memories begin: the man in the clean white suit.

I am just one man. I am just one woman.

People used to say that all the time. One man cannot stand in the path of tomorrow. And so tomorrow came. Tomorrow became today. Tomorrow just kind of . . . *happened.*

The man in the white suit. The Republic. The Prophet. The Immaculate Mother. The One Child. The Quints. Crucifixes hanging in the night sky. The Acolytes.

That old black magic.

Squad Room Shakeup

The first thing I heard when I walked into the squad room the next morning was Garvey, thronged by his fellow Acolytes, recounting the shakedown.

"The alien-worshipers were rat-holed near the wharfs. I shotgun the lock, Murtag boots the door, we barrel on in. This one freak show gets in my face"—his voice rose to a fey contralto—"'Our faith benefits mankind!' So I drilled him. They better serve banana-mush where he's headed because he won't be taking solids for a while."

The others laughed appreciatively. Most of them were ex-Brethrens, Lutherans, Southern Baptists. The hardcore faithful. Garvey himself had been a snake handler.

I sat at my desk. A portrait of Jesus Christ cradling the Lamb of God hung on the north wall. A portrait of The Prophet cradling the same Lamb adorned the south wall. Our squad room stood separate from the main station. Nine Acolytes total, divided into three-man teams presided over by Deacon Hollis. Subtle differences distinguished us from the rank and file: their badges were silver, ours gold. They wore traditional dress blues; ours were fashioned in the style of Christian missionaries: ankle-length dusters, black vests with whalebone buttons.

Eight Acolytes made roll call. No Doe.

Chief Exeter's voice came over the intercom: "Gentlemen, everyone to the muster room. Pronto."

Deacon Hollis exited his office. Early fifties with a hard flat face. His features didn't quite mesh, like an apple cut in half and put back together off-kilter.

"You heard our fearless leader," he said, fingering the beads of his wooden rosary. "Fall in line."

I grabbed my casebook. Chief Exeter stepped through a pebbled-glass door and cut a path into the bullpen. He was lean and muscular with carved-out cheekbones and teeth like elephant toes.

We Acolytes settled into the muster room, flapping the hems of our oilskin dusters. Exeter stepped up to the dais; Hollis sat to his left.

"This is a general debriefing on the department's ongoing investigations, prioritized according to threat," Exeter began. "Top priority: a 254—homicide/suicide bombing—last week in Matthew's Square, during the Up with God minstrel show. Death toll stands at seventeen. Our sketch artist has produced an updated rendering of the jihadist, provided by a survivor who recently regained consciousness."

The bomber was the classic Islamic fanatic: cheeks sharp as busted saucers, vulpine nose, eyes dark and unfeeling as rocks. Approx. 5'10", 145 lbs. I was amazed his frame could handle the 100-plus pounds of explosives he must have been packing.

Rage rippled through the bullpen as the composite circulated. Garvey spat on his copy and ground it under his heel.

"The CSI division has been working to determine the makeup of the bomb. Preliminary data based on blast radius indicate a fertilizer-based explosive with a manual incendiary igniter, possibly a road flare. This is based on CSI's on-the-scene eyeball data."

Before the Republic, CSI was an acronym for Crime Scene Investigation; it presently stood for Christian Sciences Investigation. Forensics was now outlawed as a heretical discipline: it proved the existence of dinosaurs and the like. The Christian Scientists hunted around with magnifying glasses, making deductions.

"You cannot purchase ammonium-nitrate based fertilizer without providing a Republic ID," Exeter reminded us. "Any transaction should be recorded at the store. Every home and garden store in the city will need to be canvassed."

A collective groan from the rank and file.

Exeter acknowledged the obvious. "Needle in a haystack, gentlemen. Lieutenants Toppenger and Paulsen are in charge of canvassing; officers are to work in two-man teams and report their findings to the stationhouse. Every man shall make this his primary focus until such time that a significant lead develops—"

Hollis cleared his throat and trained his slightly amused gaze upon Exeter. The Chief returned Hollis's stare, adjusted the bridge of his black-framed glasses, and turned back to the men.

"—at which point it will be remanded to the Faith Crimes unit, who, as protocol dictates, will head up the investigation. But they're going to need our assistance. Shake every tree at your disposal: every rat, every heathen lowlife. Interrogation rooms will be available all hours. Pakitown, Little Baghdad, and Kiketown scum. Rule nothing out."

Exeter asked Hollis if he had anything to add.

"No, you've summed things up very well . . . chief."

Everyone could hear the lower-case *c* in Hollis's *chief*.

Exeter said: "Dismissed, then, gentlemen. And Prophet's blessings."

Plainclothesmen filed out. Exeter leaned across the dais, regarding Hollis coolly; Hollis was tipped back in his chair, just about rubbing the shine off his rosary beads. Body language told the tale. Exeter: never upstage me in front of the men again. Hollis: your tin-badge sheriff's act doesn't scare me.

Hollis held up his hand. "Acolyte Murtag—a word with you."

"Exeter is a damned fool," Hollis said once we were settled back in his office. "Canvassing the city with a charcoal sketch of a fanatic—a fanatic who's already blown himself to bits, I don't need to remind you—asking, 'Did this swarthy bastard purchase bomb-making material at your shop?'"

He pulled a bottle of wine from his desk drawer and poured measures into water-spotted glasses.

"Did you know Exeter used to be an Episcopalian? I'd as soon blow my brains out as follow an Episcopalian into battle. And *slippery*: Exeter's the only man I know who could enter a revolving door behind you and step out ahead of you. Mind him, lad. You mind him, hear?"

I sipped Hollis's wine, so acidic it stung my gums.

"Dispatch sent word. Acolyte Doe won't be in today."

I looked up from my glass sharply—too sharply—and saw Hollis considering me over the rim of his own glass.

He set it down and knitted his fingers on the desktop. His hands were huge, scarred, knuckles grown together like crushed roots. A staunch Irish Catholic before conversion, Hollis had been tabbed as one of the first Acolytes. His reputation rested on a legendary story that took place at the start of his service career.

He'd been patrolling when dispatch had radioed a 533: *Failure to Conform*. In the early days, heathens shacked up in their domiciles to practise outlawed faiths or scientific disciplines. In this case, a family of Mormons were bivouacked in a farmhouse off RR #7.

Hollis's knock was met with gunfire. He flanked the house and kicked in the back door. Father, mother, eight children:

Hollis killed them all. For his actions he received the Star of Gilead, awarded for "Conspicuous Gallantry at the Risk of Life, Above and Beyond the Call of Duty, in Upholding the Ideals of the Republic."

There had been some conflict regarding Hollis's official account. Two of his fellow Acolytes claimed to have found no weapons in the farmhouse save a single-shot rifle and a pitchfork; this conflicted with Hollis's report of being met with "a fusillade of gunfire." Friction marks on the victims' wrists indicated they had been bound, perhaps upon their surrender, before being shot. The youngest heathen, a girl, was found draped over the barbed wire fence at the property's edge. Her throat had been slit.

But anyone who disputed Hollis's account was by now either dead or rendered low on charges of Moral Turpitude—charges levied by Hollis himself. The official incident report had since disappeared: Hollis had burned it, or it had been purged by an emissary of the state.

All that remained was the Star of Gilead resting in its frame above Hollis's desk. That medal shaped the collective memory of an event nobody properly remembered anymore. That medal said Hollis was a hero of the Republic.

"Everything went alright last night?" Hollis watched my face for a betraying tic. "By the book?"

"You've got my incident report."

He tapped the carbons I'd left on his desk. "Tight as a vise, as always. But reports don't tell the whole tale."

Reports never did. Fire Teams erased all physical evidence, leaving the reporting Acolyte free to massage facts: no report should admit wrongdoing on the part of the Acolytes and, by inference, the Republic.

Hollis's face took on a paternal aspect. "I worry about my unit, you understand. Especially Doe. Call me old fashioned."

I tried not to grimace. Hollis worried about us the way a farmer worried about his prize Guernseys—only so much as it affected his own ambitions.

"They'll all be rotting in Reconditioning Centres," he said of the rounded-up criminals. "Except Timothy McSweeney—the leader of the poofter brigade."

McSweeney. The name was familiar. "Son of Alex McSweeney . . . ?"

"Minister of Cultural Codes McSweeney," Hollis confirmed. "His son'll toddle off to bugger again, but at least we've got ourselves a favour owed."

He smiled. The points on the Star of Gilead above his head twinkled.

"I need you to cover a spot of off-hours security tonight," he said. "The Prophet's eldest daughter, Eve—"

"Babysitting duty, you mean."

Hollis fixed me with a look. "It's a touch more serious than that, lad. The Prophet has enemies—deluded wrecks whose only worth is sacrificial. If they can't strike The Prophet directly, they'll strike at those close to him."

"Where at?"

"One of the downtown establishments. The Manger."

"Fun," I said.

"The Prophet appreciates your sacrifice," Hollis said dryly.

The Manger

Babysitting duty.

The car: special issue, picked up at Central Dispatch. A stretch Buick: bomb-proof floor plates, reinforced chassis, self-sealing tires, bulletproof glass.

I pulled up at a quarter past seven: with midnight curfew, a night on the town gets started early. I nodded to the pair of off-duty officers at the gate and rolled down the crushed gravel drive to the estate. The healthy oaks stunned me: we'd been on water ration for years. Last summer's drought turned every tree in the city into husks.

The mansion: 120 rooms, banquet hall, gold-trimmed toilet fixtures—or so I've heard. The courtyard was dominated by a fountain: a statue of The Prophet, twenty feet high and carved from alabaster marble, water welling from his cupped palms. The plaque at its base read BESTOWER OF ALL THINGS.

A trio waited at the top of the terrace stairway. The Prophet's eldest daughter and a pair of famished sycophants.

Eve, the daughter: tall and lithe and gorgeous in a white evening dress. A gold crucifix drew attention to her cleavage. Her constant companion, a teacup Chihuahua named Erasmus, sat in a handbag at the end of her arm. A crucifix had been bleached into the fur between the little dog's eyes.

"You're late," she said as I opened the car door for her.

I tipped an invisible chauffeur's cap. "Forgive me."

She disappeared into the backseat, flanked by her human lapdogs: two girls as skinny as tent poles, arms jutting from the puffy sleeves of taffeta gowns. They looked identical: when people reach a critical point of malnutrition, they all look the same. Their heads were just skulls wrapped in crepe paper.

I piloted the Buick into the city. The sun sank over the downtown core, reflecting off the skyscrapers. I cut down Gilead to Iscariot, skirting Kiketown. A thirty-foot-tall razor wire fence ran round the ghetto's perimeter: Jews were permitted to work in the city proper but otherwise confined from ten o'clock at night until five the following morning within their ghetto.

"Jimmy Saint Kincaid is playing tonight," I heard Eve say. "I simply *adore* him."

"Oh, yes," said one of the taffeta-clad hand puppets. "He is *sooo* pious."

"Have you heard his newest song," said Eve, "'Nailz Thru My Palms'?"

"Love it, just love it," the other hand puppet said. "I can feel the Lord's love shining through his music."

"Eehhh." Eve sounded bored. "He's got a great ass, give him that."

The two hand puppets covered their mouths, shocked. They sat on either side of Eve: a pair of spindle-thin bookends. The Prophet's wife, Effie—The Immaculate Mother, Virgin Mother of The One Child—was their idol. The Immaculate Mother looked like a driftwood skeleton; she was so wan you could see her facial veins magnified on the three-storey SuperChurch JumboTron TV every week.

The Immaculate Mother said the Lord had come to her in a dream and told her that the devout must prove their piety through deprivation. Her profile graced bottles of the city's best-selling beverage, Purity Purge. Ingredients: water, lemon juice, a mild laxative agent.

I cut down Jericho and into the club district. A Daily Benediction Booth on the corner did brisk business. At a cost of two gerahs, the faithful could duck into the city's many DBBs to receive a videotaped blessing from The Prophet. For an extra cost, the booths dispensed a thumbnail-sized wafer and a wine lozenge.

We reached The Manger.

I parked down a side street to avoid the front-door crush. My rap on a corrugated steel delivery door was answered by a huge black bouncer in a crisp white suit.

"Bring her in," he said.

I guided my charges through the prep area and out a swinging service door into the club. High-ceilinged and well-lit—darkness breeds vice, you see—and packed with bodies.

Music pulsed from the speaker system. Musicians in the Republic were not permitted to compose music with a tempo in excess of sixty beats per minute, as accelerated tempos encouraged "licentious bodily motions." The current song, heavy on church organ, inspired a general malaise: patrons plodded the dance floor like woolly mammoths struggling in a tar pit . . . not that woolly mammoths ever existed.

The bouncers had roped off a booth. I checked the sightlines: decent. Scoped the crowd: young/Caucasian.

I took an inconspicuous position. An awestruck waitress took their order: Purity Purges for the hand puppets, RC for Eve. Every club in town sold one kind of alcohol—Republic Claret—and had a sign prominently displayed above their bars: 2 DRINK MAX. Those rules flexed for Eve. I'd seen her down twelve glasses in a night. And I'd hosed her vomit out of the car's back seat afterwards.

Someone touched my elbow. I turned to see Doe. She was in uniform, her dark hair cut regulation-short and slicked back like a man's. Her oilskin duster was parted; I saw the butt of her Volver 927 in its shoulder holster.

"I'm filling in for Garvey."

"You're alright?" I slid my hand down her arm, then self-consciously pulled away. "I rang your place—"

"I'm fine." Her gaze flicked off across the dance floor, settling on Eve. "How's Queen Bee tonight?"

Eve was working on her second RC. She fed some to the dog, Erasmus: wine dribbled down its muzzle, staining its fur.

I said, "Her usual charming self."

Stagehands tested sound levels for the upcoming concert. An MC strode onstage.

"All you true Followers," he intoned, "put your hands together for the one, the only, the incomparable—Jimmy Saint Kincaid!"

Thunderous applause. Breathless squeals. Jimmy Saint Kincaid strode on stage barefoot in a purple velvet robe. He flashed a smile: diamond crucifixes graced his upper front incisors. He launched into "You Take Control."

You are my guide
You take control,
You are the one
I embrace you

See me let it go
You are in control
Suffer as we grow
Holding nothing

A pair of hooded figures banged matching brass gongs. The crowd raised their arms, swaying.

"I'm going up there," Eve told me. "Get me up there."

"My instructions are to—"

"I don't give a damn."

"Difficult to ensure your safety—"

"Don't give a . . . D-A-M-M," she said forcefully.

"But your father—"

"I *really* don't give a damn."

I relented. We made an Acolyte sandwich: Doe, myself, Eve in the middle. Erasmus cradled in the crook of Eve's arm. We guided Eve to the edge of the stage. I shoulder-blocked a weedy guy in a vanilla suit. Doe kidney-punched a goon wearing a glittery Jimmy Saint Kincaid concert tee. Kincaid whined:

You define me
With your identity
Lose my life in You
I can take—I'll take what it costs me . . .

We reached the stage. The footlights dazzled.

"Step back," Eve said to me. "I want to dance. *Alone.*"

"Absolutely not."

She slapped me—open hand to the face. Erasmus yipped.

I leaned in close to her and spoke over the music. "Absolutely not."

She slapped me again.

"As much as you need," I told her squarely. "You just let it out, now."

"If you don't step back, Acolyte Murtag"—I was shocked Eve knew my name—"I'll tell my father you attempted inappropriate liberties with me."

Her hand moved down her stomach between her legs, a move so lascivious it stunned the blood in my veins.

Should she follow through on her threat, I'd be exiled by tomorrow. Cowed, I stepped back. Doe did the same.

Kincaid's voice reverberated into silence. The audience applauded reverently; adoring fans tossed pocket Bibles and rosaries.

Kincaid invited Eve up for his signature ballad, "Spear in My Side." Eve squealed in delight.

Doe and I stood back-to-back against the stage. Doe covered the crowd; I kept an eye on Eve. Kincaid knelt to serenade her—*she* was the spear in his side.

One of the robed gong-bangers on the stage spread his arms, Christ-like, a few yards behind Eve and Kincaid. I assumed it was part of the act until the lead guitarist hit a sour note and I keyed on his expression, which was one of startled confusion.

Only then did I see it, down to the tiniest detail: the twist of DET cord snaking from the robe's sleeve. The slender detonation plunger. The bulging stomach layered with explosives.

The mania in those hooded eyes: the eyes of a martyr.

I grabbed Doe and yanked her beneath the stage overhang, shielding her, issuing a schoolboy's prayer—*Please, Lord; pleasepleasepleasePLEASE*—as I struggled with one inconceivable fact:

The bomber was the wrong colour.

The bomber was *white*.

Boom

The explosion lifts me up like a plastic bag in an updraft. I feel no pain. I feel nothing at all. Everything unfolds slowly, gracefully.

The bomber is vaporized: nothing but a fine mist of blood that boils away in the heat of the blast. The only part of him to remain is the charred steel plate he'd strapped to his back to direct the explosion toward the crowd; I can't help but think, *What a clever idea*.

Eve and Kincaid are incinerated: the explosion sizzles the skin off their bones, melts them like wax effigies before a secondary blast reduces them to ash.

I peer down at myself suspended in the air. Floating. Weightless. My arms look pretty awful: red and shrivelled like smokehouse pork. I realize, without much surprise, that the stark rods glowing through the shrivelled mess are, in very point of fact, my bones.

Shrapnel fans out over the crowd. A young woman with a delicate china face gets ripped apart like a paper doll. Is Doe safe? Is she alright? Please, God.

A white-hot ball bearing rockets at my face. It punches through my head above the ridge of my eye socket. The bone buckles, splinters, fragments, turns to powder. I feel it moving through my head, coring out my skull, out the back with a dim *pop!* My head feels so much lighter. I'm not thinking straight. I'm not thinking much of anything. Still searching for Doe as the world turns black, a dark shade pulled against the light and then I'm falling or flying, can't tell which, at phenomenal speeds.

"—nah. Come, Jonah. Come on back to me."

My eyes snapped open. A face swam out of the smoke: Doe's face, brown with soot. The glow of a streetlamp ringed her head in a golden halo: she resembled a Saint in a stained-glass cathedral window.

"You're okay." I smiled—dopey, grateful. This sound in my ears like bacon sizzling.

"We're both okay. Me a little more than you."

I was propped against the wall of a shop across the road from The Manger. My duster and vest were shredded. A ball bearing was buried in the Kevlar weave an inch from my heart. Otherwise I felt okay . . . okay*ish*.

I was coated in a fine layer of grey ash. A fine layer of *Eve*.

"How—?"

"I dragged you out." Doe said. "Couldn't tell if you were alive."

"And Eve?"

"Dead."

"Then we're dead."

Doe acknowledged the possibility with a nod. Black, meaty-smelling smoke poured out of the club's casement windows.

"Your hair's gone," Sweat tracked down Doe's face, leaving clean rails through the soot. "And your right arm's bad."

A thin trench slashed a quarter-inch into the flesh of my biceps. It burned fiercely.

"Looks like a guitar string or something in there," said Doe.

Truth: we were alive, Eve dead. What could I say? That I didn't have the time to react? I was caught off-guard? That Eve wasn't worth saving? I'd made a choice. Angela over Eve. Probability: we'd be booted off the Faith Crimes unit. Ritually mutilated. Exiled. Even executed.

I said: "How many dead?"

"Dozens," Doe said. "Packed like sardines in there. The stage overhang saved us."

I kept the bomber's skin colour to myself. I doubt anyone else had noticed. Two prowl cars peeled into the lot, followed by an ambulance.

Doe said: "We need to get out of here."

"Flee the site?"

"You're injured. Eve's dead. Nothing more we can do. CSI will handle it."

"Where?"

"My apartment, for now."

Doe's place.

A small clean efficiency. The window overlooked the south side of the city. Ten blocks distant, cones of flame continued to rise from The Manger.

Doe led me into the kitchen. She grabbed some shears and cut the straps of my bulletproof vest. The seams had melted in the blast, bonding it to my chest.

"Like a Band-Aid?"

When I nodded, she gave a hard yank. I sucked air through tight-clenched teeth. Doe wet a cloth and blotted up the blood.

She disappeared into the bathroom and returned with iodine, tweezers, and a bottle of pills.

"For the pain."

The bottle's label read: VICODIN. Originally prescribed to a Mrs. Penny Thacker for severe pancreatic distress. The expiry date was years ago.

"Where did you get—?"

"Evidence lockup."

The manufacture, sale, and/or use of prescription medication was illegal in the Republic, so ordained by the Divine Council at New Kingdom.

I popped a pill into my mouth. "Make it two," she said. "They're *way* out of date."

She swabbed my arm with iodine before tweezing out the coiled metal. Pills or not, I screamed. Down amidst the city grid: sirens. Sirens didn't bother me. When the hunters came for you, they didn't come with sirens. They came silent as death. We both knew that. We'd been hunters.

She led me into the bathroom to dress the wound. My reflection in the mirror: every hair burned away save a few crispy threads that fringed the nape of my neck.

I returned to the front room and sat on the sofa. Walls bare: no portrait of Christ or The Prophet. Not even a cross hung above the door. Doe was still in the bathroom. I leafed through the mail on the coffee table, a snoopy force of habit.

A white manila envelope, no return address. Inside was a check; on the memo line was written: *Love you always*. Doe had been getting this same check, the same amount, for years. She guessed it was her birth parents, some too-late act of atonement. She'd tried to have them traced through the mail system, but never with any success. She never cashed them but they arrived steady as clockwork.

Love you always.

Doe stepped into the room. Face clean, hair wet, terrycloth bathrobe on. I stared: the drugs made me brazen. Her cheeks were pink, her eyes the colour of antifreeze. She was barefoot. Her second toes were slightly longer than the big ones.

She padded over to the CD player. The song was familiar—not from constant radio play, but because it was on the banned list. "American Pie," by Don McLean. The lines about the Father, Son, and the Holy Ghost catching the last train for the coast suggested that the Lord might travel on such shoddy earthbound conveyance as a train.

"Evidence lockup again?"

Doe nodded. Song notes drifted out into the night. Someone might hear them and ring the Heretic Tipster line.

Both Doe and I were orphans of a sort. She'd never known her parents—quite stereotypically, she'd been left on the front steps of the Republican orphanage in a raft made of reeds. My own mother had been taken away for heresy, an effective abandonment. Angela's last name, Doe, was the one given to every orphan.

We had kicked around different child-care systems and first met as teenagers at Kids on Fire, a charismatic Christian summer camp and by that time a Republic-mandated summer rite. I remember her face lit by burning effigies labelled "Homosexual" and "Abortionist" and "Darwinist" at our nightly bonfires. I remember how she'd fall to the floor during prayer meetings, quaking and kicking and jabbering in tongues, possessed by the power of the One True Faith.

My first impure thought had been of her. I'd glimpsed her stepping from Atonement Lake one June morning, the water's chill hardening her nipples under the standard black bathing suit before she covered herself, mortified.

That night I'd lain in the darkness of my own cabin, hands clutched between my legs, whispering to myself: *Think no vice. Think no vice. Think no vice.*

We met years later at the training academy. We were posted to the New Bethlehem force and later became Acolytes—Doe was the first woman ever so ordained. How, I often wondered, had a parentless orphan secured such a gift?

I lead a charmed life, Doe herself often said. We were partnered together. Our paths seemed oddly bound.

Could I be blamed for feeling it was all somehow part of God's plan?

She said: "Could we run? Somewhere they won't find us?"

"Anywhere we go, they'll follow," I said. "If we stay on the lam for a few months, they'll dispatch Trackers. Maybe even the Quints."

"Think they'll be lenient?" she wondered. "Amputations?"

"I doubt leaving the scene helped."

Don McLean sang about good ole boys drinking whiskey and rye. Wind whistled through the room bearing the scent of autumn.

"How long?" I asked. "How long since you stopped believing?"

She met my eye, unembarrassed. "It's not like asking someone when they lost their car keys, Jonah."

Following a span of silence between us, she said: "When you're a kid it's simple. God is good. Followers do good work. When you're older you learn about The Prophet and The Prophet is good. You go to SuperChurch, watch the fireworks, they trot out The One Child and you feel all that energy and think, I'm blessed to be a part of this. But that's just the stage dressing. And when you find yourself behind the stage backdrop with the rusted pulleys and frayed ropes—when it's your *job* to pull the strings and rig the guy wires . . . you realize how fake it is. You know what we do, Jonah. The games we play and why we play them."

"To keep the citizenry sedate. Maintain equilibrium and social harmony—"

"Don't quote The Charter at me."

I said, "You can't mean this, Angela. We're . . . we're the Chosen People."

"Everyone thinks they're the chosen people."

"But," I told her, confused, "we really *are*."

She smiled in a way that conveyed sadness, or confusion, or both. "You can take nearly everything away from people—every right and freedom, every want, most every need. But you can't take their Gods. We're killing their Gods, Jonah."

I recited the departmental boilerplate in my head. *Moral Turpitude: a critical loss of faith severely affecting performance of duties, potentially injurious to oneself and one's unit. Any Acolyte suspecting a fellow officer of Moral Turpitude is beholden to report these suspicions to their Commander.*

Angela came to me. Extended her hand. "Dance with me?"

To dance alone in the darkness with a woman to whom I was not betrothed was an act of abject sacrilege. . . .

I gave her my hand.

Her body still held the latent heat of the explosion. I was clumsy, nervy; she placed my palms round her waist. Her wet hair smelled like a doused campfire. She sang with her chin rested on my shoulder, her breath prickling the hairs there. Don McLean sang about flames climbing high into the night and Satan laughing with delight.

Doe unfastened the sash of her robe. I glimpsed that smooth cut of skin. She shot a hip to one side, a pantomime of sexuality she must've seen someplace. After all, what did she really know? What did either of us know? We were both virgins . . . weren't we?

"Are you . . ." I was grinning like a child. "Trying to corrupt me?"

"Are you willing to be corrupted?"

Doe slid the robe off her shoulders, old knife wounds crisscrossing them, down the toned ladder of her rib cage. A bullet scar on her left thigh, the deep impression like a core sample. Her body a map of the roads she'd travelled in service of the Republic.

"Do you love me, Angela?"

"I don't love anyone, Jonah," she said. "But I probably could have, had the world unfolded differently. Is that good enough?"

"No."

"Will it be good enough for tonight?"

Lips soft, tongue soft, but the body hard. I still didn't know where to put my hands on her—those scars, the injuries, that hardness. Where do you put your hands on somebody who is broken all over?

No protection: prophylactics were banned. She hissed in pain but there was no blood: afterwards she told me her hymen had burst during a fistfight with a Sikh who'd been resisting arrest. We rocked together slowly. Angela locked her legs around my back, grasped the bedrails, gyrated against me.

I closed my eyes and saw Eve's face turning to ash and watched it blow away in a superheated wind. I wondered who the hunters would be and guessed old mates: Henchel, Applewhite, Garvey. I saw the Star of Gilead twinkling above Hollis's desk and thought about the face under that hood . . . the wrong colour. The *wrong damn colour*.

The Sack

I sat in a folding metal chair facing my apartment door. I'd left Doe's apartment hours ago. The hunters usually caught you in bed—figured I'd surprise them. Every light off, eyes closed: I wanted to hear them coming.

It had been Angela's decision: *Let them come for us separately. They might be more lenient*. So I'd left her.

Steps outside in the hallway now. I felt them out there: the pressure of their bodies, the violence of their intent. A crumpling blast was followed by a superheated wind that raced low across the floor, blistering my ankles. Later on I'd catch my reflection in the interrogation room's one-way mirror: face and neck acned with pinpricks of dried blood, shallow racing grooves on my skull where debris had scored a path.

Shapes moved in a haze of cordite smoke. One of them said, "Over here—in the chair." A few mordant chuckles and then a Scots brogue whispered, "Fancied we were coming, did you lad?" and I smiled or at least tried to, couldn't feel my face, then someone slipped the Sack over my head and I got real scared.

Every hunter was familiar with the Sack. Black burlap, the word HERETIC printed across the front in yellow block letters. I'd slipped it over a fair share of heads myself.

The drawstring cinched tight, cutting across my windpipe. A fist drove into my gut and knocked the air out of me. Another punch tipped the chair back and spilled me onto the floor, where I puked a wretched stream of bile into the Sack.

The blade of a box cutter slid between my collar and the skin of my throat. My shirt was slashed away, belt and trousers, my underwear. Hands gripped my armpits and dragged me into the hallway naked and shivering.

"Heretic!" the hunters called for the benefit of my rubbernecking neighbours. "Traitor to the Republic!"

They tossed me in the back of a meat wagon. My skull caromed off the floor plates; melting-hot constellations exploded in the stinking blackness.

Someone was in the meat wagon with me. I heard his ragged breathing.

"How could you let it happen?" someone said.

"Garvey?" I croaked.

"How could you let Eve *die*?"

The Sack was wet with blood and puke, glued to my face like cling wrap.

"I didn't . . . the guy wore a hood . . . thought he was part of the band . . ."

"She was The Prophet's *daughter*. Did you get a good look at the guy?"

He was white, Garvey, I thought. *He was* us.

"No," I said. "The hood. Are they going to kill me?"

"I think so," Garvey said, rocking with my head in his lap. "I won't be able to step in, either—you know the rules."

"Doe?"

"We took her in first. Same rules apply."

Panic seized me: a thousand fiddleback spiders scurrying the walls of my gut. "Listen: she had nothing to do with it."

"Hey." His voice that of a master shushing a yappy dog. "*Hey*."

Angela mutilated. Exiled. *Dead*. I pictured her lying face-up in a shallow hole, quicklime eating into the cool green of her eyes. . . .

The meat wagon wrenched to a stop. Hands grasped my ankles and dragged me out. I was hauled up a staircase—kneecaps bashing each step, pain singing along my spine. The muted chatter of keyboards, telephones ringing. The precinct?

"Take him to number three and strap him down," I heard Hollis say.

Interrogation room number three. They sat me in the Confessional. Same shape as an old-fashioned gynecologist's exam chair: my legs split, ankles shackled head-high.

The door eased shut; the soft outrush of air pebbled my skin. A box cutter's blade slashed through the blackness a quarter-inch from my eyes. Stark light flooded in.

Hollis's rosary beads went *clikka clikka clikka*. . . .

"We'll be needing to get to the bottom of things, you and I. Down to brass tacks."

My eyes adjusted. Hollis was the only one in the room. A burlap bag, the same dull grey of the walls, lay at his feet. It was Hollis's infamous tool bag.

"I don't know what you want me to tell you." My voice was a dead thing. "I don't know anything."

Hollis said, "You know The Prophet's daughter is dead. You know that what's left of the poor dear couldn't fill an ashtray. You know you fled the scene of an investigation—you, an officer, a primary witness and now, it must be said, a suspect. Most of all, you know the procedures of our department so I can't imagine any of this comes as a shock."

He pulled a deck of cigarettes from his vest pocket, shook them at me. I hadn't smoked in years but it was high time to get reacquainted with bad habits.

Hollis slashed a new vent in the Sack and poked a cigarette

between my lips. I coughed it out on the first inhale: it dropped to my chest, where Hollis let it sizzle through the sheen of sweat before poking it back in my mouth.

"Go ahead, lad. Tell me what happened. Spare not the slightest detail."

"I picked her up after seven," I said. "It was Eve and two friends. The Manger, she said—some singer she was keen to hear. Jimmy what's-his-nose."

"Saint Kincaid."

"It went like any other duty: frisking cocktail waitresses, keeping gawkers at bay. There was no—"

"The bouncer," Hollis backtracked. "Involved?"

"Can't say. Wouldn't think so."

"He the only one guarding the service entry?"

"Yes."

Hollis cut a look at the one-way glass and nodded. Sometime tonight the bouncer would be roused from his bed, shackled, stripped, and Sacked.

"When did Acolyte Doe arrive?"

"Shortly after the girls were seated."

"And you were glad she was there," Hollis said archly.

"I was glad to have the appropriate backup, if that's what you mean."

I stared at Hollis through the ragged slash of burlap. Hollis pinched the cigarette from between my lips.

"Filthy things." He crushed it under his boot. "They'll kill you, you know."

"A lot of filthy things might kill me."

Hollis smiled at that.

"You allowed Eve out into the crowd."

I said, "She's The Prophet's daughter."

"*Was* The Prophet's daughter."

"What Eve wants—*wanted*—Eve got."

Hollis said, "Yet you realized how badly that would compromise her security."

"I made her aware of that. She wanted to dance, and didn't

want me anywhere near while doing so. I refused to leave her side. She slapped me."

Hollis sneered. "And that was enough to melt your mettle? A slap from a nineteen-year-old girl?"

"It wasn't the power of the slap. It was the power of the slapper."

Hollis nodded with a look of patently fake understanding. Friendly Uncle Hollis. I don't know why he bothered. Did he want to elicit something approximating the truth before beating a false confession out of me? The honest truth before the official lie?

"Did you want her up on stage, alone, without protection? To save your own skin against the blast you knew was coming?"

I said, "Is that how we're playing this?"

"This isn't a game, son. Nobody's playing."

"I was nearly killed myself."

"But you aren't dead."

"Not yet."

"And your accomplice, Doe—she's not dead, either."

I said: "If you want to spin this that I dropped the ball and got Eve killed, okay—could be that's true. You want to play it like I orchestrated it all and see that I get my head chopped off on National Republic TV, fine, I'll read whatever script you hand me. But first I want it known and I want it witnessed: Doe is clean. So get Chief Exeter and let's get on with it."

Hollis grinned a death's head grin.

"That's altogether dashing of you—Jonah Murtag, the self-sacrificing hero of any dime store romance." Then, speaking softly so the interrogation-room mics couldn't it pick up: "You've lusted after Doe for years—I know you've always wanted to fuck her." His voice was pure snake venom. "You craved her sweet *cunny*, isn't that right?"

Before I could protest, he barrelled on.

"The bomber. The heretic jihadist. Catch a glimpse of his face?"

"No," I said after a beat. "It happened too fast."

"Too fast? He was on stage for fifteen minutes."

"He wore a hood."

"So you couldn't see, or you purposefully ignored?"

"I had my attention on Eve. The most credible threats were coming—"

"From *you*, isn't that a fact?"

"From the crowd. From—"

"No. *No*. From you." Hollis shook a rosary-wrapped fist in my face. "You, Doe, and your accomplice set it up: allowing Eve up on stage, encouraging her even, saving your own hides when any true Follower would've sacrificed themselves on her behalf. Isn't that right?"

"No!"

"Shshsh. Shshsh." Switching gears: placating, honeyed. "Let's go back to the bomber. When did you recognize the malice of his intent?"

"Too late."

"Don't get smart. When, precisely, did you appreciate his threat?"

"He came up behind Eve and Saint Kincaid. He spread his arms, this . . . crucifixion pose. I thought it was part of the act. Everyone did. Then I saw a DET cord sticking out of his sleeve. Half a second later . . ."

Hollis bent beside his tool bag. He pulled something out.

"A question for you, lad . . ."—stalking my blind side—". . . if you acknowledged the threat, why-oh-why weren't you blown to bits in your attempt, however fruitless, to throw yourself between the bomber and Eve? How come you found yourself in the only place in that club where anyone could have survived the blast?"

"Get Exeter," I said. "I'm ready to confess."

Hollis's voice dripped cold rage. "You're ready when I say so, you filthy bastard."

The steel prongs of a cattle prod sent 10,000 volts flooding through my body. Next I was snorting blood and choking against the strap fastened round my throat. I saw an off-white chip stuck to my knee with bloodied saliva and realized, without much shock, it was one of my teeth.

Hollis was fulminating like an Old Testament Prophet:

"I am the Divine sword of justice, searching out villainy and excising it!" He broke into the Book of Revelations, spittle shining his lips: "*And in those days, evil men shall seek death, and shall not find it; and shall desire to die, and death shall flee from them!*"

He socked the prod into my throat and sent another jolt hammering through my system. No pain, only this terrifying sense of confusion: my brain sucked out and the empty skull case stuffed with squirming black beetles.

"*—the four beasts had each of them six wings about him; and they were full of eyes within—*"

A new voice joined Hollis's. Choked and childlike. My own.

"The lord is my shepherd; I shall not want . . ."

Zzaap!

". . . maketh me lie down in green pastures; he leadeth . . . me in the paths of . . . of righteousness . . ."

Zzzzaaap!

". . . Yea, though I walk through the valley of the shadow of death, I will fear no . . ."

Zzzzzzzzzzzaaaaaaaaaaaaaap!

"My cup . . . my cup runneth . . . my cup . . . my cup . . . my . . ."

A spark. This fizzling blue pop in the darkness. And another. I willed myself toward the spark only to find I couldn't: I was back in my body, arms and legs strapped. Then a voice:

"What do you mean, clemency? We're talking about the man responsible for the death of The Prophet's daughter. He's all but admitted it."

I was still seated in the Confessional. The voice belonged to Hollis, who spoke on the interrogation room telephone. The spark came from his cattle prod, which he kept firing off in agitation.

"No . . . now wait a bloody minute." *Zzap.* "This man was part of my unit and we police our own. And if you even think about crossing swords, Exeter . . ." *Zzap.* "No, that was not a threat: that was a precise foretelling of future history."

Was Chief Exeter intervening on my behalf? I wondered, *Why?*

"Gabriel wept!"—a snowball-sized spark—"Do you think I won't request an audience with Him myself? And when I do, do you think your bollocks won't be swinging from the nearest flagpole?"

Hollis hung up the phone in a rage.

"Are you a believer in miracles, Murtag?" he said. "Divine intervention?"

I said nothing. My lips were sealed with blood.

"You should," he said. "You've been spared. Word has come down from on high."

Edges of sharp metal closed round my right pinkie finger: tin snips or bolt cutters. The punishment was Standard Operating Procedure for gross negligence by an emissary of the Republic. It was the lightest discipline I could expect.

Hollis said: "Don't flinch. I don't want to have to cut twice."

Steely pressure, a crunch of bone, the hiss of blood. When Hollis trained a blowtorch on the wound to cauterize it, I blacked out from the pain.

I regained my senses sometime later.

I had been strapped to a gurney in a well-lit room. The smell of antiseptic. Everything clean and polished and white. Nurses bustled here and there.

Angela was strapped to another gurney ten yards away.

Smiling wanly, she mouthed, "Okay?"

I mouthed, "Okay."

She raised her hand, a clandestine wave. The sight heartened me.

Hollis had taken my entire pinkie finger.

He'd only taken the tip of hers.

RECOVERY

I opened my eyes. Ashy afternoon light streamed through the hospital windows. Garvey sat at the foot of the bed.

The fingers of my right hand were wrapped in gauze to the knuckles. A plug of yellow wax had been melted over the stump of my pinkie. The skin was purple and infected. I hoped it wasn't gangrene.

"What's happening?" I croaked. "What's to become of me?"

Garvey chawed on a ball of tobacco. He worked it from one side of his mouth to the other and said, "That's need-to-know info and I don't need to know. But as I take it, you've been spared."

"By who?"

His eyes rolled heavenward.

I said: "The Prophet?"

"You're alive and within city limits." Garvey shrugged. "Be thankful."

Blisters on either side of my ribcage: electrical burns from Hollis's cattle prod.

"Am I still an Acolyte?"

Garvey said, "So it seems. You and Doe both. But the two of you are under me now."

He came round to the head of the bed. Bracing his hands on the mattress, he knelt so his face was level with mine.

"We've been through plenty together, yeah?"

"Yeah, Garvey."

"Faced the heathens, fought side by each—you've saved my life more than once and I appreciate that. I love you as a brother under Christ. And I don't know what happened in that club, with Eve."

He paused, thinking maybe I'd divulge something. When I failed to do so, his hands clenched into fists and pulled the bedsheets taut.

"But if you ever give me reason to doubt your belief, I'll kill you dead. You mustn't ever test my loyalties; you'll lose every time. Fair enough warning?"

"Fair enough."

"I know you're a man who appreciates straight dealing."

Garvey reached for a squeeze bottle at the bedside. "Nurse said give you a squirt of this. Knockout sauce, put you back to sleep."

I closed my lips around the plastic tube. Sweet fortified wine washed down my gullet. I caught the bitter taste of mandrake root and was gone again.

I awoke sometime at night. This time Hollis sat at the foot of the bed, smiling at me. In the withered light his teeth looked as if they'd been filed to points. He'd pulled the privacy curtain round the bed.

"What I did to you was my job. My duty." He smiled again.

"Your duty," I said in a way that indicated I could accept it. "Are we going to be able to continue forward on a . . . professional basis, you and I?"

"Depends on you, lad. I was simply doing as I was told, no malice intended. You left a crime scene. I am a god-fearing man, and god-fearing men do not carry unjust grudges. Do you carry a grudge?"

I shook my head no.

Hollis said, "If I'm going to be stabbed, I'd prefer it in the chest, not my back."

I willed my face into a mask. "No grudges."

He stared at me for a long time. "We have been put on this earth to spread the One True Faith. We are on the same side, are we not? Those things I said while you were in the Confessional . . ."

"Duty."

"You and Doe have been reprimanded and thus expiated. You may still need to mend fences with your fellow Acolytes, but I'll do my best to help. We need to maintain a unified front in light of recent events."

A horrible sense of loneliness enveloped me, spurred by the understanding that the monster at the foot of the bed might be as close to an ally as I had left.

"I only cut off the tip of Doe's finger." He held this fact out, an olive branch. "Could've taken it all. It was mine by right."

I fluttered my eyes, feigning exhaustion. Hollis opened the privacy curtain. The moon hung low in the black sky. Eerie orange-tinted light bathed the rooftops and cathedral spires of New Bethlehem. I shut my eyes.

Morning came. Sunspots sparkled off dangling IV bottles. The sunlight felt wonderful where it touched me. I needed to relieve myself. Fiercely.

The duty nurse was in conversation with Chief Exeter, who saw I'd awoken.

"Acolyte Murtag." Exeter eased himself into the bedside chair.

"If it isn't the ghost of Christmas future."

He smiled obsequiously. "How are you feeling?"

Better, but I wasn't going to say so. "Got to piss like a racehorse."

Exeter's throat flushed above his collar. The man's prudishness was legendary. The nurse came over with a bedpan.

"Would you like me to . . . ?" Exeter said. "Shall I turn away?"

"Don't bother." I knew it would embarrass him more than it would me, and it'd be wise to put him on the defensive. "It's the standard plumbing."

I swung my legs off the mattress and fished myself from the slit of my hospital gown. Exeter sat with eyes averted, legs crossed, clasped hands resting on one knee.

The book on Exeter: overeducated—Master's in Civic Faith Services from Oral Roberts, matching doctorate from Pat Robertson University—but under-experienced. Naturally, I loathed him—despite the fact that, so far as I knew, he was the one who'd saved my skin. But I doubted very much it had been out of the goodness of his heart.

I said: "To what do I owe this honour?"

Exeter sighed. "Can't say as I was expecting graciousness, but I could do without the outright hostility."

"Recent events have temporarily put me in an un-Christian spirit."

He polished his specs with the hem of his vest. "Are you speaking of your failure to protect The Prophet's daughter?"

I took a shaving mirror off the bedside table and consulted my reflection. The sight did nothing to improve my mood: hairless, skin pale as candle wax, eyes surrounded by black rings like washers. My front tooth had broken off during Hollis's interrogation session. I probed the empty space with my tongue and marvelled at just how witless I looked.

"You're alive," said Exeter. "No broken bones, no internal bleeding. Besides, your duties do not require you to look good." He aimed for a levity that didn't suit him. "A scar or two, roughened features—who says those aren't a plus?"

"And I take it you're the reason why I'm not six feet under."

To his credit, Exeter's expression revealed nothing; he finished polishing his specs and slid them onto his test-pattern face.

"I overheard Hollis on the phone in the interrogation room," I went on, "in between jolts from his cattle prod. Figure I should be thankful."

"I don't figure as you should be anything at all," Exeter said after an introspective pause wherein I sensed he weighed the benefits and drawbacks of telling the truth. "I wasn't aware what was happening to you. As you well know, your unit operates behind a veil of autonomous secrecy."

"So, who?"

He waved my question off. "Does not factor. Suffice it to say, I found out and put an end to it. There was never any intention to have you or Acolyte Doe executed. And that"—he indicated the stump of my finger—"is regrettable, but Deacon Hollis took it as his right. The investigation into the bombing is ongoing. You and Doe are witnesses, which makes Hollis's actions not only hotheaded but borderline treasonous. What if one of you had been killed? What were you doing in the Confessional in the first place—an oaf with a blowtorch can get whatever admission he wants."

The nurse retrieved the bedpan. It was filled with red broth: as much blood as piss.

"The trend continues," Exeter said. "Another bombing last night."

"Two nights in a row?"

He shook his head. "You've been here three days. They've had you medicated on ether and that"—a nod to the bottle of fortified wine and mandrake root—"so I'm not surprised you're foggy. Nevertheless, two bombings in four nights is an alarming trend."

"Where?"

Exeter's brow wrinkled. "It happened in Kiketown. An eight-storey storage facility." In the ghettos, there was no differentiation between warehouses and apartment complexes: all were zoned as storage facilities. "An explosion on the third floor. Seventeen tenants burned to death, another dozen dead of smoke inhalation."

Had the explosion taken place in the city proper, the damage would not have been so extensive. But the fire department did not respond to storage facility fires.

"So . . . it was random?"

Exeter nodded. "And it's looking more like The Manger was random. That The Prophet's daughter was killed can be construed as an unexpected tragedy or bonus, depending on which side you're on."

Random. The most terrifying word in a lawman's dictionary. If heathens had a *modus operandi* you could stake out potential targets and zero in. But if they had no specific enemy—if they were aligned against humanity in general—all bets were off.

Exeter said: "The Prophet will be addressing the death of his daughter during his weekly sermon two days from now. It's in your best interests you be up and on duty before then."

"I'll be back by tomorrow."

"I imagine it may be difficult easing back into things. You Acolytes are an insular crew, and some may harbour a grudge. So if there's anything I can do in futu—"

A shockwave trembled through the hospital. Beds jounced, ceiling tiles cracked, IV bottles shattered. Exeter rushed to the nearest window.

Off to the east, smoke was already rising into the cloudless morning blue. Greasy black streaks were joined by grey funnels spiralling from wreckage too far away to glimpse, yet which I could still picture in my mind's eye: heat-warped girders blown apart and laying at jigsaw angles, flames shooting from shattered windows, disconnected arms and legs roasting on the blackened brickwork. And screaming. Lots and lots of screaming.

Exeter said: "That's in Little Baghdad. My God, even the bombers are being bombed."

The lack of civic response told me he was correct. I heard no sirens because no emergency vehicles would be dispatched.

My blood was buzzing. "This makes no earthly sense."

Exeter's pager went off. He glanced at the number and shut his eyes.

He would keep his eyes shut for quite some time.

Article II:
He Falls the First Time

6 MOM

I checked myself out of the hospital sometime during the witching hour. A trio of charge nurses knelt round me reciting the standard fare-thee-well prayer. One of them gave me a lump of cornbread covered in blue-green mold.

"Eat it all," she said. "Helps with your infection."

I flagged down a cab. The cabbie dropped me at my apartment building. No key so I hauled myself up the fire escape, cracked my window and clambered awkwardly through. Stink of cordite smoke. Black ash climbing the walls.

I found the wrapped box in the closet. Mom's present.

Raphael's Roost was a rest home for Cure cases. A squat tri-levelled building in the shape of a U, flaking paint the hue of a diseased liver. Lawn burned so badly all that remained was a fuzz like that covering a tennis ball.

Inside the Roost, wall sconces burned feebly. The hallways smelled somehow forlorn, as if the emotional states of its inhabitants had impregnated themselves upon the physical bearing of the Roost itself, layer upon crazed layer.

The overnight orderly was a bovine-looking character. His nametag read: REMO PALLADINI, TRAINEE.

I set the wrapped box on the inspection table. "My mother's here. This is for her. Her birthday."

Palladini said, "It's well past visiting hours, Mr. Murtag."

"Officer." I flashed my badge. "Officer Murtag."

"Right. Officer. Past visiting hours."

"I won't wake her. I just want to leave the present so she wakes up to it."

"You can leave it at the desk." His lips skinned back from his teeth as if to suggest even this would be putting him in a tight spot. "Maybe the dayshift orderly can get it to her."

I asked if he had pen and paper, and when he gave them to me I looked at his nametag before carefully copying his name down.

"What's that for?" he said.

I slipped the paper into my pocket. "Oh, this? It's nothing. Every so often I get someone's name and run a background check. The department encourages it."

Palladini's face blanched. His nostrils dilated.

"Why would you do that? What for?"

"That's the whole point. It's random, totally random. The same way policemen in cruisers run the licence plate of the car ahead of them at a traffic light. Ninety-nine percent of the time they're clean. I'm sure you're clean—right?"

Palladini's jaw tightened.

"Five minutes, Officer Murtag."

My mother was asleep, her white hair fanned over the pillow.

Honeycombed shadows from the security window sectioned

her face, which was pinched with tension. While awake, her face was as placid as a pool of water. That placidity had been carved with the blade of a scalpel.

I set the box on her dresser. She stirred in agitation, and the smell of the room—sick, same as the hallways—rushed at me, and in the darkness I swore I saw the layers of sickened psyche peeling right off her, thin as onionskin paper.

01 Wholesale Slaughter

Back on duty.

Just after 7:00 a.m. I'd come to the stationhouse straight from the Roost, changing into my spare uniform in the locker room.

Sitting at my desk, its frosted-glass gooseneck lamp the only light in the squad room, I jammed the hunk of mouldy cornbread in my mouth. Fibrous fuzz tickled the inside of my cheek. The natural penicillin should help.

I walked to the Ongoing Investigations corkboard.

Kidnapping/Attempted Murder. Female victim attacked in Lower Jerusalem near St. Matthew's Way. Unknown male assailant slashed victim's throat and took her infant son. Assailant: mulatto with pronounced negroid features. 20–30 yrs. Threat: low. Priority: med. Investigating Acolytes: unassigned.

Manufacture/Possession of Banned Religious Artifacts. Hindu sect minting statues of Ganesha, Brahma, Shiva and other idols in a 3rd-storey walk-up on Shepherd's Court. 10 fugitives: 6 captured; 4 remain at large. Threat: low. Priority: low. Investigating Acolytes: remanded to rank & file.

At 7:45 my fellow Acolytes began to filter in. Martel Applewhite, a god-fearing ex-Baptist who I'd been sworn in beside, didn't even acknowledge my presence. The others offered poisonous glances.

When Garvey arrived I braced for more of the same. But he surprised me by pulling up a chair next to me. He carried a fresh hint of superiority. He had a bottle of murky yellow liquid, which he drank off before slapping my knee in a gesture of camaraderie.

Doe came in last. Her skull had been shaved. The sight stirred a fleeting panic—*they've cut out a piece of her brain*. But there was a reassuring clarity in her eyes, and when her head swivelled I saw no incisions or catgut. She went to the cistern and poured a cup of decaf.

"Anyone got anything to say?" she said. "Pipe up now, fellas."

Doe spoke with her back to the room. She turned and held her left hand in front of her face. The stump of her pinkie finger was inflamed. Staring through her remaining fingers, she regarded each man in turn. Nobody said a word.

Hollis entered to offer the daily debriefing.

"First off, let's welcome back Doe and Murtag." When nobody said a word, Hollis rapped his knuckles on the desk. "I said, let us welcome a pair of fellow officers back into the eternally forgiving bosom of the unit."

After a round of halfhearted applause, Hollis went on: "Here's the skinny, lads: you've all been officially detached from whatever priors or unsolveds you were working and attached to the bombings. We need every shoulder to the wheel on this. Applewhite, you were first on the scene at yesterday's bombing in Little Baghdad. What have you managed to ascertain?"

Applewhite stared at his notepad.

"The target was a Republic-run bottling plant. They bottled Purity Purge, mainly; also Sin Burner with ephedra and Soul Glow, a raspberry-scented detoxifying facial cream. Aside from management, the workforce was Islamic. Death toll stands at fifty to fifty-five—"

"Spare us the numbers," said Hollis.

Applewhite flipped a page. "The quarter-acre plant was levelled. CSI's preliminary findings indicate a nitrate-based explosive compound is not feasible. It would've taken somewhere in the neighbourhood of five-hundred square cubits."

"Why is that not feasible?" Hollis's lips pressed into a thin bloodless scar. "Back a cube van up to the front door and blow yourself to Kingdom Come."

"The blast pattern suggests the explosion was triggered inside the plant. The northern and southern walls are intact. There's a scorched crater at the heart of what was the bottling line."

"All of which means . . . ?"

Applewhite cleared his throat nervously. "The bomber or bombers were armed with a more potent and concealable incendiary compound. The blast went off near a pressurized vat of liquid chromium—the active skin-lightening agent in Soul Glow—and set off a secondary explosion. This means the initial detonation was hot enough to melt metal."

Hollis rubbed the back of his neck, as if a pebble had set up shop at the tip of his brainstem. "Anyone remember the days when all the loons could get their hands on were match-head pipe bombs? Used to be part of a loon's moral fibre. How are they laying their hands on high-level gear?

"That's . . . undetermined," said Applewhite. "We'll need to—"

"Stuff it, lad," Hollis cut him off. "The real question is, why are the bombers bombing themselves?"

A pall settled over the squad room. The question struck at

the heart of an uneasiness that gripped us all. On one hand, this was a scenario we had always envisioned: Muslims were war-loving, sword-waving fanatics whose lunacy was so directionless that they would eventually become outraged with even their own kind, falling upon, cannibalizing, and ultimately destroying themselves. But that should only happen once they had achieved their goal of wiping all infidels off the map.

Unless the bombers weren't Muslims, spoke an insistent voice in my head. *Unless they were . . . Followers.*

An accident report chittered off the Teletype machine. Garvey tore off the printout.

"Traffic wreck outside of town. A semi full of animals pegged for the shrines run off the road. Says here the driver was murdered."

"Rank-and-file can handle it." Hollis said. "It's a hijacking gone awry."

"Sacrificial animals?" I said. "It's an odd shipment to hijack."

Hollis looked flummoxed before easing into a grin. "Acolyte Murtag, so nice to see your investigational wheels spinning again. And while I believe they're spinning in mud with this one, you and Garvey go check it out."

Hollis then turned his attention to the remaining Acolytes.

"Applewhite, you and Doe head to Little Baghdad; canvas the neighbourhood, find out if anyone saw or heard anything to give pause. Everyone else fan out and bring back leads we can work with. Dismissed."

Garvey signed out a prowl car from the auto pool. We headed south. Garvey drove. He shot me a distracted glance, drumming his fingers on the wheel.

"You should have kept your mouth shut. You don't dictate what assignments we pick up anymore. Now we're driving all over hell's half acre chasing this wild hair. It's a waste of time and gets us no closer to Eve's killers."

The streets were all but deserted. We passed a billboard for Sinless Sheen shampoo. Tagline: *Lather, Rinse, Repent.*

Garvey stopped in at a Puritan's Pantry. Returning to the cruiser, he tossed me a bottle of water and a packet of Hallelujah Energy Boost powder.

"Mix that up for me, will you?"

I eyeballed the ingredients: *life-enriching flavonoids, age-defying spiritual compounds, vitamin V for Vitality, secret spices, guar gum, dye #29 for robust colouration.*

Garvey cut down a side street, goosing the horn to scatter foot traffic, merging onto Falwell Memorial Boulevard. The on-ramp arched past St. Mark's Cathedral, home of the Sacred Whores. Young women lounged in opulent glass-fronted picture boxes strung round the turreted church at eye level. Crimson spots backlit each box. Beautiful and untouchable: their availability was restricted to top-ranking officials; one-time use by Republic-affirmed servants was also permitted in recognition of exemplary public service.

Garvey slugged back his Hallelujah Energy Boost. "That'll put lead in your pencil. As The Prophet says: healthiness is closer to Godliness."

The odometer had clicked off 162 furlongs when we pulled up to a tractor trailer lying half-on, half-off an uninhabited rural route.

The rig's rear wheels were mired in the soft muck of the ditch. The trailer portion had smashed through a barbed wire fence and lay overturned in a weedy field. Huge curls of vulcanized rubber lay across the tarmac.

A pair of legs jutted behind the left front tire.

"Highwaymen," Garvey said, surveying the scene. "Ten to one."

The Highway Patrol had been decommissioned years ago due to budget cuts. The "zone of guaranteed public safety" terminated at the city limits. Out here was the Badlands: so named not because of any geological traits or scarcity of vegetation, but because the people who roamed it lacked the correct faith.

Highwaymen—some heathens, some once-devoted Followers who had forsaken the path—now patrolled these empty stretches of highway. Nomadic, they lived in tents or makeshift shanties or vacated farmhouses. They preyed on unescorted shipments cut off from the safety of a convoy. Truckers fought back by outfitting their rigs with self-sealing tires and bulletproof glass and by bolting cowcatchers to their grilles to bust through claptrap roadblocks. The roadsides were littered with the hulks of flame-eaten, bullet-riddled vehicles.

The air was clean and bracing as I stepped from the car. I hadn't been this far outside the city in a long time. The breeze shifted and a new smell hit me, raw and ripe and bloody: as if I'd stumbled downwind of a slaughterhouse.

Dr. Calvin Newbarr, an old saw with the CSI team, had beaten us to the scene. Now in his late sixties, Newbarr had been a county coroner in the days before the Republic. A genteel throwback, he always dressed impeccably: crisp dark-sable suit, Windsor-knotted tie, a brushed felt hat. His unkempt eyebrows hung like silken draperies before his eyes.

"Prophet's blessings," he greeted us.

"From the Lord's lips to His," I said. "You shouldn't be out here on your own."

He shrugged. "What would a highwayman want with an old string like me?"

The legs sticking out from the back of the rig belonged to the trucker himself. He was fully clothed and lay facedown on the road. His head had been run over. The pressure of the five-ton truck had flattened his skull. His scalp had been lifted off and was stuck in the tire treads. His stark white skull had the look of a plate that had been stepped on and broken into pieces.

Newbarr removed his hat and held it at his belt buckle for a moment before replacing it on his head.

Garvey said: "You got a spatula, doc?"

The coroner unsnapped his medical kit. "Poor taste, son."

"Lighten up." Garvey spat into the nettles. "Not like he's bound to register the insult."

Garvey wandered up the road to reconnoitre the outlying

scene. Newbarr tugged on latex gloves and did some exploratory feeling around. He made notes into an old-style Dictaphone. I heard: "Massive depressed skull fractures." I heard: "Cranial epidermis removed as a result of blunt force trauma." I heard: "Identification via dental plate match not feasible."

"Wipe my brow?" Newbarr held up his bloody hands as a plea. With my handkerchief I dabbed sweat from under his hat brim.

"I heard what happened with The Prophet's daughter," he said. "I'm very sorry to see you in such poor shape."

I waved it off and said: "Doesn't it seem a lot of needless trouble?"

"Meaning?"

"This trucker was a big guy. Liable to put up a fight. Why not just shoot him? As it stands, must've been one guy driving the rig and two-three others holding the guy down so they could run over his head—why bother?"

Newbarr pushed his hat up to expose a liver spot. "You're saying it was a gang?"

I shook my head. "Highwaymen generally act alone. It's their misanthropic nature that drives them out here in the first place."

Newbarr nodded. "Even if it was only two men, one of them had to be freakishly big and strong."

"What I'm saying is, what if it wasn't a highwayman at all?"

"Who else?"

I came back with another question: "Sacrificial animals? How do you offload them? It means heading into the city, exposing yourself. Any licenced shrine requires paperwork, too. It's hardly worth the risk."

I clambered into the cab while Newbarr chalked an outline. A ragged hole was blown through the passenger-side floorboard. I spotted a hand grenade in the cup holder.

In the glove box I found insurance papers with the trucker's name: Irvine B. Coughlin. Address in New Nazareth, 1,500 furlongs southeast. I flipped the visor down: smiling photos of a boy and girl paper-clipped to the sun-bleached felt. Above them a snippet of Matthew 28: *I am with you always, even to the end of the age.*

When I swung down from the cab, Garvey was making his way back.

"The driver's side door is back over that hill. A pair of punctures in it."

"Bullet holes?"

Garvey shook his head. "No, punched from the inside out. I'm guessing someone chucked a grappling hook through the window and ripped the door off."

"Anything else?"

"Skid marks of differing widths. More than one vehicle was involved in the hijacking."

Having wrapped his preliminary investigation, Newbarr said, "Nobody's certain this was a hijacking. For it to be a hijacking, something has to have been taken." He threw an apprehensive glance at the overturned trailer. "Let's hope it's been ransacked and everything's gone. At least that would make *some* sense."

As bad as the driver had gotten it, his trailer got it worse.

It had broken free of the rig and skidded across a field wet with morning dew. The undercarriage had dug a twisting scar into the earth, now filling with groundwater.

We stepped over snapped fence posts and snarls of barbed wire. Garvey had a shotgun; Newbarr and I carried flashlights.

The trailer rested on its side; one of its cargo doors lay open like a drawbridge. Sunlight slanted through low-lying clouds to highlight the patina of blood on the door, the weeds and grass, still soaking into the dirt. Feathers—white, brown, yellow, most bloody—dotted the scene.

The head of some animal, a goat or sika deer, lay where it had been hurled in a thatch of cockleburs. The ragged neck wound indicated its head had not been cleanly sliced but rather wrenched and partly torn off. Its hide was stuck with burrs and its eyes gone filmy: they looked like marbles rubbed with sandpaper.

Coming from inside, their origin obscured by darkness: rustling sounds, scrabbling sounds, the odd peep. I pulled my revolver from its shoulder rig. It felt ungainly in my pinkie-less hand.

The second cargo door hung down like a flap of skin. I bent underneath it, easing myself into the trailer. The stink hit me like a closed fist: not decay, as not enough time had passed—just the high, giddy smell of death.

My flashlight beam was joined by Newbarr's. They illuminated wholesale slaughter.

It looked as though a wind of razor blades had blown through the trailer. The compartment was crammed full of animals. Goats, deer, rabbits, guinea pigs, birds of many species. Most had been caged but some had obviously been roped to the walls; when the trailer flipped on its side these ones—goats, a few llamas—were strangled on their leads: they hung in the muggy darkness like heavy bags for boxing.

The cages had been forced open, steel rods bent and mangled, the animals plucked out and subjected to far worse than the goats got.

Someone had fed rabbits into the trailer's cooling fan—it had remained operational even after the crash, judging by the red spray on the walls. The whicker birdcages had been stomped to splinters, birds and all. The hanging deer had been gutted and their chest cavities stuffed with dead guinea pigs.

A bluebottle bounced against my head, rendered sluggish by this bounty. Thousands of them created a maddening buzz. Below the buzzing, other noises: confused and pitiful.

"Who?" Garvey was seething. "Who would commit such sacrilege?"

He snatched Newbarr's flashlight and stalked deeper into the trailer. I staggered back and heard a brittle, jaw-clenching crack. Training my flashlight down, I saw I'd stepped on the skull of a pale blue budgie. I blessed myself and inspected the ground for footprints, finding not a single one—how was that possible?

A fresh realization stung me. These animals hadn't been killed outright: most had only been mutilated. Birds with wings torn off, rabbits with their feet snipped off, all left to bleed out and die. The mutilations were careful, meticulous; it must have taken hours. A wingless dove lay in a pile with several others, still horribly alive. Biting back a sob, I stepped on its head, too.

"How much more do you need to see?" Newbarr said softly. "This all seems nothing so much as . . ."

"Some sort of a message," I finished for him.

Garvey let loose a scream. His shotgun blew a ragged hole into the death-box, and another, and another. He stormed the length of the trailer and shouldered past Newbarr out into the field.

When I took a hesitant step forward, the old coroner gripped my elbow. My ears were ringing from the shotgun volleys but I could read his lips well enough:

"You don't want to see it."

And he was right: I didn't want to. But I needed to.

The flashlight reflected tiny glassy eyes, piles of wings and paws and hooves, lit up a decapitated llama head with its mouth stuffed full of bullfinches. The air was so thick with blood the feeling was narcotic; I swanned into a suspended carcass and gaped in horror as severed rabbit heads tumbled from its stomach to patter at my feet. I swung around, revolted, heartsick, and saw what had set Garvey off.

Two deer sat in a shaft of sunlight coming in through the holes Garvey's shotgun had punched in the trailer. One young, the other older: a mother and fawn. The young one was dead: someone had almost but not quite sawn its head off. The older one was licking its neck as if this might somehow resurrect it. Licking tenderly but obsessively: the hair on the little deer's throat had been licked clean off.

I chewed the air to stave off the deep rootless panic rising in my chest. The deer stared around aimlessly. Did it see me? Could it see anything? Sunlight streamed through the holes and touched its soft brown coat. It was then I noted, with the kind of sick attention to detail peculiar to only the most profound nightmares, that all four of its legs had been broken. Bones shorn through flesh as if someone had snapped each one over a knee like kindling. It scrabbled on those useless legs, inched itself forward, shielding the little dead deer from me. It licked and licked and licked and it licked.

I cocked the revolver's hammer. I didn't know that my bad hand would be strong enough to handle the kickback. It had better be.

Afterwards I heard a frantic chirping outside the trailer.

Off to my left in the long grass and dandelions: a fitful flash of blue. I knelt and saw what it was: another blood-spattered budgie. It didn't look hurt; the weight of blood on its feathers merely prevented it from flying.

I covered it with my hands. Its wings beat against my fingers. I picked it up, let its head poke through the circle made by my thumb and pointer finger. Eyes bright and alert. Twittering away. I laid it into my wide duster pocket.

Garvey knelt in the field, head bowed, gripping his skull with both hands. Newbarr stood nearby trying to light a cigarette but his hands were shaking so badly he couldn't touch flame to the tip.

I touched the back of Garvey's neck. "Garvey, it's okay. I . . . I took care of it."

Newbarr joined us. He'd managed to get his cigarette lit, but it jittered between his lips. "Those animals will go to Heaven," he assured Garvey. "They deserve that."

Garvey braced his hands on his knees and straightened his spine. The skin ringing his eyes was puffy and red.

"Hell's not good enough for the men who did this. Some of those animals are still alive. We got to *do* something."

I said: "It's still technically a crime scene."

"You won't see me back in there," Newbarr said.

"Okay," I said.

I headed to the truck. Stepped over Irvine B. Coughlin's white-sheeted corpse to retrieve the grenade from the cup holder. Garvey taped it to the prowl car's emergency jerry can with white medical tape from Newbarr's kit.

Newbarr said, "You boys better take a look here."

He directed us around back of the trailer. Written on the overturned roof in six-foot high letters spelled out in dried blood:

LET YOUR SINS GO UNPUNISHED.

Newbarr flicked his cigarette into the weeds. "What do you figure it means?"

"It's a threat." Garvey slammed the trailer with his fist. "Can't you see? Some sick twists killed these animals so they couldn't be used to wipe out our sins."

Newbarr and I crouched by the semi as Garvey pulled the pin and heaved the jerry can through the trailer door. He'd hotfooted it fifty yards before an explosion bulged the trailer's hull and threw him to the ground.

Newbarr came over and set a shaky hand on Garvey's shoulder.

"It is my seasoned medical opinion that nothing could have survived that blast. Dangerous, foolish, but effective."

Before making our separate ways back to the city, Newbarr drew me aside. "I'll need you to drop by the pathology lab. I've been putting off Eve's coronary report—figure you'll be able to fill in some blanks."

I assured him I'd stop by in the afternoon. Garvey set the car in gear and pulled out of the breakdown lane. Those five words kept turning over in my mind.

Let your sins go unpunished.

I couldn't quite draw a bead on it.

Was it a threat . . .

. . . or an entreaty?

11 Seditious Materials

Garvey stopped at a Puritan's Pantry on the way back. I went to a roadside callbox and fished in my pocket for a two-gerah coin. Eve's nickel-plated profile glared up at me from its face. I fed it into the payphone.

I rang dispatch and was patched through to the DMV. An office drone took Irvine B. Coughlin's name and licence number and spat info back: no pink slips, no priors, an overdue parking ticket charged to his family minivan. A dead end. I rang dispatch again and got patched through to the New Nazareth Hall of Public Records.

A clerk said, "Who's requesting?"

"Acolyte Murtag, NBPD badge number 1099. Criminal background check, one Irvine B. Coughlin, 28 East Ark Avenue, New Nazareth."

"One minute."

The clerk put me on hold. I listened to a recorded sermon on abstinence delivered by The Prophet of New Nazareth: each major metropolis had its own Prophet, instated by the Divine Council.

The clerk clicked on. "Not much to relay. He fell behind on civic tithing seven years ago but has been prompt since his warning. No Reconditioning jolts. A good Follower."

So the killing had been random. After briefly summarizing the crime, I said, "You'll have to send someone round to deliver the news to his next of kin."

"Will do." The clerk's voice maintained its chipper tone. "Give all glory to God."

I rang dispatch and ran a check on the location of the accident report call. The operator scrolled through the daily log and told me it had been placed from a payphone on Pilate Street.

"Kiketown?"

Dispatch affirmed. "Just inside ghetto limits."

When I relayed this to Garvey, he stiffened. "The heebs had something to do with it?" Fat beads of sweat dotted his upper lip. "Isn't Goldberg's shop on Pilate?"

Tibor Goldberg was a snitch who ran a vintage record store in Kiketown.

We motored down the Bakker expressway. The budgie chirped in the backseat; I'd put it in a shoebox with holes punched in the lid.

Garvey mashed the gas and juked in and out of traffic. He thumbed the cap off another bottle of Hallelujah Energy Boost, chugged the yellow goo and hucked the bottle out the window.

"We are gonna lean hard on that filthy snipcock," he said, speaking of Goldberg. "Lean until his ankles snap."

I tried to ease him down. "The call came from Kiketown, but that doesn't mean anyone there had anything to do with it. Could be the perpetrators knew it was going to be logged, and dialled from the ghetto purposefully to throw the dogs off their heels."

"Could be," he said. "Could be the sun god Ra descended in

his golden chariot and dialled the number with one flaming finger. Could be any wacko supposition. That's why we lean on Goldberg and get some answers."

Garvey was only the palest shade shy of totally unhinged—in his current state, he'd peel Goldberg like a banana.

He tuned the radio to RBJC and cranked it. The song was "Less Than Nothing" by Jimmy Saint Kincaid; the station was airing a memorial marathon. He took the first Kiketown exit and badged his way through a ghetto checkpoint.

In the early days of the Republic it was concluded that to eliminate all heathens would be imprudent. It would wipe out a city's workforce. Instead they were to be segregated—*quarantined* was the official nomenclature. Heathen families were allotted a single child and all children were to be indoctrinated into the State Religion. These policies ensured that over a span of generations all impure faiths would cease to exist. *Be eradicated* was the official nomenclature.

The car bounced down a cobbled road, through potholes filled with oily water. The buildings were squat and trollish, clad in a layer of soot that pumped ceaselessly from a solid waste incineration plant nearby.

We pulled up across from Divine Discs. Pilate Street's lone payphone stood directly in front of the store.

Garvey said, "Where's the golden calf?"

I hunted it out of the glove box; Garvey slipped it into his pocket. We headed across the street.

✠

Divine Discs was long and narrow with a high popcorn ceiling. Racks of vintage LPs, carefully organized and labelled, ran down both sides. It was dimly lit with forty-watt bulbs on account of Kiketown's energy restrictions.

The bell jangled as Garvey plowed through the door. The lone customer took one look at us and made a beeline for the exit.

Tibor Goldberg stood behind a glass-topped counter. Tall and handsome in a malnourished sort of way, wearing black except for the red ID band round his left arm.

"Here he is, sitting Shiva." Garvey's tone was more frightening for its mock-sunniness. "Busy collecting your pound of flesh, Goldberg?"

Golberg laughed nervously. "Aboveboard and lawfully, of course."

Garvey tucked his chin and pooched his lips, nodding sarcastically. "An upstanding rat such as yourself, a guy who'd squeal out his own grandma for a few pieces of silver—why would we question your integrity in matters of commerce?"

"Officers, it doesn't have to be like this." Goldberg said. "You want some skinny? That can be arranged. No need to pump me like the town well."

I insinuated myself between them, hoping to keep Garvey's hands at arm's length.

"See that payphone out there?" I said. "At eight forty-seven this morning someone placed a call from it. You need to tell us who."

Goldberg looked confused. "Some guy?" he said hesitantly. "Some phone call?"

I stared him down. "I didn't say some guy, did I? Said some*one*."

Goldberg flushed. "I don't know anything about any call about any crime."

"Who said it was a crime-related call?"

"That's right, Goldie," said Garvey, flipping through a rack of LPs. "Could be the guy was phoning in his winning lottery numbers."

"When's the last time a Jew won the lottery? We can't even buy a ticket. I keep my ear to the ground but my eyes down, you know? Now what I do know is, a family over on Zundel Avenue's got a box full of menorahs—"

Garvey pulled an old record: *The Very Best of Christopher Cross*.

"Mind if I give 'er a listen?"

Garvey centred the LP on the turntable and dropped the

needle. Some guy started to croon about sailing. Garvey snapped his fingers and bobbed his head to the beat . . .

. . . then, with one finger, he started to rotate the disc backward, tortuously slow.

Mmmwwuooubbrooouuueeeeegertuaahhuueeeedddaaaa . . .

"Ah, man," Goldberg whined. "You'll ruin the vinyl."

"Hear that?" Garvey cocked an ear. "It's saying . . ." His eyes went wide. "Deliver your soul to the dark lord Satan."

Goldberg's face fell. "Officer, now wait, there's no way—"

Garvey rotated the disc faster.

Ggggooouuuwwweeeeiiiislllllooouuuugheepher . . .

"Now it's saying . . ."—hissing this through clenched teeth—"heave your grandparents into the roiling lake of fire! You heard that, Murtag?"

"Sorry to say"—I bit my lip to deadpan the delivery—"but yes, I did."

"Selling seditious materials, uh?" Garvey was fired up, his tongue coated in a yellow film of Hallelujah Energy Boost. "Corrupting youthful Followers with subliminal messages—is that your angle?"

Goldberg appealed to me. "Christopher Cross was a devout Baptist. His songs played on easy listening stations."

I tut-tutted: "The devil assumes beguiling guises."

Garvey snapped the record over his knee. Goldberg moaned. I rifled the stacks and picked *East of Midnight* by Gordon Lightfoot, and handed it to Garvey.

"That's a first pressing LP in its original jacket," Goldberg pleaded. "Mike Heffernan on keyboard, Sheree Jeacocke singing backup vocals, produced by the incomparable David Foster . . ."

"Relax." Garvey switched gears, went fatherly. "That other album was an anomaly, right? Your entire shop can't be packed with treasonous propaganda, *can* it?"

Garvey rotated the Lightfoot album slowly, tortuously against the grain.

Hhhuuoooooaaaarrrdddurtaaaassssstttrrreeeeoooiinnnwwwoo owwow-woaaaaii . . .

"You picking up anything?"

I shook my head. Once I saw the relief wash over Goldberg's face, I said, "Wait . . . wait, I hear it now. Coming in clear as a bell. It's saying, *Oh dreidel, dreidel, dreidel, I made it out of clay—*"

Goldberg cradled his head in his hands.

"*Oh dreidel, dreidel, dreidel, now dreidel I shall play.*"

Garvey busted *East of Midnight* into shards. Goldberg yelped.

"So help me, I'll tear this den of sin apart!" Garvey shouted.

"I can ease him off," I said. "Just tell me who you saw."

"If I saw anyone I'd say so," Goldberg grovelled.

Garvey seized a record at random and broke it. A valuable one, judging by Garvey's anguished reaction.

"I don't believe you," I told him. "And until you make me believe, my partner's gonna persist with this bull-in-a-china-shop routine."

"Well, well, well," said Garvey. "What do we have here?"

Now he was displaying the golden calf idol, which he'd discreetly tucked behind a stack of 45s.

"That's not mine," Goldberg said dejectedly.

"I found it in your shop," Garvey went on, "and possession is nine-tenths of the law. Unless this is a tiny little milking cow. Is it a milking cow, Goldie?" Garvey turned the golden calf over, inspecting it. "Jeez, sorry, no teats. So we've got you on intent to distribute seditious materials and possession of a false idol. Enough to send you away for a long time."

Goldberg rested his forehead on the countertop. "If I tell you, can you promise immunity?"

I said, "We'll do our best."

"I don't mean immunity from you," he said. "Immunity from *him*."

"From who?" Garvey wanted to know. "You recognized this guy?"

Goldberg straightened up. "I never seen him before. Or ever want to again."

Garvey looked very interested now. "*Speak*."

"I was opening this morning, at a quarter to nine. This guy shoves past me—couldn't do otherwise, seeing as he was wide as the sidewalk."

I prompted him. "So?"

"So he goes to the callbox. This guy was so huge he couldn't even wedge his shoulders inside. Then before he leaves he opens the callbox door and just stares at me. Marking me, it felt like." Goldberg shivered. "He looked evil. The most vile evil I'd ever seen."

I thought back to the trailer scene. Whoever had perpetrated that did indeed possess a core of perfect evil. "And then?"

"And then he's gone. And now, a few hours later, you guys're here."

"You got a clean look at his face?" When Goldberg nodded, Garvey said, "Lock up. You got a date with our sketch artist."

21 Human Remains

Garvey hightailed it to the stationhouse with Goldberg in the back seat. I led Goldberg down the hallway and through a set of frosted swinging doors, up a flight of stairs past the evidence lockup into an empty room housing a draftsman's table. The artist wasn't around so I shackled Goldberg to the radiator.

"Sit tight, Tibor. You're a heathen in a police station; everyone's armed and nobody will think twice."

Goldberg tipped his chin at the portrait of The Prophet on the wall. "I am rendered paralyzed by his mesmerizing countenance," he said sarcastically.

I left him and put the bird on my desk. It was chirping animatedly in its box. I dug a pack of sunflower seeds out of my desk drawer and dropped a few in for it. Then I took the elevator down to SB2: Sub Basement #2. A cramped corridor led to a pair of swinging galley doors: PATH written on the left hand door; OLOGY on the right.

I shouldered through into a large, antiseptically white room. Meat-locker cold: the chill amplified the intensity of the halogens popping and fritzing above. Storage vaults lined the walls. Red tags detailed their residents: H. GOTCHALL, M, FOLLOWER / B. FALGUNI, F, HEATHEN. The clatter of water pipes made it sound as if the cold corpses were knocking their metal cells in an effort to free themselves.

Newbarr entered, followed by Doe. My heart trip-hammered. I thought back to the last time we'd been alone together, her naked in the moonlight. . . .

"You're both here," said Newbarr. "Marvellous. Let's get down to it, shall we?"

He led us to vaults tagged EVE, F and J. S. KINCAID, M. When he rolled out the slabs there wasn't much to consider: a pair of four-gallon Tupperware containers filled with charred debris, plus a Ziploc bag holding a sizzled lump of fur with the words "Canis—Erasmus" written on the plastic in black Sharpie.

Newbarr acknowledged the slim pickings. "It's basically guesswork. Bits of Kincaid could be mixed up with bits of Eve—even bits of the bomber."

"How did you separate them out?" I said.

Newbarr gestured to Kincaid's container, shrugged, said, "I put the most artistic looking pieces in there?"

Doe barked laughter.

Newbarr pried the plastic lids off. The expelled air smelled like rain-sodden cigarettes. He stirred through the meagre evidence with a speculum, turning over knobs of bone, melted dental bridgework, flame-scored costume jewellery. A diamond crucifix winked in one fire-blackened tooth.

He plucked a slim metal ring from the ash. "Surgical stomach band—one of them had gastric bypass surgery."

I said, "Eve?"

Newbarr shrugged. "Judging by his press photos, Kincaid

wasn't carrying any extra weight."

He rubbed his chin with the speculum. "I haven't been acting coroner on many suicide bombings, but in those cases the bombs were homemade jobs, and badly botched: in the first case the bomb misfired and tore the bomber in half; in the second it exploded early, killing only the bomber's accomplice. But this recent rash has been lethal: hundreds dead, hundreds more critically injured. There's a chilling professionalism to it."

He shut the vaults and opened one tagged JOHN DOE, HEATHEN. Two more containers: one of ashes, another of charred metal balls. Beside them were a pair of steel-toed boots—with a pair of burnt and blackened feet still inside them. Next to them lay a scooped metal plate pitted with tiny bowl-shaped dents.

Newbarr said, "The explosion was baffled by this." He rapped the metal plate. "It ensured the bomber's body and debris were blown forward, toward the crowd. Rebound effect. The blast was so fierce it snapped the ankle bones and tore the lower legs from the feet."

He picked up a boot and displayed the wax-smooth tread. "Melted to the stage. I had to cut them off the boards with a knife."

He rattled the container of balls. "Tungsten. The metal with the highest melting point. Iron or steel would've liquefied. The plate's tungsten, too."

Doe said, "Can you give us a reconstruction?"

Newbarr said: "Give me an intact corpse and I could examine the stomach contents, give an idea of that person's heritage, make presumptions regarding their last seventy-two hours on this earth. Give me a crime scene with blood spatters, a murder weapon, tissue samples, footprints, fingerprints—Lord, *anything*. That's the problem with bombings—the blast erases everything. No trace to work from. Back when we used forensic science, I could've scraped a shred of meat from the boots and gotten a DNA fingerprint. But never mind that. Here's one thing that still confuses me."

Newbarr pointed out a series of burnt discs climbing like ladder rungs up the tungsten plate. "The vertebrae of the bomber's spinal column—they're fused directly to the metal."

I said, "What's so odd about that?"

"If his chest was girded with explosives, it's hard to see how it could occur. The combustion should've scoured every vestige of tissue and bone."

Newbarr grabbed folders from a file cabinet. "I need your John Hancocks on these evidence reports. Eve's remains need to be interred in a state burial, plus Kincaid's manager has been hassling me."

The doctor gave a disgusted snort. "Apparently he's packaging the ashes in crucifix-shaped ampoules for fans to wear round their necks. A sick little piece of Kincaid-iana. He wants the remains pronto, before his client's star goes on the wane."

Before leaving, I handed Newbarr a packet of Hallelujah Energy Boost.

"No, thanks," the coroner said. "I'll stick to rotgut coffee."

"Could you give me a breakdown of the ingredients?"

"Says here it's packed with vitamin V," he said, examining the ingredients archly. "What more proof do you need?"

"If you'd rather not . . ."

"I'll see what I can do. No promises, son."

Doe and I rode the elevator up together. It was the first time we'd been alone since the night I'd said in a roundabout but sincere way that I was in love with her.

She stood very still, watching the elevator buttons light up floor by floor. Shallow incisions radiated from her left eye; I could only speculate as to which of Hollis's subtle tortures had inflicted those.

I said, "You were in Little Baghdad this morning?"

She nodded.

"Everything okay? I thought the residents might have been angry, on account of all the casualties. I . . . I was worried about you."

She performed an ironic curtsy. "Don't you go worrying your pretty head."

A trapdoor opened in my belly. I'd never told a woman I loved her, not once—was this how it worked? You told someone you loved them and they did an abrupt about-face, dismissed you and made cynical quips?

The elevator doors eased open to admit Chief Exeter.

"Acolyte Murtag. The very man I was looking for."

He guided me out into the hallway. Doe slipped past us and was gone.

"The boys giving you a rough go of it?" Exeter set a hand on my shoulder. "No fun being on the outside looking in, is it?"

I resisted the urge to crack him in the mouth and leave him spitting up his pricey enamel crowns.

"I'm fine," I told him, keeping it diplomatic. "Busy."

"Anything I should know about?"

"It's Acolyte business."

Exeter bristled. His veneer slipped. I glimpsed the razor-toothed leer that lurked beneath his empty smile. It struck me there was little difference between Hollis and Exeter: both were wolves. Exeter wore his sheep's clothing more convincingly was all.

"A man on a tightrope should ensure he's got allies on both sides." He gave my shoulder a sly tweak. "Otherwise he risks finding his rope cut one day."

I held his stare. "The Lord is my keeper. There but for the grace of He go I."

"Yes, well . . . you have been summoned."

"By whom?"

"The Prophet."

I couldn't keep the astonishment out of my voice. "Why me?"

The angle of Exeter's cocked head said I was an idiot for asking.

"You were the last servant of the Republic to see Eve alive. I expect he wants to allay any lingering unease in his mind that his daughter's final moments were overtly traumatic."

I wasn't convinced. Men were sometimes invited to hold palaver with The Prophet only to vanish. And it wasn't simply a matter of disappearing—they were retroactively erased from being. Names cleansed from public rolls and clipped from newspaper archives, medical records excised, life histories overwritten, their every vestige wiped out of creation. And it had always worried me, more than the tortures those men most certainly endured or even their unlovely deaths: the prospect of being unborn.

"When?"

"Tomorrow, before High Mass." A sharkish grin from Exeter. "Dress reverentially."

The Prophet. A face-to-face with the conduit of God.

When I returned to the squad room I was met with a skeptical glance from Applewhite, who was eyeballing the composite the sketch artist had sent up.

"You'd better go wake your snitch." He folded the paper in half and handed it to me. "The guy's been dreaming up perps."

The sketch was nightmarish. According to Tibor Goldberg's recounting, the perp had a bald wedge-shaped head like a *V*, nose crushed flat over off-kilter cheekbones, ears like open Buick doors, and a forehead like a grocer's awning, sheltering pisshole-in-the-snow eyes—one of which was completely white: no cornea, no iris. The physical dimensions Goldberg guessed at were absurd: 6' 10"; 420 pounds.

Applewhite groaned. "You expect us to canvass town for the Jolly Green Giant?"

"Goldberg did say the guy was big. *Freakish*, was the term he used."

"That's certainly a freak. Circus left town last month, mind you."

I said, "What about Livingston?"

Applewhite frowned. "Henry Livingston, the Wiccan ringleader?"

"He's massive, isn't he? Mug all screwed up from some nerve disorder?"

Applewhite said, "Gigantism. That was the reason the witches and warlocks followed him: he scared the bejesus out of them."

"Scared—past tense?"

Applewhite nodded. "He's dead, Murtag. Executed. His freak head hacked off."

I considered the other sketch on the board. The Muslim

extremist, as witnessed by the sole survivor of the Up with God Minstrel Show bombing. On a whim, I picked up the phone and dialled Mount St. Mary's Healing Hands Centre. After airing my credentials I was forwarded through to the ICU charge desk.

"How may I help you?" a nurse said.

"The bombing victim from the Up with God Show. He still alive?"

"He is, officer. He was making progress but has suffered a setback. Infection of the lungs. We're praying for him round the clock."

"Is he awake?"

"The poor dear goes in and out. We have our most fervent practitioners sitting at his bedside."

"If I were to stop by, what are my chances of finding him lucid?"

"Who can say? Only God. Prayer is a powerful curative but—"

I hung up on her, irritated. I stuffed the sketch composite into my pocket. Rooting through my desk, I rounded up my set of plastic devil horns and a tube of spirit gum. My phone rang. It was Newbarr.

"I've figured something out," he said.

"Go on."

"I've been working from the theory that the bomber was wearing a dynamite vest or some such. In which case, how was he not spotted?"

"None of this is new information, doc."

"No, but this is: what if the bomber was packed *with* explosive?"

He gave it a second to sink in.

"Those spine fragments set me off," he went on. "They were fused to the metal plate, meaning the explosion had to originate from somewhere inside the spinal column. The human intestinal tract can accommodate seven to ten pounds of foreign material, so long as it is malleable. The stomach can hold roughly five pounds itself."

"So you're saying . . . ?"

"I'm saying C-4 is malleable. I'm saying it is possible for a man to ingest, or be force-fed, five pounds of tungsten ball bearings. He'd be the most uncomfortable man on earth but if he felt his cause was worthy he could put up with the discomfort."

I gaped. "So you think the guy *was* a bomb?"

"And perfectly concealed. Metal detectors wouldn't be able to ping through the skin, fat, and stomach lining."

"What about a detonator?"

"Just a wire and a battery. It would be a simple matter of slipping the wire up his, er, you know what, and triggering the blast."

13 Calling Dr. Satan

My apartment remained a shambles—door blown off, copious smoke damage. So Hollis arranged for me to be put up at the Harbinger's Harbour motel a few blocks from the stationhouse while my landlord made repairs. Doe was here, too. Just down the hall.

My room's window overlooked an alley strung down the rear of the motel. Crucifixes glowed on rooftops on the west side of the city. A lot fewer than usual: dark gaps in the skyline where lit crosses once stood. My gaze trailed down the alley mouth. . . .

Something was spray-painted on the grimy brickwork.

Let Your Sins Go Unpunished.

I'd stopped at a store for a birdcage and a sack of birdfeed. I removed the rescued bird from the shoebox. Its wings were still gummed with blood. I spritzed it with warm water from the tap. It sat docilely in the sink, shaking bloodied water from its wings until it was clean enough to flit around the bathroom. I lined the cage with newspapers. It flew into the cage of its own accord, perching on the swing and chirping happily enough.

I threw myself onto the sprung mattress. Roaches skittered in the wall behind my head.

Angela. I couldn't shake the memory of her in the moonlight: the knife wounds and bullet scars. Couldn't shake the softness of her body or the steely bent of her mind.

I got up. Put on my shoes. Doe's room was down the hall. I found myself lingering outside her door, pacing a strip of balding Astroturf. From inside: voices. It took a moment to parse one from the other: Angela and an unknown male. A needle of ice penetrated my chest.

I rapped on the warped door. The sound of feet padded toward me.

Bisected by the security chain, Doe's face flashed relief.

"What's going on? Something the matter?"

"The matter? No." My left foot twisted nervously into the Astroturf. "It's just, we haven't talked lately except for those few words in the elevator today, so I thought we could—"

"I'm sorry, tonight's no good."

The investigator in me, the habitual snoop and invader of privacy, stole a glance over her shoulder. I caught a long thin shadow cast on the chowder-coloured carpet.

"Got a hot date?"

A voice said: "Who is it, Angela?"

The voice was as glossy as a cultured pearl. It spoke her Christian name. The needle of ice in my heart grew into a tenpenny nail, into a railroad spike—

"It's nobody."

—into a sharpened spear that screwdrivered out of my back and left me gasping.

"Nonsense. Invite him in. I'd love to meet one of your friends."

The room's other occupant stood at the foot of the bed

clocking me with an expression that existed free of overt emotion.

I'd never seen anyone quite like him. Tall and ethereally thin. I found myself looking for the bamboo pole he must've been yoked to, same as a tomato plant.

He said, "Prophet's blessings be upon you, my friend."

"From the Lord's lips to His," I said stiffly. "I can't recall if we've ever met."

The guy was not handsome in a traditional sense but his face was striking in its angularity: it could've been chipped from a block of basalt. He wore boxy sunglasses with wraparound armatures custom-fitted to admit no light.

"I don't imagine we should have," he said. "I am in all respects a law-abiding citizen, so there's no need for our paths to have ever crossed."

I sensed two things immediately. Number one: he was lying. Number two: he was mocking me. Or not mocking *me*, exactly—mocking all I stood for.

"Nice digs, huh?" I said to Doe, purposefully ignoring him. "Hollis went all out."

"We shouldn't have expected any better." She slopped Republic Claret into a motel Dixie cup and slugged it back. Her teeth were stained with the stuff. "See how they treated us today? At least lepers had the option of a colony."

"It'll blow over."

The stranger said: "If you don't mind me asking, how do you feel about your recent treatment?"

I faced the guy head-on, chin tilted at an aggressive angle. "It's got zero to do with you. Acolyte business. And who are you, if you don't mind me asking?"

He took not the slightest offence. "Thomas Swift. Tom, to my friends."

I shook his hand out of custom and immediately wished I hadn't. His bones were clad in the slimmest stretching of skin and his grip mildly predatory: like shaking a bat's wing.

"Where are you from, Swift?"

"Please—call me Tom. I've lived here and there. Most recently

New Beersheba, until that city underwent a massive upheaval."

Very little had been reported regarding the situation in New Beersheba. Apparently there had been an outbreak of civic strife. The Divine Council dispatched a delegation to quell it.

"The Quints?" I said. "Isn't that who was sent?"

Swift nodded. "Heaven's own bagmen."

"And you were given a dispensation to relocate here? You must be well-placed."

He waved my question off and sat on the bed. The way he smoothed his hands over the coverlet raised my hackles: a possessive gesture that spoke to future intimacies.

It was then that I noticed a shape hovering outside the room, behind the filmy curtains. Enormous: it looked as though a maintenance man had wheeled the motel's soda machine in front of the window—an assumption that might have held if not for the subtle rise and fall of those blocklike shoulders.

I turned back to Swift, who regarded me behind his dark glasses. A tear tracked down Swift's face. "Beg pardon," he said. "I'm leaking again."

He eased his glasses onto his forehead. His eyes were of palest blue. His bottom left eyelid was sliced in the dead centre, skin parted in a glistening *V* an inch down his cheek. He wasn't crying. His eye was leaking the ichor of a wound that was never likely to heal.

He dabbed at it with a crusted white handkerchief.

"Years ago, I might have made a fine living." He folded the hankie into a neat square, stimulated the necessary facial muscles to trigger a smile, and clarified: "On the freak-show circuit."

Angela gripped my elbow and guided me toward the door. I didn't want to leave.

"I need to talk to you about—"

"Not tonight," she told me. "I'm busy."

"Busy with what?" I winced at the plaintive note in my voice.

"We'll talk tomorrow, okay?"

I dropped my voice. "How do you even *know* this guy?"

"We're friends. Old friends, that's all."

Swift kept eyeing me—not with malice, but rather the wry curiosity of a man watching a simpleminded zoo creature fumble about an unsuitable habitat.

"I trust you're a gentleman?" I said. "A pure Follower?"

Swift laughed so hard I thought his paper-bag chest was going to explode.

"Pure as the driven snow, Acolyte Murtag."

He eased his sunglasses over his eyes again. Doe shut the door.

I drove streets slick with night rain.

I felt more awful than I could ever recall. Humbled and broken-hearted and moronic. How could I have let that slit-eyed sideshow curiosity rattle me?

My reasoning was idiotic: it had struck me that the man, Swift, ultimately lacked some critical essence of humanity—the essence commonly known as a soul.

Tom Swift. Lately of New Beersheba. I'd be running a background check on that fine fellow right quick.

As I idled at a stop sign not far from Trinity Square, a homeless wreck shambled up and tapped the glass with one frostbitten finger. I unrolled the window and the stink of his mouldy flannels filled my nostrils.

"Spare a shekel so a down-at-his-heel Follower might receive his daily benediction?"

My eyes followed the black stump of his finger to the DBB across the street. I was less than surprised to find five words graffiti-tagged across it:

LET YOUR SINS GO UNPUNISHED.

I dug into my pocket but instead of a crumpled shekel I came up with the sketch composite from earlier today. I tossed the poor shambles a few shekels from my duster pocket and set off for the Healing Hands Centre.

Fifteen minutes later I pulled into the parking lot. The Centre was all steel and glass and calculated angles. Dark at this hour save the odd square of light burning in the upper galleries and a stained glass portrait of Saint Luke, patron saint of physicians, backlit above the revolving entry doors.

The air lacked that antiseptic undertone, everything constantly wiped down and sterilized. Instead the sweet, slightly cloying scent of frankincense. You would find not a single medical instrument—not a thermometer or an enema bag, not saline solution or calamine lotion or baby aspirin—at The Healing Hands Centre. Patients were treated with the power of prayer alone.

I walked down a hallway past speakers piping out madrigals. When I dinged the bell a charge nurse parted a pair of thick purple drapes separating the desk from the ICU ward. Her nametag read: HEAD PRAYER-MASTER.

I informed her that I came with questions of great importance to the Republic to pose to the witness of the Up with God minstrel show bombing. She guided me through the drapes.

A contingent of off-duty Prayer Maids lounged in the break room near a punch clock. Young, female, dressed in diaphanous crimson robes, they were rented out at an hourly rate to offer bedside prayers of succour. The richer you were, the more Maids you could afford. The Healing Hands Centre administered exclusively to males; the Maids' garb was purposefully revealing to ensure a patient's last days in this fleshly realm were palatable. But the Maids were devotees of the Immaculate Mother, quaffers of Purity Purge, and so most of them resembled little more than ambulatory anatomy charts.

The witnesses' room was the last on the left, next to a broom closet. A Maid knelt at the man's bedside.

"Leave us," I told her. "I need to talk to this man alone."

I scanned the clipboard hung off the foot of the bed. Jack Hanratty. Devoted Follower. Sixty-four years old. A retired bookkeeper last employed at a Republic munitions factory.

Hanratty had been hit broadside by the bomb's blast. Snarls of shrapnel were embedded in his skin: any other hospital would have teased them out, but at The Healing Hands Centre it was the Lord's will to expel them . . . or not. The fluids pumped out by his immune system had leaked over the twisted bits of metal, oxidizing them: they'd all gone the fungoid green of coins after a thousand rainstorms.

I closed the door and locked it. Holding fast to the doorknob, I steeled myself against what I'd have to do next. The trick was to convince yourself that you were only doing your duty—acting for the good of the Republic.

I pulled up a stool and hiked back the sheets to expose Hanratty's right foot. Jamming my thumbnail into a wrinkled groove on his big toe, I grasped firmly and applied steady pressure. The toe went white from blood loss. I squeezed so hard that my thumb joint cracked. My nail bit in. Blood squirted.

Hanratty's eyelids fluttered.

"Alice?" he said dazedly. "Alice—that you?"

I wiped my bloody thumb on my trousers and said, "Who is Alice, Jack?"

His eyes achieved a temporal clarity. "Who's asking?"

"Acolyte Murtag. I'm here to ask a few questions."

Hanratty's eyeballs twitched up and down my body. "My wife. I thought . . ." he hacked weakly. ". . . she'd come to visit . . ."

Hanratty shifted and all that shrapnel shifted with him: this tortured grinding, metal squalling against bone as his body struggled to eject all that foreign matter.

When I showed him the police sketch he said, "Yeah, that's the son of a bitch who did it."

"You're sure? Must've been a lot of confusion."

"That's him. Some turbaned fanatic who blew himself up because another cuss told him he'd go to the land of milk and honey to canoodle with virgins if he did."

"Tell me how it happened."

"Already told the other fellows who came round."

"One more time. In light of some new information we've received."

"I'll give you the short version. Get your little notepad out and let's get it ov—"

Hanratty embarked on a prolonged coughing jag that

culminated with him ejecting an oyster of blood-veined phlegm and passing out.

I wiped the mucous off his chest with a Kleenex and thumbed one of his eyelids open: nobody home. I was set to give his toe another tweak when he switched back on just as abruptly as he'd flicked off.

"Who are you?" He cast his eyes about, bedeviled. "Where's the Maid?"

"I've introduced myself . . . sir, we were . . ."—momentarily bedeviled myself—". . . we were just speaking, weren't we?"

Hanratty showed not a whit of comprehension. So far as he was concerned we were meeting for the first time. Evidently Hanratty's brain seemed to have decayed in a very specific way: it appeared he couldn't remember this minute from the last. Otherwise he seemed pretty lucid. This was bad for him. But it was good for my interrogation.

"Who the devil are you?" he asked again.

I made it up on the fly: "I'm with the Centre. A Maid's assistant. I'm going to ask you a few questions, some of a personal nature if that's alright, so the Maids might incorporate them into prayers on your behalf."

"Anything that might help. Lord knows I can use it."

I flipped to a bare notepad page and took down pertinent details. Middle name: Olen. Children: Ellen and Franklin. Childhood pet: a beagle-hound cross named Bandit.

There was an old scar on his right knee; I asked how he'd gotten it.

"You think that's important?"

"We believe in being thorough here."

"I was splitting logs for the woodstove. Axe stroke." He made a feeble chopping motion with his hand.

"This last question is a tough one. The information stays confidential; only me and your Maid will ever know. Mr. Hanratty, tell me the worst mortal sin you ever committed."

The old guy looked at me a long time. "What's the use of that?"

"The Maid needs to know the offence to offer up a prayer of

absolute penitence. To be honest, nothing else is working."

Hanratty sucked his teeth and said, "Water."

I grabbed the plastic jug beside the bed and guided the straw to his lips. He finished drinking and flopped back onto the pillows, staring up at the ceiling slideshow: bugling angels and sunlight spearing through dark clouds.

"My wife and I married young: me twenty, she eighteen. You've never seen a prettier bride; my heart nearly burst at the sight of her coming down the aisle." His hand bunched up the sheets. "But there are things you can't ask from a wife. But not being able to ask doesn't mean you don't still crave."

He turned his face away and spoke to the wall. "There's a stretch near Preacher's Row where you can buy, rent—*have* a woman for an hour. I didn't know her name and didn't want to. I wanted . . . only flesh. She took me to her place. I remember the wallpaper, these shiny bumps in a wacky pattern . . . then one of the bumps skittered up the wall. A boy sat in the front room. Her son: they had the same red hair. She told him she needed to talk to me about a church bake sale. In the bedroom."

Hanratty's voice went throaty. "I didn't want to see her face so we did it that way. Sad truth was, sometimes I didn't want to see my wife's face. I hated myself for loving it so much. We're in mid-rut and her kid comes in the door. I'm peering into his startled saucer eyes and they're just flaying me bare and I scream, 'Get out, you little bastard! Get the hell out!' and he screams back at me, a tortured yowl like I'm murdering his mother and so she tells him real soft and sweet that she's okay, she's okay, just go wait in the front room, baby. The weirdest part is, I don't know what I feel more shame over: the adultery or the way I screamed at that young boy."

"Thank you for that honesty, Mr. Hanratty."

"Won't be able to look that pretty young Maid in the eye again, now that she'll know that about me." He crossed himself and said, "Get me through this and I swear I'll make amends."

We talked a bit longer. I was only waiting for him to pass out again, which he did after a while. Then I went to work.

I patted my pockets and located the plastic devil horns I'd

pocketed back at the stationhouse. They were an inch long, weathered-looking as deer antlers. I slicked my hair back, applied a blob of spirit gum to each horn, and affixed them to my forehead. Standing on the stool, I pried open the overhead light fixture and unscrewed the bulb so the contact points touched intermittently: the light flickered on and off. I filled a plastic cup with ice then stuck the index finger of my left hand inside it.

All Acolytes were instructed on this interrogation method at the Academy; the course was called *Coercion Through Satanic Threat*. I'd received the highest standing; my instructor said I had a gift for invoking a demonic aspect.

The technique worked best on suspects whose minds were untethered. Hanratty, on death's door and suffering from memory lapse, fit the MO.

A cheap illusion, but if you were a skilled illusionist—if you made a man *believe*—well, it would make him more candid than any Confessional chair.

I waited. Before long Hanratty's eyes trembled. He awoke in Hell. Or this was my hope.

I let him get a clean look at me, a glimpse of the horns—yes, yes, there it was: an expression of mortal fear. This was when I leaned forward and in a soft mocking voice said:

"Jack . . . Olen . . . Hanratty."

"Wh-wh-who are you?"

"I go by many names."

The light fritzed and popped; the room lit up then plunged into darkness. Hanratty gulped. Hanratty's lip quivered. Most crucially, Hanratty *believed*.

Plenty of Acolytes would've blown the illusion by chortling maniacally or something. But restraint was the key. I smiled the most ghastly smile in my arsenal and said, "Hello, *Jack*."

Hanratty's eyes rolled wildly in their sockets. The man was petrified. I felt horrible. This was cruelty beyond measure, perpetrated on a sick man. But he knew things I needed to know.

"What did I do?" he wheezed. "I've led a good life."

"Oh?" Cocking my head. "Do you think you can hide secrets from me? I know everything about you, Jack Olen Hanratty. I know your wife, Alice, and your children, Ellen and Franklin. I even know about your cur of a childhood dog—what was that mongrel's name? Ah, yes: *Bandit*."

If there was a doubt left in Hanratty's fraying mind, I'd erased it. But I needed to go beyond belief to the realm of sheer psychic horror. God help me.

"I know you got this scar . . ." I pulled my finger from the cup I'd kept hidden and ran that ice-cold digit over his knee ". . . chopping wood for the stove."

Hanratty's chest heaved. He was on the verge of hysteria.

"I'm a devoted Follower," he protested. "I've done nothing wrong."

"You are an adulterer. An adulterer and a *whoremonger*."

That took him over the verge. He sobbed uncontrollably, chest hitching as tears rolled down his face.

I said: "The truth is, Jack, Hell is overflowing. Every day sinners pour in from all points of the compass. Men like you are on the borderline: one foot in Hell, the other in . . ."—I spat the word out like a bug I'd swallowed—". . . *Heaven*."

"How? How can I go to Heaven?"

And there it was. The moment of truth.

"A person is currently roasting in Hell for the mortal sin of suicide." I unfolded the sketch and held it up. "This is not that person. You purposefully misidentified the perpetrator and lied under oath about it—didn't you?"

"Yes. . . *yes*."

"The person is—" A calculated guess: "Caucasian."

Hanratty began to nod uncontrollably. "She was white. A beautiful white girl. Blonde hair, wearing a funny old-looking white hat. She couldn't have been more than a teenager."

That took me a moment to absorb. "So the . . . woman was not a Muslim, as you told investigators. Why did you lie?"

Hanratty looked helpless. "Followers . . . we don't *do* that to ourselves."

A predictable wave of exhaustion rocked me: it always did after I'd broken a slew of Commandments to accomplish my ends. Guilt prickled my forehead, a pair of searing white dots where each horn was stuck.

"You are not an evil man, Jack," I said softly. "Your motives were pure. And for your honesty you shall surely go to . . ." Spitting the word out again: "*Heaven*. Now go to sleep."

Not surprisingly, he did just that.

61 The Heaven-sent Hero

I awoke at the Harbinger's Harbour motel. The bedside clock read 10:19 a.m. I was scheduled to meet The Prophet before High Mass.

I showered quickly. The water was ice-cold. I stepped shivering from the stall and towelled off.

I sat on the bed and switched on the Republic News Channel. The anchor had a face like a crumpled paper bag.

"Late last night, a freak fire struck a plant where the wildly popular Hallelujah Energy Boost is packaged," he droned. "The Lord protects The Prophet and his workers; thus, there were no casualties. Faulty wiring was responsible. Followers who have come to rely on The Prophet's patented energy formula, fear not:

to ensure there are no shortages, the base of operations has moved to a temporary facility. Blessed are those who walk with the Lord. Blessed are those who follow His Prophet."

Faulty wiring was how they had decided to spin it, huh? Jesus wept.

The electrified wrought-iron gates at The Prophet's compound swung wide. I piloted the car down the crushed gravel lane, recalling that the last time I'd covered this terrain it was to pick up a spoiled young girl whose remains now resided in a Tupperware bin.

The mansion was majestic. Sunlight gilded the marble colonnades and made them shine like covenant silver. But the courtyard fountain was shut off and the water dotted with bright green algae blooms.

A peacock staggered from the honeysuckle. Its plumage was in tatters, tail feathers snapped so when it fanned them the sight was ghastly, like a broken pinwheel.

A robed servant answered my knock. The foyer shone like a Kruggerand mint: everything was gold-flaked, gold-leafed, gold-dusted. Marble staircases descended from either side of the grand entryway, twining together like snakes. Portraits of The Prophet and Immaculate Mother graced each wall; their eyes met in the dead centre of the foyer.

The servant beckoned me down an arched hallway into a regally appointed room dominated by a mahogany dining table.

I sat on a padded leather chair, fidgeting anxiously with the whalebone buttons of my duster. Footsteps echoed on the polished tiles. The door opened with the softest *click*, and I was in the presence of God's earthly mouthpiece.

"Acolyte Murtag. My blessings be upon you."

It was him. The Bosom of Love. The Heaven-Sent Hero. The Prophet.

I knelt, head bowed. "Humbled in your presence, Your Grace."

"Rise up, my son. Sit."

He was taller than he appeared during sermons—but as my seats were on the second tier of Stadium SuperChurch, I'd never seen him this close. He was dressed in his trademark vanilla sharkskin suit and black spats. He tugged on a pair of latex gloves from a box on the table and took my chin in his hands; tilting my face up to meet his own, he inspected my injuries and with a sigh that turned my insides to hot gelatin.

"You absorbed this trying to protect my daughter?"

Even the whitest of white lies would reduce me to ash. "Some, yes. Others were received as punishment for not protecting her."

He yanked the gloves off. I couldn't help but notice he wiped his fingertips with a clean handkerchief, which he then smoothed across his chair before sitting down.

"Chief Exeter told me about your trials," he said. "Had I known, I would have put a stop to it. But while God's eyes see everything, mine, alas, do not always. I cannot hold you wholly accountable, as sometimes the Lord chooses to pick a rosebud before it blooms. Tell me what happened, my son. Tell me how."

I recounted the evening of the bombing, sparing few details. I finished by saying how the bomber materialized out of nowhere, before anyone understood the threat.

"Eve had no conception of the danger she was in. It was merciful. It was . . . quick."

The Prophet chewed over my story. "The Lord always lived in my daughter's heart, but too seldom was He reflected in her deeds. What happened was perhaps unavoidable and surely part of the divine plan."

The Prophet seemed somehow relieved. The perpetual embarrassments Eve had inflicted upon the Divine Family had come to an abrupt and—if my intuition was correct—not totally unwelcome end.

A pair of robed men entered silently and spread documents on the tabletop. One handed The Prophet the official stamp, which he wiped with one of a seemingly endless supply of linen handkerchiefs before pressing it to an inkpad. It was impossible to help noting how tired he appeared: every one of his fifty-seven years. While I still believed he'd outlive Methuselah and fulfill his own prophesy, he looked ancient right now.

"Heavy is the head that wears the crown," he said with a wan smile. "I will always be thankful to the Lord and the Divine Council for entrusting me with the spiritual health of New Bethlehem, but some days I pine for the open road, the travelling revival show."

The Prophet's rise from the revival circuit to New Bethlehem's highest office had been well documented. Years before the Republican regime he'd toured as a faith healer: he and his wife, Effie—later known as The Immaculate Mother—each driving a van, hauling trailers with the makings to throw up a revival tent. They ministered to the working poor in woebegone burgs and hamlets. The Prophet's sermons were famously soul-quaking. He cut a swath of religious fervour across all the dark and empty spaces of this land, leaving Followers in his wake.

When word leaked he was in the running for the position of Prophet, opposition was strong. The Divine Council's usual choices were ex-priests and monsignors; the idea of a scripture-thumping, brimstone-spouting faith healer taking the reins did not sit well with many. Critics claimed there was a healthy dose of the sideshow barker in him: he was a tin-pan man peddling old-time religion. A shark in a sharkskin suit.

Butchers' daughters and sharecroppers' wives from the out-of-the-way places he'd ministered had even stepped uneasily forward to tender accusations of a fleshly nature against him; some even had sons who bore a striking resemblance to The Prophet. But since paternity sciences had long gone the way of the Episcopalians, nothing was ever proven.

All criticism ceased once The Prophet took office—largely due to the fact the critics themselves ceased to exist. Ruthlessly, all of them were eventually un-born.

The Prophet smiled at me benevolently and produced a teak smoking pipe from his pocket. He filled the bowl with sweet cherry tobacco, tamped it down, affixed a length of surgical rubber tube to the stem and lit up.

"Different times back then. A different life altogether. We'd roll in during the dead of night, nail up crossbeams and drape a tent over them, stake it all down and shake a bucket of sawdust over the muddy earth—come sunrise we were ready to speak the Lord's will. Though it may sound blasphemous, tuning in the Lord is like tuning in a radio station: easier to accomplish in wide open spaces."

He puffed reflectively.

"For a while we toured with a freak show. Dr. Ebenezer Wonderlic's Not-So-Human Oddities. Wonderlic was no doctor; his Christian name was Roger Cornwall. Ex-con, boozer, a five-time loser whose sole talent was in collecting curious specimens: men with congenital deformities and women with congenital idiocies that were so lonely, so shunned, they grasped at the dubious life preserver he tossed."

I had no clue why he was being so candid. A knot of unease locked up my gorge: if he was set to dispose of me, he could say whatever he liked.

"These freaks Cornwall assembled were the most benighted bunch you'd ever seen. He had a flair for monikers. Henrietta the Mule-Faced Woman, Dogboy Jones, Francis Rutledge: Heroin Monster, Pliny the Pinhead. He'd lock Dogboy in a cage and let gawkers toss rotten fruit at him for a buck a throw. Other times he'd have Dogboy caper and jig and gurgle and act the fool. Cornwall understood that all spectators wanted was to feel wholly superior: to understand there was a pecking order and that, despite their having a harelip or a clubfoot or rampant hair loss, in the grand order of things they weren't so bad off. The freaks functioned as a barometer of sorts: they were the lowest, most unlucky and unloved ebb one might descend to. Everyone went home feeling better about themselves because it could be worse, and the proof of that stood before their eyes.

"The mongoloids and mental feebs didn't understand they were being abused. The ones with mangled bodies but working brains—*they* got it. One night Pliny visited me. Pliny's head was no bigger than a grapefruit and his features outsized: squeezed onto that tiny head, they gave him the appearance of a too-big baby. He'd come to me for a Divine remedy. I could lay hands upon Pliny so God might bless His defective creation with the forbearance to accept his imperfect nature, but a cure? Not possible. But I also told him this, which I will tell you now: the Lord hovered around the poor souls of Wonderlic's Not-So-Human Oddities. Never have I felt so strongly the presence of the Lord as I did in those days—His gaze was trained nearby; I needed only direct it my way. And *do* I miss that, my son. That Divine closeness."

Next, the Immaculate Mother breezed in through the half-open door—it was cracked open no more than fifteen inches and it opened not an inch farther with her entry. She wore a violet robe of brocaded satin. Her arms resembled nothing so much as the fetlock bones of a horse skeleton.

"The day's blessings be upon you, Good Father," she said to The Prophet.

"And you, Dear Mother," he replied. "This is the Acolyte who was with Eve on her final night."

She gave me a long, considering glance.

"Your partner," she said. "What is her name . . . ?"

"Doe." I was surprised she'd know anything of her.

"Angela," the Immaculate Mother said. "Angela Doe, yes. Is she . . . alright?"

"Yes," I said. "She's recovered nicely."

The Immaculate Mother looked genuinely relieved. "That's wonderful. So important to see those entrusted with the public's safety are themselves safe."

Servants entered with plates. Olives, green grapes, sliced cantaloupe and apple. I couldn't remember the last time I'd tasted fresh food. The Immaculate Mother did not eat a bite: instead she punctured the fruit with one long fingernail and inhaled its scent. She was following her own dictum to "Taste with one's nose, not one's mouth."

The Prophet bit into a cantaloupe slice and tongued the juice dribbling down his chin. To me he said, "I won't insult your intelligence by rehashing the recent happenings in our fair city. Since, according to Chief Exeter, little progress has been made on securing culprits, the duty now falls to me. I have sat in council with the Lord these past two days and nights, eating naught but bread and drinking naught but lemon water. On the second night God did come to me as a ball of Heavenly light and guided me as to how we shall cure the affliction that has lately plagued our city."

I pushed my plate aside and leaned across the table, straining toward The Prophet as the Man beckoned me do.

"The Lord directed me to enact the second of the seven deadly plagues, my son. He said it is time to set His works in motion."

"When did the Lord say to do so, your Grace?"

"Tonight, my son."

I said: "Who's heading things up?"

"Exeter and Deacon Hollis both. Apart from the pilots and the Chief, it will be an Acolyte-only affair."

"Do it for Eve's sake," the Immaculate Mother said to me.

A tear rolled down her cheek. It was the most patently fake display I'd ever seen. She was like one of those dolls that ejected a crocodile tear when you squished its stomach.

I said, "Will you prophesize its coming?"

"At today's sermon, yes." The Prophet spread his hands to me. "It is God's will, after all. We are merely providing the lightest push."

"You'll advise people to stay indoors and off the street?"

The hue of The Prophet's eyes darkened the way the sky scudded over before a storm.

"That is nothing at all of your concern, Follower Murtag. What I say or do not say is no less than the Lord Himself has instructed."

A servant removed me from their presence soon afterwards.

I was led down the hall in a daze. In the foyer sat The One Child's processional bier; my heart performed a funny little flip-flop at the sight of it.

The bier was an ornate box with royal purple curtains draped down each side. It sat on the tiles, cherub balloons bobbing from the gold-inlaid curtain rods—could The One Child be in there?

The One Child was the greatest mystery and most honored personage in the Republic. No other city boasted anyone quite the same. He or she—the sex of The One Child was unknown; it was deified as a pansexual being—had been born through divine intercession. It lacked a mortal father: its father was *Our Lord and Father*. The Lord had come upon the Immaculate Mother back in the revival show days and sown his flawless seed in her womb. She had woken overcome with hysteria at the painless heat emanating from her belly until the face of the Lord appeared in her morning oatmeal—a manifestation made somehow more reasonable for its curiousness—to assure her it was He who'd planted the seed within her.

The seed had ripened at an unnatural rate and seven months later The One Child entered the world: Republic birthing records indicate it was born at the stroke of midnight on a moonless, starless night. The midwife died during the delivery: an autopsy report showed her eyes had been burned from their sockets and her hands turned into salt.

Nobody had laid eyes upon The One Child since: not The Prophet, not even its own Mother. To look upon The One Child was to behold the face of the Almighty made flesh: a sight beyond any mortal's capacity to bear. Its handlers wore blindfolds at all times and even the highest state dignitaries wore blacked-out glasses in its presence.

A photographer claimed to have snapped a shot of it from the crotch of a tree overlooking The Prophet's compound using a telephoto lens, but when he opened the camera the insides were melted and the film turned to ash. The rogue shutterbug had been executed later that same week.

Eyes downcast, I hurried past the bier. I didn't look back.

Outside, the famished peacock made another tortured rush at me. I held my ground as the starvation-crazed thing pecked my boots, tearing at shreds of the leather flaking off the toes and eating them hungrily.

I reached into my duster pocket for the grapes I'd surreptitiously stashed from The Prophet's table and scattered them on the grass.

The bird ruffled its tail feathers and stared at me with sad, grateful eyes before bending over to eat them.

51 Sermon

I joined the sluggish traffic streaming toward the Stadium SuperChurch. I parked in the St. David section, 1-B, under a light stanchion bearing the Saint's picture. I dodged the crowds gathered round devotional street performers and made my way to the ticket boxes.

"Your ticket has been upgraded," the wicket maiden said. "Check at will-call."

After presenting my ID at the will-call booth I found I'd been upgraded to third row aisle, a mere twenty paces from the stage. The ticket envelope was stamped BY SPECIAL INVITATION OF THE PROPHET.

I was given an invasive pat down before being ushered onto the thick red carpet of the cathedral-level lobby. Men and women I'd seen in the *Wining and Tithing* section of the New Bethlehem Bugler mingled, bowing or receiving bows according to their position.

I grabbed a program and scanned today's sermon: "Wages of Sin, Taxes of Retribution."

1. Prophet's Introduction
2. Funeral Procession for the First Daughter of His Heavenly Mouthpiece The Prophet
3. The Immaculate Mother Addresses Her Devotees
4. The Prophet's Weekly Forecast
5. Collection Baskets
6. Healings (time permitting)
7. The One Child's Song

The SuperChurch rose in sloped tiers like ancient Greek amphitheatres. Each level was barricaded with Plexiglas and loops of razor wire to keep each social strata separate. Every year when tithes were toted, families moved up or down tiers depending on their contribution.

The Prophet's introductory music—Wagner's "Ride of the Valkyries"—boomed over the speaker system. Neon laser-lights wheeled across the dome roof.

"Ladies and gentlemen," the announcer intoned, "devoted Followers, arise for your Heaven-Sent Hero and Bosom of Christly Love . . . The Prophet."

The Prophet emerged from the sacristy, moving across the stage to a glass altar. I saw the sweat glistening on his forehead and the slim microphone friction-taped to the side of his face.

"Harken to me, my children; hear the word of God. Who amongst us cannot say that these past weeks have brought woeful tidings? Seeking answers, I fasted and prayed for three days, eyes cast Heavenward in search of an answer. And lo, the Lord did come to me and His wrathful gaze stripped me to the bone and He delivered a prophecy that froze my soul. He said,

'The Devil has come to New Bethlehem.'"

A low moan rippled through the congregation. An old woman in the front row was so overcome she passed out; she slid bonelessly from her chair swaddled in the folds of her fur coat.

"I speak nothing but the gospel truth, Lord's lips to mine. And when I asked why the Devil has come to New Bethlehem, how he'd come to insinuate himself within the city walls, the Lord did not tell me to blame the crafty Jew or the heathen cow-worshipper or the fanatic who exterminates himself in the name of Allah. The Lord said it was *He* who sent the Devil to New Bethlehem!"

The congregation swooned.

"He did so to test the truly faithful. For while it was written in Jeremiah 15:21 that the Lord shall deliver Followers out of the hand of the wicked and redeem them out of the hand of the terrible, first He must know His people are worthy of redemption. I spoke unto the Lord and asked how we might spot the Devil—what guises will he take? And unto me the Lord saith the Devil's name is Legion, he contains multitudes. Thus, he might be glimpsed in anyone's face: your wife or husband or grandfather or teacher and even your sons or daughters. The great deceiver Satan may live in every one of you; it was your lack of piety that let him in!"

A funereal bagpipe dirge dripped out of the speakers. A pair of swinging doors were flung open and Eve's coffin emerged onto the stadium floor. Eve's face was projected on the big screen: virginal, serene, ringed by a shimmering halo.

"Rise and pay respects to my precious daughter, swept away in the tide of blood that has washed over this city. Eve laid down her life for New Bethlehem, dying for the sins of those gathered under this roof."

A pandemonium of sadness gripped the assembly.

"Eve!" The Prophet lamented. "Sinless Eve, we thank you for your sacrifice, and beckon you: spread your eternal beacon over our besieged city in this, its darkest hour!"

The Prophet took a knee, exhausted, mournful. The

Immaculate Mother exited the sacristy to drape him in a purple robe. The choir sang "Nearer My Lord to Thee."

Next, The Prophet's shoulders hitched and he threw off the robe just as the choir kicked into a rendition of "When the Saints Come Marching In."

At this close vantage I could see his eyes. They were dry as desert stones.

"Eve-*ah*!" he hollered, re-energized by the light of the Lord. "*Praaaaise* you, Eve-*ah*!" He danced on the balls of his feet. "Your death shall not be in vain-*nah*, because the people of this city are set to reform their wicked ways and root out the Devil-*lah*, root out the great scourge Satan-*nah*!"

The stadium exploded into wild cheers and cries of "Hallelujah!"

The Prophet was running in place, high-stepping, knees whapping his chest.

"Now you tell me-*ah*, we gonna run from Satan?"

"*NO!*" the congregation replied.

"Now you tell me-*ah*, we gonna let him take our city-*yah* down the path of Gomorrah?"

"*NO!*"

"Are we gonna make this city pure-*ah*; are we gonna prove to the Lord we are worthy of redemption-*nah*?"

"*YEA!*"

"And are we gonna catch the Devil wherever he lays-*sah*, close our hands round his venom-spouting throat-*tah*, and crush the life outta that fulsome serpent-*tah*?"

"*YEA!*"

"Can I hear a 'God is Great, Amen'?"

"*GOD IS GREAT, AMEN!*"

The Prophet ran a circuit of the stage, fists pumping. Laser lights strobed and danced. A chain of fireworks went off, bathing him in a shower of golden sparks. Eve's coffin had nearly completed its tour of the stadium floor.

"Can I get a 'Praise be to God, Hallelujah Amen'?"

"*PRAISE BE TO GOD, HALLELUJAH AMEN!*"

The coffin passed through the swinging doors unnoticed—

it was as if Eve had been some bombing vaudevillian given a merciless hook. The show went on.

I tuned out the Immaculate Mother's address to her devotees. Same old song and dance: abstinence, denying want, pure body equals pure soul. She ceded the stage to The Prophet, who emerged in a kingly robe.

"Followers, this week's prophecy is grave. Evil has infested our town and made it unclean. We pray to the Lord for answers in this time of need."

We said: "Lord, hear our prayer."

"The Lord saith we shall be visited with a punishing plague because, just as the heathen Pharaoh of old, our hearts have been hardened. The Heavens shall pour forth pestilence; so saith the Lord. We can only pray for respite—so let us pray."

"Lord, hear our prayer."

"And I sat in council with our Lord, and he did repeat unto me Luke 4:23—Physician, heal thyself. He shall help those who help themselves. Whomsoever might spy a man acting in an ungodly manner, defacing city property or conspiring in league with Satan, must alert the authorities. Give us strong men, devout men, to ferret out the disease festering within these city walls. We ask this in the name of the Lord.

"Followers, this is my prophecy," The Prophet went on. "It is immutable. It is the Word of the Lord."

The One Child was borne onstage. Its bier was rigged for sound and it began to sing . . . unearthly, that voice. The One Child's songs were wordless—it had no need for words. Its language was one of evocation: of love, of triumph, of spirit and empathy and hope. Hearing its song, you knew this was no creature of our world. This was a Heaven-sent gift. Undeniable proof that yes, God existed and yes, He cared deeply for his creations.

The One Child's song ended. We filed out of the stadium silently. A hundred thousand shaken shells.

PLAGUE #2 RAIN OF FROGS

That night I waited outside the motel for Garvey. His car slewed up and over the curb. Its bumper sticker read: *I'm Pro-Choice . . . I choose to keep my PANTS UP!*

He hoofed the passenger door open and leaned across the seat.

"How much you charging, sweetheart?"

I slid in and said, "Your soul."

"Awful steep, even for a purty little tulip such as yourself."

He was in an upbeat mood. This, I noted, could be due to his having consumed an enormous quantity of Hallelujah Energy Boost. Empties rattled round the floor. He had that telltale Energy Boost 'stache: gritty yellow crystals clung to the stubble of his upper lip.

The sky was scudding over with a layer of low-lying thunderheads. The perfect night for our sort of devilry. Mother Nature graciously providing camouflage.

Years ago I found myself in conversation with a Jew who'd made his living as a film producer back when Hollywood was still called Hollywood. He told me about a radio show that had provoked mass hysteria when he was a boy. It began with a newscaster stating in a calm stentorian tone that aliens—saucer creatures, he called them—had landed on Earth with the intent to enslave humanity.

Panic had broken out in the streets. Listeners rioted; they ran for the hills. Why? Because people are imminently deceivable. In a masochistic way they *want* to be deceived, so long as the deception proves the existence of an unquantifiable entity they've harboured a longstanding belief in.

Like aliens. Or God.

A razor wire fence ran round the airstrip's perimeter. Garvey nudged the unlocked gate open with the car's bumper and we drove cracked ruts along the airstrip's edge, wheels kicking up bone-coloured dust. The hangars sat like steel tortoises on the alkali flats.

Exeter was tapping his watch as we pulled up. Hollis, Applewhite, Henchel and Brewster, and the rest of the crew were there—and, standing outside the circle of men, arms locked across her chest, was Doe.

"Long night ahead of us," Exeter told us. "We've got somewhere in the neighbourhood of ten tons to get from there"—he pointed at the hangars—"to there"—pointing at the trio of B-17s.

I'd been part of this plan from the jump: I'd laid out waterproof netting over the hangar floors and distributed the plastic pools which were filled with trucked-in swamp water; I'd dumped in the tadpoles and shut the hangar doors. Every week someone had driven out and tossed in a few sacksful of food pellets. Now we'd harvest the fruits of that labour.

We donned hazmat suits and split into teams. Garvey, Doe, Hollis and I got the nearest hangar. When Hollis shouldered the door open we were hit with a wave of swampy stench. Frogs—thousands and thousands of them. They were piled ankle-high. All of them were blind after a lifetime in darkness: their eyes were tiny pearl onions socked into their faces.

Our task was to cart chains to the far end of the hangar and hook them to the net-grommets; the opposite ends would be rigged to the hitch of a flatbed driven by Doe. The frogs would then be winched into the B-17's payload bay *en masse*.

We forged into the hangar with loops of heavy-gauge chain over our shoulders. My hazmat suit didn't come with an air purifier; the stink was a full-bore punch in the face. Most of the toads were alive but some were long dead; their rotted carcasses blended with waterlogged food pellets and algae-scummed brine and roughly five tons of decaying frog dung to create a nauseating stench.

Progress was slow through the quivering, squishy swampland. Frogs bounced off every part of me with sloppy smacks. A dozen species: huge horned toads and warty carbuncled ones, plus hundreds of small red-eyed frogs. I spotted a massive blind bullfrog with the rump of a small blue-bellied frog poking out of its mouth. The small one's legs were still kicking.

I reached the net's end, hooked the chain through the eyelet. Hollis's face glowed with wry good humour behind his face-shield.

"Aren't we forgetting something?"

"What's that?"

He pointed upward. My eyes trailed up into the cavernous blackness just as Hollis hit the hangar wall with the sledgehammer he was carrying. The vibration caused all the sucker-toed frogs clinging to the ceiling to tumble down: thousands of fat, squirming teardrops.

I backpedalled madly and, as luck would have it, I trod on a plump toad that burst underfoot with a busted-accordion wheeze. I righted myself and stared hostilely at Hollis, who just laughed.

Doe set the flatbed in gear, goosed the gas, and the net doubled upon itself: this massive green omelette folding over.

Hundreds of throat bladders burst like tiny wet balloons. Doe jerked the flatbed and this sudden pressure squeezed frogs through the bonded nylon—a sight reminiscent of cooked potatoes sent through a masher.

"Ease up!" Hollis called to her. "You're slashing the poor darlings to rags."

We transferred the chains to the winch and hauled the huge sack onto the plane. The teams reconvened beside a recently arrived van bearing the pilots. Three middle-aged men, ex-commercial airline pilots by trade. They looked jumpy in their clean shirts and trousers, ringed by Acolytes in flesh-splattered hazmat suits.

"Listen up," Exeter said. "Windy tonight; decent vectors but it's a tiny window. We're aiming for the city's densest population centres. We'll be going up four-and-a-half thousand feet and looping over the Badlands to slingshot in from the north. Engine power halved once we hit fifty furlongs from the city—fly over silent as death."

Three B-17 Flying Fortresses lifted off from an alkali-whitened runway shortly after ten o'clock. Their payloads held roughly ten tons of toad meat.

The plane banked west over the Badlands. My ears felt clogged with wet cotton batten. I worked my jaw until they popped. Wind shear and whining rotors and the crazed croaking of toads were the only sounds.

Doe joined me where I sat against the fore bulkhead. I kept quiet. She hugged her knees to her chest—the cabin was cooling as we gained altitude.

The plane pitched with turbulence, throwing Doe against me. She lay there an instant before righting herself. The shape of her body lingered on my flesh the way the sun's imprint kept burning at the back of your retinas even after you'd looked away.

Garvey and Hollis emerged from the cockpit. Hollis tossed us harnesses.

"Strap yourself in. Pilot says it's bound to be a mite gusty."

We clipped our harnesses to steel rods down in the payload well. Garvey and Doe on one side, Hollis and me on the other.

The toads were quiet: something about the altitude must have narcotized them. A lot of them were frozen stiff, coated in a fine crystal frost.

The engines cut short as the pilot switched to phantom power. The cabin and wing lights blinked off and the ramp lowered. Below us lay an undulating, crested darkness: the topside of night clouds.

The cover broke and there was New Bethlehem. The power grid demarcated the haves and have-nots: the SuperChurch a magnified white ball, whereas light ranged from fitful to nonexistent in the ghettos.

The pilot opened the fore vents. A high-altitude wind blew ice pellets up the gangway. Wind shear robbed the breath from my lungs.

Hollis gripped my shoulders. "Come, my young prince of New Bethlehem!" The man was grinning like a satyr. "We've got a plague to unleash!"

I hacked at the net with a box cutter until a flap of netting gave way. A clump of half-frozen toads lifted free and smashed into my face. I stumbled as toads bounced off the bulkhead, broke apart, and were gone.

The net came loose as the top portion of the green, lopsided, flesh-boulder of toads—frozen, suffocated, some fitfully alive—was released into the star-salted sky. However, the bottom portion remained stuck to the frozen gangplank.

"God rot these filthy things!" Hollis roared, kicking the chilled toads with his brogans.

We all rucked in, booting at the frozen frogs. Doe's foot broke through into its clammy core and she jerked back, revolted. The cabin was dark and the wind howled and ice pellets ricocheted off the hull. A tiny frog fell from overhead—the wind must've blown it up there—and wriggled down the collar of my suit.

For a moment we stopped and stared at one other, sweaty and panting and high on adrenaline, grinning like school kids who'd just flushed a cherry bomb down the toilet. There was something murderously, hideously *fun* about all of this. Our band of merry pranksters were the only ones in on the joke.

The frogs loosened from the gangplank and slid in a solid block, down the loading ramp. What looked to be another blackout was only the plate as it fell through the night, breaking apart and disseminating, and as it did the city lights shone once again.

Back on terra firma the mood was jubilant.

The other two planes had already landed by the time ours taxied in. An oil-drum fire stoked with hazmat suits raged; bottles of RC circulated round the flames.

We tossed our suits on the fire and swigged from the passing bottles. A few lucky toads croaked amidst the B-17's landing gear. Hollis threw an arm around Daniel Applewhite's shoulder and in a rich Scots brogue sang, "Oooh, Danny boy, the pipes, the pipes are cah-hah-liiiing, from glen to glen and doon the moon-tayn-saaayde. . . ."

Amidst the backslaps and laughter, borne on a soft breeze over the Badlands and drumlins south of here, from the direction of the city, came the wail of sirens.

The pilots were thanked for their service and escorted to their van. I noted the rear windows were smoked out. I also noted the glance that passed between Exeter and Hollis before Exeter gave the slightest of nods and stepped into the van behind them.

The pistol shots were not especially loud. Could be the van had been padded for that very extenuation. The windows lit up: three flashes in quick succession, followed by two more. The van rocked on its axles. Something thumped against the frame.

This evening's events must be kept secret. And the most effective way to keep any secret was to cull the number of ears it had been whispered into.

Exeter exited the van. His waxen face displayed not even a vestigial hint of emotion. He summoned Henchel, wiped away the blood speckling his lips and said: "They'll need burying. They were good Followers and deserve proper regard."

Exeter retrieved a pair of shovels from his car and singled out Doe and me.

"You two. Get digging."

We accepted this as further penance and found a patch of soft soil. Applewhite rigged the planes with C4. Hangars were splashed with kerosene. The site was sanitized.

Garvey deposited the pilots beside us. Once the grave was dug we hauled them in by their ankles. Garvey was less than approving.

"You call yourselves grave diggers? I wouldn't bury my canary in that marble pit."

We dug deeper. The pilots went in. Dirt went over. We drove back to the city.

Bedlam reigned in New Bethlehem.

The cacophony of sirens intensified so that by the time we'd reached the outskirts my head was throbbing.

The main road was blocked. Temporary quarantine, we were told by a whey-faced plainclothesman. Garvey flashed his badge and we passed into the downtown core.

The city was in ruins. Toads, like most living things, were seventy percent water: they'd frozen solid during their long free-fall.

A convertible had smashed through the plate glass window of an upscale boutique due to a frog that had torn through the cloth roof, splattering the driver's skull over the steering wheel. Mannequins in sequined dresses were crushed over the hood at paralytic angles. The accident scene was so elegant in its gruesomeness and so static in appearance that it put me in mind of a museum exhibit.

Garvey butted over the curb to avoid the ruins of a hotdog cart—the proprietor's body battered and lifeless—and veered into a Puritan's Pantry. The shop's smashed windows were not the work of frogs but rather a band of opportunistic looters.

Garvey fired a few shots in the air; the looters fled with pockets full of ice cream bars and pretzels and Hallelujah Energy Boost.

We drove past Little Baghdad. The power grid was shut off. The occasional shot rang out while shapes dashed frantically in the streets. An ambulance was speeding the wrong way down a one-way street only to be clipped by a fire engine that hurtled out of a blind intersection. The ambulance spun on its axles, flipped onto its side, and careened into a bus shelter.

Badging through another roadblock, we hit an undamaged stretch. The toads had fallen unevenly: some blocks devastated, others untouched. Followers knelt on the sidewalks, wailing, hands clasped in prayer.

The Harbinger's Harbour motel was unscathed. God's hand at work.

Back in my motel room, the blue budgie flitted in its cage. I opened the cage door so it could fly freely. I stripped for a quick cold shower. Afterward, I flicked on the TV.

The news was predictable. God's wrath had descended, as prophesied by His mouthpiece. Death toll in the hundreds and mounting. The Prophet, Immaculate Mother, and their compound was left unscathed by the Lord. Blessed are those who tread meekly before God. Blessed are those who follow his Prophet.

My attention was drawn to the shirt I'd worn tonight, draped over a plastic chair beside the door. A small head poked out of the breast pocket.

The frog was no bigger than a sand dollar, green with red suction-cup toes. It sat deathly still in my palm, sides heaving like a tiny bellows.

I filled the bathtub with an inch of water. The budgie flew into the bathroom and perched on my shoulder. I was feeling a bit like Noah.

The frog hopped off my palm and paddled circles around the drain plug. I was reasonably certain it would survive.

By the time dawn arrived, the city's air would reek of its rotting brethren.

Article III:
Aftermath

21 Hallelujah

Normalcy—or the curious status quo we had come to equate with normalcy—was restored in New Bethlehem.

Toads dropped. Bombings stopped.

Toads fell from the sky. Civil strife ended. The citizenry was properly penitent. The Prophet's word and rule of the Republic was once again unquestioned.

There remained, however, the ticklish chore of disposing of the toads. As with a great many inspired if feckless plans, it had been designed to achieve instant impact with precious little attention paid to the aftermath.

In this case, ton upon ton of putrefying toad meat.

The frogs were scooped up, scraped off, hosed away,

disentangled from whatever organic matter they'd knit with, and disposed of in heavy-duty sacks dispersed free of charge. Sanitation crews compacted and burned them at the Jewtown incineration plant.

Despite a city-wide cleanup effort, the smell lingered. Amphibians exuded sundry slimes and ichors that, regardless how much hosing or scrubbing was done, impregnated whatever surface they splattered across. The city experienced an unseasonable hot spell a week after the drop; the air was nearly unbreathable.

Death toll: 1,438 Followers. Nobody of importance, although a Deputy Deacon was killed when a toad crashed through his skylight while he was enjoying a bubble bath—an excessive and vaguely feminine luxury that, it was whispered in rectory chambers, had been the cause of his freakish demise.

My apartment was repaired. I bade farewell to the Harbinger Harbour and moved back in with my bird and frog.

I'd never had pets. Ours was a society where animals were commonly viewed in terms of sacrificial value. But these ones had bucked the odds. I felt compelled to make their remaining days enjoyable.

They made fine companions. They had no opinions of their own, or not that they could express. I liked that. I set the bird's cage and the frog's aquarium in front of the window before leaving so they could soak in the sunlight.

That was life for a while. Me. The bird. The frog.

It wasn't much. It was . . . it was just nice.

During the apartment repairs some mistrustful soul had bugged my telephone: the telltale *tica-tica* overlapping the dial tone told me so. Couldn't say I was surprised: the Manger bombing would make me an object of casual suspicion the rest of my career.

As I contemplated the irony of bugging a phone that rarely rang, Doc Newbarr called.

"It's about those tests you wanted me to run—"

I cut him off. "Nice night, isn't it? Meet me for a walk?"

We convened at an all-night bakery. I sprung for coffees and a bag of sweet rolls.

Newbarr said, "Why the cloak and dagger?" When I explained he nodded and said, "Never going to live that down, son."

We huddled in the doorway of a condemned apartment complex. He handed me a printout: the component breakdown of Hallelujah Energy Boost.

"Most of it's worthless," he said. "That's to say, nothing about Hallelujah Energy Boost is beneficial to the human body. Sugar and corn starch, mostly. Empty calories. Trace amounts of vermin feces . . . sadly, that's the most nutritious part. Finding the one outstanding ingredient required a bit of guesswork. I saw the way your partner Garvey slurps the stuff down. He's not the only one—half the stationhouse is hooked. I scanned for addictive substances in powder form. Codeine. No. Methadone. No. Cocaine. Nope. Heroin. Nada. Then I tried this little beauty."

He pointed out a chemical string: C10H15N.

Doc said, "Methamphetamine."

"Garvey's hooked on this garbage," I said. "He'll be okay?"

"So long as the supply continues. I consulted an old pharmaceutical guide; my guess is it's a derivation of Desoxyn, once administered to patients suffering from extreme obesity."

"And if the supply runs short?"

"He'll be clawing the walls along with everyone else in the precinct."

"You think The Prophet's ever taken a slug of it?"

Doc smiled sadly. "You figure Hitler popped his head in a gas chamber just to check if it worked?

My body healed over time. Hollis's cattle prod left dime-sized scars all over my torso. I carried a lot of them—scars. Never did get a fake tooth to replace the one he'd knocked out, either: I didn't mind the way the gap made me look. A little hardened.

A month went by. The citizenry of New Bethlehem settled into complacency. Things went back to the way they were—the way they'd always been.

Until one day they weren't.

81 School Bus

Mount Galilee elementary school gymnasium. Five hundred school kids sat on the polished hardwood floor, eyes oriented on the stage. On one wall, a mural depicted the crucifixion of Jesus on the mount of Golgotha. On the other: a humorous mural portraying Charles Darwin, his features rendered in simian fashion, locked in a cage with a bunch of gorillas.

I stood backstage while the headliner worked the crowd. The Rappin' Disciple was his name. He wore a rhinestone-bedazzled robe, long mane of hair, a big four-finger ring like a knuckle-duster in the shape of a Cross.

"What is it we all want?" The Rappin' Disciple's arms went punch-punch. "We want to live *authentic lives*! We got to find redemption! And let me tell you, gang, even at your ages, you've sinned. Oh, yes!"

Punch-punch went The Rappin' Disciple's robed arms.

"You eat too many sugary snacks—and that's a *sin*, my young brothers and sisters; the sin of *gluttony*! You loaf inside when God's shining His sunlight all over the world, playing your video games"—The Rappin' Disciple pronounced video as *videar*—"and it's my duty to tell you, that's the sin of *sloth*!"

His voice grew fatherly: "But hey, that's fine, that's fine as cherry wine in moderation. Because I was once like you, boys and girls: a *sinner*. I used to stay up all night staring bug-eyed at the TV until I was thinking more of Mario than I was of Mary Magdalene! But now I love my God and my Prophet more than ever—and love is *obedience*, little Followers and Follower-ettes!"

He broke into a rap song. Strutting around, arms going punchy-punch-punch, rhinestones flashing. I gave him points for rhyming "frankincense" with "abstinence." When he ceded the stage, I stepped behind the dais and cleared my throat.

"Prophet's blessings, everyone."

Five hundred well-trained mouths replied, "From the Lord's lips to his."

I was here as part of a Republic-sponsored community outreach initiative whose aim was to warn children about potential Faith Code infractions happening in their own households. The program worked in partnership with the Ministry of Eugenics and Social Stratification, a two-pronged attack to weed out seditious traitors and preach the dangers of cross-pollination with mongrel races.

On a folding table sat an array of banned artifacts. The teachers and children *oohed* and *aahed* as I'd produced them.

I picked up a yarmulke and asked, "Does anyone know what this is called?"

Scanning the assembly, I saw coffee-skinned kids, twenty or so Asians, even a few red Indians. Ghetto children were permitted to attend Republic schools—education being the first step to eradicating bastard faiths.

I spotted a girl in the front whose nametag read *Alona Cohen*.

"Alona, have your parents or grandparents ever worn the yarmulke?"

"My grandparents are dead," she squeaked.

I picked up a menorah. "How about lighting candles in this?"

Alona tucked her chin to her chest and shook her head vigorously. "We don't have those in our house. They're bad things."

"Look at me when I'm speaking, please."

She lifted her head obediently.

"Now, Alona dear," I said, "you would tell me if you'd seen these items before, wouldn't you?"

She sniffed. "Uh-huh."

"You do understand your duty to the Republic, don't you? What is it, Alona?"

"Te . . . te . . . te . . ." Alona blubbered before choking up.

"It's okay, Alona," I said, softening, unwilling to reduce her to tears.

The principal rallied the assembly with, "Come on, guys, what do we do when we see a faith crime being committed?"

"*TELL!*" the assembly chorused.

"That's right," I said. "Tell a fellow Follower. Call the anonymous heathen tip line. Or you're welcome to come down to my office and tell *me*, okay?"

The kids were elated at this personal invite. Imagine walking into Acolyte headquarters with a hot tip! Most of these boys probably daydreamed about becoming Acolytes.

"Remember, the people committing these crimes are sick. They may not seem sick, but they're very sick up here." I tapped my skull. "If someone was sick and could be cured, you'd want to help them, wouldn't you? That's all we do: take them away and fix them. Once they're fixed, they come home. Good as new." A confiding wink. "Better."

The presentation continued. I showed off a Scientologist's E-meter. I produced copies of the Koran, the Gita, and the Torah, all of which I set fire to in a trash can. I torched a copy of Darwin's evolutionary chart, which had been soaked in creosote to help it burn more cinematically.

"Any questions?"

Only one hand went up.

"Yes, you. Speak."

The boy didn't look particularly well. His skin was the colour of pot roast forgotten in the back of a fridge; balls of sweat ran down his neck, soaking into his parochial vest.

"You were here last year," he said. "A few weeks after, I found one of the books you talked about in my Dad's closet. You said people could be sick and not show it and my Dad sure seemed that way—he wasn't talking to me or Mom much. He was calling in sick to work a lot."

The boy tapped his forehead, just as I'd done.

"But maybe he was sick up here. So I phoned the tip line. They came and took Dad away."

"That was the right thing to do," I said.

"You said he'd be cured," he said. "But they brought him home in a wheelchair and his hair had gone all white and he couldn't speak anymore. He just sat by the window and watched the snow. One night Mom shook him and shook him and she was screaming so loud that our neighbour made a call and they took Dad *and* Mom away."

Had we been in private, just the boy and I, perhaps I'd've spoken about my own mother: not to allay his guilt at an act he could've felt tricked into doing—tricked into by *me*—but only so he'd know he was not alone. But to say so here and now, publicly, in my role as an ambassador of the Republic?—I couldn't.

"Do you believe The Prophet would let that happen unless your parents deserved it?"

The boy shifted on his rump and winced. "It was just a *book*."

A shocked gasp rippled through the assembly. I raised my hand for silence.

"Just a book? By that argument, son, the serpent in the Garden was only a serpent. A book is never just a book. Do you think we can simply allow people to go around reading whatever they choose? There is no God but God, and The Prophet is his mouthpiece."

The bell rang. Assembly dismissed.

Ten minutes later I stood in the school's quadrangle doling out cheap plastic badges: shiny silver, APPRENTICE ACOLYTE stamped on the foil plating. After receiving their badges the children shouldered their book bags and made for the yellow busses in the parking lot. The grey-faced boy had left the gym as soon as the bell rang. I kept an eye out for him, thinking perhaps we could talk.

The principal approached across grass gone brown from lack of watering. She wore the same grey her students did—heavy steel-grey dress and cable-knit sweater, a pewter cross pinned over her heart.

"Tough crowd, huh?"

"I was looking for the boy with the missing parents," I told her.

"Jeremiah. He rides a bus, but I couldn't tell you which one. Shall I check?"

"That's fine," I said, unsure of what I might say should Jeremiah be summoned.

A storm was homing in from the east. The sky darkened in stages, waves of blackness rolling over it like a filthy shade drawn over the day.

"He's in a home," the principal told me. "After his parents were taken. A charity home, but a respectable one. Children are so very resilient."

"You should go inside," I told her. "Catch your death out here in the rain."

My eyes rose over her shoulder to watch the busses filing out of the school lot. Their windows were open and the sound of laughter and shrill catcalls drifted across the quadrangle.

In the final bus I spotted Jeremiah. He was kneeling on his seat, staring out the window at me.

"If you'd like," the principal said, "I could find the address of Jeremiah's home. . . ."

The boy knelt on the bus seat, face set in an expression far too resolute for his age. He wasn't wearing a plastic badge. He waved to me. The bus was pulling away, picking up speed. Jeremiah clutched something in his free hand; I squinted, trying to make it out.

Jesus Christ.

I sprinted toward the departing busses. Jeremiah now stood at the back of the bus, one hand balanced on the emergency door catch. Still waving.

The bus swayed as it picked up speed. My feet flashed over the sidewalk as I waved back to Jeremiah: *It's okay, son, whatever you're going through, whatever hardships you're experiencing, God is always with you. You know that, don't you?*

He raised his other hand. A twist of DET cord snaked from his pallid grey sleeve. That tiny red button. His belly was swollen from swallowing ball bearings. His face ashen from all the poisonous C4 stuffed inside him.

The bus gained ground. The children laughed and hollered. The explosion tore the air apart. A ball of polar whiteness expanded from the boy's chest and the crumpling blast was so loud, hitting sonic registers beyond my capacity to bear, that I heard nothing at all: blank ongoing silence punctuated by the throb of my heart in my eardrums.

The windows blew outwards, glass fused into molten blobs as the roof curled back in a rip curl like the lid pried off a sardine tin. A superheated fist knocked me off my feet. A pocket Bible pelted through the air and glanced off my forehead.

I dragged myself up and staggered after the bus, by now nothing more than a fire-scored shell on flaming wheels wobbling out onto the road past the other busses who'd bumped over the curb to avoid it and on through an intersection where students waited—older ones wearing reflective orange sashes in their role as crossing guards—the blackened carapace rolling past their shock-filled faces, flames spitting from its empty window sockets, shedding crisped seats and flame-shrivelled shapes.

Traffic stood at a standstill, drivers riveted behind their wheels while this horror show lurched past their windshields and into a manicured garden beyond the intersection, crashing through a waist-high wrought iron fence to strike a statue of the Immaculate Mother.

By the time I arrived, a few motorists stood, shell-shocked, around the flaming wreck. A man made a useless attempt to douse the flames with a water bottle, droplets spitting off the bus's white-hot flanks. Another woman had a blanket, as if she hoped to wrap a shivering survivor in it. The scorched skeletons of the children not vapourized outright sat heat-fused to their seats in positions they'd held when the bomb burst: some sitting straight, others blackly frozen in the midst of horseplay. Flames licked from the domes of their charred skulls and I thought, awfully, of Vespers candles.

The witnesses looked at me, the agent of civic peace, as though I might be able to fix things. What could I possibly do? I had no magic to bring these children back. What could I say—*Disperse, people, nothing to see here*? There was *everything* to see here.

So we stood there, us good Followers of New Bethlehem, round the flaming hulk of a school bus in the driving rain. The Immaculate Mother's arm outstretched, an oxidized copper dove cradled in her palm—and hooked over the statue's arm was another: a severed child's arm that hung like a shrivelled black boomerang.

Another explosion ripped the air, the sound of roof beams snapped between giant hands. Shielding my eyes from the rain, I saw a building tumble through the sky less than a block east. Dust clouds puffed, forming a gauzy cocoon that the building collapsed into, straight down, as if a gallows trapdoor had sprung beneath it.

Blasts rocked other city sectors like distant artillery fire. Everything was falling down; everything was breaking apart.

61 Chaos Theory

Eleven explosions would rock the city that afternoon.

The targets shared no obvious commonalities. The school bus and the building nearby—which had been a condemned fireworks factory, of all things. The midtown Ecclesiastical Library. A municipal bus. A downtown fitness club. A raw sewage treatment plant in Little Baghdad. The technical wing of Trinity Divinity College.

Eleven explosions. No trace of connectivity. Some explosions took not a single soul; others took dozens. Final death toll stood at 179 Followers. Nobody saw or claimed to remember anything—faces, voices, names. Eleven roads leading nowhere.

The Immaculate Mother was kidnapped that same afternoon.

Every week she had her nails done at Zoila's Salon in Jewtown. She was driven to the salon in a bulletproof town car accompanied by a pair of armed guards.

The guards' distress signal came at 3:13 p.m. When the officers arrived in the alleyway behind Zoila's Salon they found the chauffeur and guards dead, shot in the face. The guards' gun-arms had been broken, bones punched through the skin; they looked to have been manhandled by an incensed gorilla.

The Immaculate Mother had managed to trigger the car's automatic locks but her kidnappers cut through the door with a plasma torch. Officers found the empty car with the motor running, seat still warm where the Immaculate Mother had sat. Her abductors had not made contact. No ransom note. No concrete proof she was even alive. The Prophet released a tersely worded statement exhorting the kidnappers to seek the Lord and return their captive unmolested.

New Bethlehem had become a killing jar. Not a single hole was punched in its lid.

The day following the explosions saw me bedridden.

My decision to chase after the bus earned a heap of injuries. Shoulder dislocated by the blowback and resultant fall. A deep purple bruise radiated halfway down my arm and across my chest. Also, I must've been weeping when the boy detonated: the tears boiled away in the blast and left me with thin inch-long scars under each eye. I looked a little like a sad clown.

Hollis called that afternoon.

"Holding the fort alright, lad? Heard you were scraped up."

"I'll be in tomorrow."

"Don't bother. Until further notice, all Acolytes are on

their own reconnaissance. Us all gathered under one roof is an invitation to the loons," he said. "If you've any leads, follow them on your own. At such time that one of them blossoms into a traceable thread, we'll reconvene the unit. Contact the others privately if you wish."

I hung up and lay on the sofa dabbing aloe vera lotion on my blisters. The bird twittered in its cage. The frog hung upside-down from the aquarium screen. I closed my eyes but all I saw was that white ball expanding from Jeremiah's chest. Someone had convinced the boy to press the button. Someone had orchestrated it. That same someone was surely behind the Immaculate Mother's abduction, which had likely been the end goal all along. The explosions were only a distraction.

✠

The next morning I headed to the Municipal Hall of Records.

The sky was purpled like the bruises ringing a hanged man's throat. The streets were deserted. Closed signs hung in store windows.

I'd never set foot in the Hall of Records. That such a small building could house the archived historical records of New Bethlehem and select sources from other Republican cities seemed absurd until you considered how much had been censured, doctored, or burned over the years.

The matronly clerk's hair was arranged into a bun that pulled each follicle tight as a guitar string. She had the emasculating glare specific to librarians and museum curators and those whose orderly systems were continually under assault from a slovenly public.

"May I help you?"

She was not much impressed when I showed my badge.

I said: "I need to look over any records you have coming out of New Beersheba."

"And why's that?"

"Official investigation, ma'am."

I was led to a staircase that spiralled down two stories before exiting into a catacomb-like hallway. The air was bone dry. We arrived at a steel door, which the clerk unlocked with one of two dozen keys on a ring hitched to her waist. Beyond the door was a cramped room housing a microfiche reader and a single unpadded chair.

"Sit," she ordered.

She set a slim padded sleeve in front of me. "We haven't received anything else from New Beersheba in over a year."

Once I'd managed to manoeuvre the slides onto the reader, it became apparent there was little to be gleaned. The New Beersheba newspaper had been subjected to the customary censures: the local censor blacked out anything deemed inappropriate for out-of-city viewers, the New Bethlehem censor blacked out anything deemed inappropriate for local residents, and an official Republican censor waved his pen over whatever else might cause strife. Entire lines had been erased. I riffled through a months' worth of papers and found nothing. They stopped on July 24th of last year; the final weeks were so heavily blacked out I couldn't help but wonder, *What the hell had happened in New Beersheba?*

The record keeper returned. Her eyes fell to my notebook, lying open next to the microfiche reader. Different spellings of the same name were written in block letters:

TOM SWIFT, THOM SWIFT, TOM SWYFT.

"That's who you're searching for?"

"You know him?" I said, surprised.

"He's not anyone you can really know. I can find him for you, though."

My hand shot out, fingers tightening on her wrist. "You know where he is?"

"You're . . . you're hurting me."

I eased off. Massaging her wrist, she said, "Follow me."

She led me to a set of stairs that terminated at yet another corridor. The room I found myself in next was larger. I followed her down rows she navigated seemingly without need of sight.

Her fingers roamed over book spines, alighting softly before moving on.

"Here," she said. "I knew we had one."

The book she handed me was titled *Tom Swift and His Motorcycle*, by Victor Appleton. The cover was badly faded but I could make out an illustration of a boy puttering down a country lane on an old-fashioned motorbike. He was wearing jackboots and a crested leather hat; from what little I could remember of their uniforms, he appeared to be a . . .

"He wasn't a Nazi." Unnervingly, the clerk had read my mind. "He was a boy adventurer, an inventor, a genius based on . . ." She searched her memory banks for a name. ". . . Thomas Edison. My older brother read all his books. I was too young and a girl—girls read Nancy Drew—and besides, Tom Swift always relied on a Jewish boy to help him out of scrapes. I didn't like that."

"Thank you," I said to her, and left.

02 The Damascus Towers

Stakeout.

I'd met Tom Swift only once, in the company of Angela Doe. If the thread wasn't particularly long at least there was an end to grab hold of.

Doe had returned to her fourth-floor apartment near Nazareth Park. I took a room at the motel across the way with clean sightlines into her place. For three days I drank rotgut joe and spied on the woman I loved. I could not deny that my snooping was based at least partially on jealousy. But it wasn't my sole motivation. People were dead and it was still my responsibility to discover who'd killed them. Tom Swift was as likely a candidate as any.

A dangerous man. Amid all the patsies and stiffs and losers I'd come in contact with in the line of duty there had been but a few truly dangerous men. Those ones you recognized right off: something in the voice, the eyes, the viperlike way they moved.

At quarter past eleven on the third night, a van rolled up. A man exited the passenger side and crossed the sidewalk. He did not push the buzzer. He had a key.

Angela's kitchen light went on. I socked a pair of binoculars to my eyes and thumbed the focus wheel. Angela and Tom Swift. The two of them smiling, Swift touching her shoulder, Angela's cheeks colouring, Swift tossing his head back in laughter.

They sat. I stewed. At some point Angela guided him to the front door.

I hustled to an unmarked prowl car in the motel lot and caught the van as it pulled away from the curb. I didn't radio for backup—none to be had, not that I trusted.

The van meandered for twenty minutes before cutting off Mount of Beatitudes into one of the tony suburbs ringing the SuperChurch. It pulled up at a stop sign. A few people approached. Some looked like they might own homes around there; others looked to have crawled from cardboard shanties.

The van's rear door swung open and the people vanished inside. When it opened again, those same people exited the van and went away down the street. Nobody appeared to be carrying anything, so what were they receiving—drugs? Benedictions?

The van hit three more neighbourhoods: Jewtown, Little Baghdad, Preacher's Row. I surveilled from afar, idling in the darkness of smashed streetlights. I counted each person entering the van: forty-three in total. They went into the van, a few minutes passed, then they got out of the van and walked away. They fit no known demographic.

It was past midnight when the van rounded down a cracked two-block stretch of tarmac leading to the Damascus Towers. The Towers had been built decades ago to house the previous Prophet, an ex-monsignor. But, seeking to distance himself from the old Monsignor and all tokens of his regime, The Prophet had ordered the Damascus Towers shut down. They remained standing, if barely. Scavengers had gutted the insides, tearing out the marble counter-tops and brass fixtures and ivory carpeting. After the easy meat was gone, the most industrious foragers had ripped out the doors and window glass and copper plumbing pipes and teak floorboards.

Like any creature with its guts yanked out, the Towers had basically collapsed into themselves. All that remained was a pair of yawning fire-gutted skeletons, upper stories crumbled on weird angles. They resembled decayed tusks poking at the sky.

I popped the trunk and grabbed a flashlight. I had my pistol and badge but otherwise bore no trace of office; in my three-day-old clothes and beaten night watch jacket, I passed for a fair facsimile of the wrecks who called this area home.

I picked a path across the shattered cobblestones, my intention being to pass between the towers to the rear parking lot where I was certain I'd find the van. This course took me past the courtyard fountain; a knee-high stone tub presided over by a headless statue of the old Monsignor. That the head had been hacked off was old news—but now a carved pumpkin had been perched atop the stained marble stump.

Two figures huddled on the street side of the fence. One struck a match while his partner cupped his hands round the glowing matchstick and touched his cigarette to the flame. Had they scissored in behind to cut me off? Or were they only a couple of rummies? I pulled my pistol from its shoulder rig and made my way between the towers. What had once been a series of manicured terraces were now risers of brittle grass littered with cracked stone flowerpots. My gaze trailed up the western face of the left tower: bricks scorched by old fires, yawning window frames consuming the cloud-filtered moonlight. Thunder rumbled nearby, filling my mouth with a dry ozone taste.

The van was parked on the decline of a loading ramp that led into the far tower. Its doors flung wide, interior empty. After checking it on the off-chance its keys had been left in the ignition—no dice—I hugged the wall leading down the ramp.

It emptied into an underground parking garage. Skids of canned food were stacked along the walls; was Swift gearing up for Doomsday? Rats skittered across sewage pipes overhead. I could hear voices or music coming from somewhere.

My shoulder brushed something. I dropped the flashlight. It spun on the concrete floor, illuminating the garage in a revolving fan. More canned food, a few cars, words scrawled on the walls that passed too quickly to read . . .

. . . and directly in front of me, a man.

I levelled my pistol. "Don't move."

He did not—not a muscle. I picked the flashlight up and shone it at his face.

Wasn't a man at all, but an effigy of our Prophet. Arms and legs made out of wheat chaff bundled with baling twine, jutting at perpendicular angles from one of the vanilla suits favoured by the Heaven-Sent Hero. Its clay face was an eerie replica of The Prophet's own, except the features were outsized and cartoonish. The sculptor gouged deep thumb-holes in place of eyes: they were stuffed full of rancid meat. Scrawled on the wall behind it:

MAY YOUR SINS GO UNPUNISHED.

"That's not for your eyes."

I turned toward the sound of the voice, my pistol coming round with me. It was engulfed by a hand so large it felt more of a paw—my mind snagged upon the scene outside Zoila's Nail Salon, those officers who looked to have been torn apart by a gorilla. I brought my free hand up in a desperate bid to smash this monster's face only to have it glance off a freakish expanse of chest. Next, something crashed against my skull and every ounce of light drained out of the world.

12 A Polite Conversation

"Well, I don't care if it rains or freezes,
Long as I got my plastic Jesus,
Sittin' on the dashboard of my car . . ."

It was dark, wherever I was now, though an ambient glow came from somewhere. My skull felt cracked open, some of its contents leaking down the back of my neck.

"Comes in colours, pink and pleasant,
Glows in the dark 'cause it's iridescent
Take it with you when you travel far . . ."

My guess was that I was in an abandoned unit in the Damascus Towers. A hurricane lamp hung from a ceiling nail. Wind howled through the empty windows. I was lashed to a chair at ankles and wrists.

"Go get yourself a sweet Madonna dressed in rhinestones,
Sittin' on a pedestal of abalone shell.
Goin' ninety, I ain't wary 'cause I've got the Virgin Mary,
Assurin' me that I won't go to Hell."

The singer sat at the edge of the lamplight. I'd heard his voice before. Tom Swift plucked a few more chords on his instrument: a milk box ukulele with a yardstick fret and fish line strings. The photo of the missing boy on the milk carton was familiar.

"Have you ever heard this song, Jonah?" he asked. "It's called 'Plastic Jesus.'"

"No," I told him. "Never."

"It's from a film," he said. "*Cool Hand Luke*. Ever seen it?"

"That's a banned work."

"Why so?"

"It valorizes disobedience of authority. It may cause people to . . ."

"Question their masters?"

I nodded tiredly.

"How many times have you seen *The Passion of the Christ*?"

Every Republican Follower was expected to watch that film yearly; it'd been playing in its own downtown theatre since before I was born.

"Thirty-five times."

"Thirty-*five* times and you've never seen *Cool Hand Luke*."

Tom Swift shook his head as if to say this, in a nutshell, was the real problem with the world. He asked if my head hurt. I asked him what the hell he wanted.

"Oh, the usual: peace for all mankind, an end to hunger, your Prophet's head on a stick." He held out his hands, wrists touching. "Want to cuff me, Jonah? I'm a heathen sinner."

"I wouldn't bother with cuffs. I'd shoot you."

He frowned. "That's no way to treat your host, is it? I should be asking what it is you want, Jonah, seeing as it was you doing the following."

I switched gears. "What's with the fake name? Tom Swift, some dried-up boy genius."

He offered a polite golf-clap. "Nice sleuthing. But you didn't answer my question—why were you following me?"

I said, "What happened in New Beersheba?"

"What did you *hear* happened in New Beersheba?"

"It's a black hole. No information coming out."

Water dripped, dripped, dripped down my neck.

"Do you love her—Angela?" The tilt of Swift's head indicated that my answer would be of purely abstract or scientific interest. "I can see why you would. She's intrinsically loveable."

I jerked my body towards him. My aggressive move prompted a pillar—or what I'd mistaken as a pillar, huge and fixed as it had been—to step forward and place a hand on my shoulder. The hand was the size of a cast iron skillet. The man it connected to had the fridge-like dimensions to match.

Swift made a soothing motion. "I'm sure our friend was only stretching his limbs, Porter. That's all you were doing, Jonah, yes?"

Lamplight curved the underside of the monster's face. I recognized it as the face from the sketch composite by Tibor Goldberg—the fairy-tale giant who'd placed a call from the payphone outside his record shop. *Freakish* was the word Tibor had chosen. No hyperbole in that choice. Measured ear-to-ear, his head must've spanned a foot.

Swift waved the man-mountain off. "Acromegaly," he said. "Gigantism, in layman's terms. Big as a house, isn't he?"

Swift made a pirouetting motion with his finger. The giant obediently turned to face the wall.

"His name's Porter Rockwell," Swift said, "but we call him Golem. You know about Golem?" When I shook my head, he said, "Why would you? It's a heathen Jew myth. A Golem was a giant shaped out of clay. Its maker wrote orders on slips of parchment and placed them in the Golem's mouth; at night, the

Golem came alive and did whatever it was commanded. Swept the hearth, mended the fence, murdered his maker's enemies . . . anything at all."

"Why make him turn around?"

"Porter's deaf. He did it to himself—screwdriver. It's partially my fault. I told him he was better seen than heard and he misinterpreted it." Swift guided an index finger toward his ear with aching slowness. "No thought, all action—that's a Golem for you. But he has learned to read lips quite well."

I thought: *How could he have placed a call from that payphone if he was deaf?*

I said, "How do you know him?"

"Oh, I picked him up along the way," Swift answered, as though the giant were a stray dog who'd opted to tag along out of loneliness or fear.

"Do you really want The Prophet's head on a stick?"

Now Swift smiled. "That was crass of me. What I meant was that your Prophet is a coward and a snake and I suppose it's my wish for people to see him in his proper light."

"How's that—by encouraging them to blow themselves up?"

"Your Prophet is a figurehead," Swift went on, ignoring my question. "Most people are such herd animals they'd prostrate themselves before anyone so long as he's been certified a holy mouthpiece by your divine council. They need a little enlightenment, is the thing."

"And you're just the man to spread that good word."

"I don't see anyone else stepping up." He spread his hands, as if in hopes that someone might absolve him his dreary burden. "I wish for people to think for themselves. Right now their lives are governed by a book of fairy tales."

"Your conviction is admirable," I deadpanned. "There are plenty of soapboxes on Preacher's Row."

He stood and walked to the empty patio window. We were high up—no lights, no rooftops.

"I do wonder," Swift said, "why it is we think so highly of ourselves. Why we're the only species with enough . . . gall? Yes, gall, to think that some part of us, some essence, must live on after we die. We are unique in this view that something within each of us is so valuable it must exist forever in some form, on some plane—heaven, hell. Insects, animals: their existence is finite. Ours, infinite. Why should we be so special?"

I had no answer to that.

"I do understand our need for belief in a clinical way: we're so fragile, our existence so uncertain, we need a centrepiece around which to orient our moral selves. One perfect being to look up to in a world where others so often act in their own self-interest. But what if there's nothing to be pious for, sacrifice for, abstain from, look forward to?"

Wind skirled between the panes of the hurricane lamp, blowing the flame slantwise. I could hear Porter Rockwell breathing heavily. When the flame licked up, I saw Swift had returned to his chair.

"My fondest hope is to be wrong. Should I die in such a manner that spares me a moment to address my sins, I promise you I'll recant. Do you want to know what the final words to pass my lips will be?" Throwing his hands heavenward. "Take it all back, Lord! I *believe*!"

The tower whipsawed in the wind.

"Something about you greatly puzzles me," said Swift. "Tell me: why don't you visit your mother, Jonah?"

My breath locked up, this feeling of cold steel bands clapped over my ribcage. How did he know these things?

"If you do anything to her . . ."

Swift's upper lip curled back to reveal teeth white and straight as organ keys.

"You must think me a rare scoundrel! What have you ever done that I would seek revenge upon your mother?"

"Then why do you care?"

He said, "My own mother is gone. Murdered. It happened long ago, when I was a boy. Yours is not. That you would let her rot away in that house of ghouls . . . promise me you'll visit her."

I said, "I will."

"I'll know if you don't."

"I recognize that. Can I ask you something?"

"Of course."

"Why are you here in New Bethlehem?"

"A reclamation mission," was his simple answer. "Reclaiming the lost, the abandoned, the forgotten and the damned."

"You want what happened in New Beersheba to happen here."

"Whether I want it or not, yes, it will happen. As it was bound to before long—if not me, some other catalyst. Tell me, Jonah. What is it you want for Angela?"

"I wish for her to be happy."

He cocked his head. "That's not exactly true, is it? You wish for her to be happy with *you*."

"And you think she'd be happier with who—you?"

"She's beyond the possibility of happiness altogether."

"You're wrong."

He stood and tapped Porter Rockwell's shoulder. The giant lowered his head while Swift massaged Porter's neck above the fringe of close-trimmed hair. Rockwell made a noise approximating the nicker of a satisfied horse.

"Golem's going to pop a pill in your mouth," Swift said. "No lasting effects, I promise. Please don't fight it; Golem's been known to break jaws."

I obeyed, thinking I'd stash the pill in my cheek until I could discreetly spit it out. But it dissolved like spun sugar the moment it hit my tongue. Swift retrieved the ukulele and plucked a couple off-key notes. I concentrated on the photo of the missing child on the milk carton. Who *was* that kid? I knew the face.

"Once a man arrives at the conclusion that humanity is a sinking ship, can he be blamed for drilling holes in its hull?" Swift said. "The question becomes: How to make an entire species self-destruct? What is the most effective system of annihilation? Religion. It's a tool, and any tool has a right and a wrong use. And this particular tool has already been mishandled and manipulated by a thousand different masters. Fear, obedience, sacrifice, fanatic loyalty: these are the fruits religion cultivates in a nurturing hand. And the greatest part is that the nurturer doesn't need to promise anything tangible: the reward is only delivered in death. It all rests on the bones of belief. And those bones are unbreakable."

I focused on the milk carton and finally recalled where I'd seen that face before. My last glimpse of it had been framed by the glass of a yellow school bus, that child's stoic expression so much different than the young smiling version that graced the carton, that long-missing boy waving stone-faced as the bus pulled away. The boy. Jeremiah.

The pill kicked in. My mind kicked out.

22 Orgy

I dimly recall being carried downstairs, Rockwell cradling me like an infant. He set me in the van, on a pile of stinking rags in the back. It jounced along the road leading from the Damascus Towers and smoothed out as we hit the main thoroughfare. Rockwell was scrunched into the driver's seat like an orangutan stuffed into a kitchen cupboard. Swift rode shotgun.

The van halted, a buzzer went off, and we sawed down a series of switchbacks. Rockwell killed the engine. He opened the rear doors and tugged a black satin hood over my head. He picked me up again—the man's strength was terrifying.

"What's the best way to grow a religion?" I heard Swift say. "By *fucking*, my dear Jonah. Loads and loads of fucking. Look at the Mormons: Joseph Smith assembled a dozen virile gents and their docilely fecund wives and told them it was their sacred duty to mint as many ankle-biters as possible. With nothing else to do on those cold Pennsylvania nights, those Mormons got down to some heavy-duty fucking."

The echo of their footsteps suggested we were in a cavernous space. Warehouse? Underground parking garage?

"An exponential equation. Joseph begat Joseph Jr., who begat Joseph the third. It's strictly a numbers game. The more you have, the more you can afford to sacrifice."

We passed through a doorway. Dark, moist, hot. Gnashing tribal music. The pill was running roughshod over my nervous system. My extremities had gone numb, or nearly so: this sensation like a million ants tunnelling through the veins of my arms and legs. Rockwell set me down. The hood came off. My eyes adjusted. I was splayed out on a bed of plush pillows; ringing the pillows were chaises whose ergonomics seemed to suit an erotic agenda. The chaises were surrounded with people. None of them spoke a word. The silence was funereal.

Swift knelt beside me and began to unbutton my shirt.

"This is my clan." His fingers worked through the sparse hair of my chest, cold as winter steel. "And while none of them are destined for this earth long enough to bear or raise anything that might be conceived tonight, I see no benefit in robbing them of that joy."

He unbuttoned my fly. Tugged down my trousers, my underwear.

"Tonight we indulge the pleasure principle. Fuck and be fucked. All those things you've been told are immoral and sinful."

✠

. . . the world phased out for a while and when it re-solidified a naked woman was sitting on my face. Couldn't see her eyes with her thighs vised round my skull and my tongue buried inside her but she was moaning in a way that suggested I was doing something right so I ran my tongue over her wondrous geography until she gripped my head, steadied it as though it were a tool contrived for her pleasure and ground herself on my face, the knob of my chin, my nose.

She whimpered, kittenish mews and said: "Do you like this?" and while none of it seemed to be designed with my enjoyment in mind, I mumbled the affirmative.

An anonymous mouth fastened over my penis—*oh!*—taking it down to the root and I grunted, my abdominals constricting and I would've sat bolt-upright if not for this implacable woman on my face. The faceless mouth was fiercely talented, a sacred whore's mouth, coaxing me toward climax while another stranger mashed herself over the busted contours of my face.

My orgasm was so head-splittingly intense it felt as though a solid rope was being sucked out of me and for a panicky drug-fused moment I feared the lion's share of my small intestines had been hoovered out through my urethra. The woman slipped off my face, slithered off to join another snaking ball of limbs and mouths. A voice came, hot and close in my ear.

"Better for one man to perish than a whole society to dwindle in disbelief. . . ."

I turned to see the Immaculate Mother wearing only a slattern's grin, body of no more substance than a wet rag hung on a hook. Her fingers skeletal, icy, breasts a pair of speckled coin purses hung off her chest and her face a macabre travesty.

"I fucked the little astronaut." She rubbed against me, her eyes fixed on some indeterminate point. "Fucked that tiny bastard and *loved* it."

For the first time that night, the first in a long while, real terror stole into my heart. She was the embodiment of our values and to see her opiated and horny and so tragically human . . . Christ, the veneer was gone.

"You're . . . you're my daughter's friend," she said, staring at me.

She began to cry, or at least was trying to, face contorting but no tears coming. . . .

". . . and everything you've ever been told is a lie. All your gods are dead."

Swift's voice addressing all of us. *Everything you've ever been told is a lie. All your gods are dead.* Perhaps this was so.

The blackness burst into sudden incandescence. That effigy of The Prophet had been soaked in lamp oil and set alight. It burned in the centre of the room, a solid cone of flame licking to the rafters. The Prophet's face pocked and bubbled, fire eating his head as that socketed meat grilled down to char.

Everybody cheered. The Immaculate Mother loudest of all.

23 Mom Again

"I want to tell you that the greatest freedom you can enjoy is obedience."

I jerked awake and my first thought was: *I've been buried alive.*

I was in a box. A black-walled box. A casket.

Except I was sitting up, the casket reeked of urine, and a buzzing picture screen hovered at eye-level. The Prophet's face lit up that screen.

"Perfect obedience produces perfect faith."

I was in a Daily Benediction Booth.

The screen faded to black on The Prophet's blankly smiling face. The auto-unlock mechanism hissed. I staggered out onto the street. The sun, stabbing my eyes like cocktail swords. The street was deserted. I wasn't far from where I'd left the prowl car.

I slumped behind the wheel. My skull felt like it was packed full of sawdust and millipedes, ladybugs, and other insects were crawling through it. I felt around my right side, hissing when my fingers brushed over a series of shallow but surprisingly painful punctures below my ribs. Nail gouges?

Faces flooded back: Swift and his gargantuan henchman, the Immaculate Mother, The Prophet burning in darkness. Angela? No, she hadn't been there.

I drove back to the motel. No doubt Swift was behind the bombings. The clues were abundant. Jeremiah's photo on the milk carton. Tibor Goldberg's description fingering Porter Rockwell for the tractor-trailer massacre. They had kidnapped the Immaculate Mother.

One questions: Why was I still alive?

After picking up Bird and Frog from the motel, I drove to my apartment. I fed them, changed the newspaper in Bird's cage, and stripped for a shower.

In the bathroom mirror I saw that five words had been written on my chest in candy-apple red lipstick. The first two words were a name:

CALEB MURPHY

The final three were either an entreaty or a warning:

VISIT YOUR MOTHER

Raphael's Roost.

Upon establishing my credentials at the front desk, electric locks buzzed to admit me into the ward. Gaily painted signs read THOSE WHO GO ALONG SHALL SURELY GET ALONG and THE PROPHET BELIEVES IN YOU.

The rooms lacked doors, lacked privacy. Patients/inmates/victims were laid out under thin sheets that couldn't hide their coma-shrunken bodies or stained skin where the feeding tubes were plugged in. Madrigals played on a constant loop. The dayroom existed in a state of suspended inertia. Residents dressed in pajamas or bathrobes tried to find their way out of the catatonic fog. Identical gaps in everyone's hairline where the old incision scars lay.

My mother sat in a folding chair before a garish mural of the Last Supper, to which The Prophet and Immaculate Mother had been added. Cherub magnets were affixed to the metal-backed mural; staff members moved the cherubs around daily and inmates were awarded prizes—hair barrettes, Fruit Roll-Ups—if they were able to spot all the little angels in their fresh configuration.

A male nurse's aide sat with my mother. Mom's eyes were downcast: either she was bored or had slipped off to sleep.

The aide smiled sunnily and said: "Is this your mother?" When I affirmed it was, he went on: "Why, she has such beautiful eyes. She should raise them to the Lord more often."

The urge to strangle him—perhaps using the quartz rosary strung round his neck as a garrotte—was remarkably strong. I requested he leave us be. I touched Mom's elbow. She stirred, glanced up, smiled broadly.

"Jonah."

Mom had been given The Cure—a method of surgical rehabilitation and a social control measure implemented not long after the Republic was founded. There were four stages of Cure. In stages one through three, brain tissue was excised based on the level of corruption, leaving criminals docile and pious. Stage fours were nicknamed "drool factories," as this was the sum total of what they produced.

My mother was a stage two. The surgeon who'd performed the operation said her IQ would be that of an eight-year-old the rest of her life. I had been nine at the time of her operation, which amused the surgeon and caused him to remark, "I bet you've always wanted to be smarter than your mother, haven't you?"

She said, "Your face . . ."

I must've looked a fright with my missing teeth and clown scars. She cupped my cheek. Her fingers were terribly warm and I wondered why.

"I'm alright," I assured her. "It was a . . . cooking accident."

The Cure had given her some of her old beauty back. During the rise of the Republic her face had become strained and pinched, windowing her anxiety. Now that tension was gone, along with every other adult concern; worry lines smoothed out, her face serene as a pool of water.

She enjoyed the diversions an eternal eight-year-old would take natural pleasure in: animal crackers and drawing ponies and the arrangement of cherub magnets on a mural. The uncomplicated, unquestioning love of the Lord.

"You look nice, Mom."

"Oh." Her hand went to her hair, touching the barrettes an aide had pinned above her temples. "Th-th-thank you so much."

I remembered what Doe said about certain things existing beyond humankind's capacity to destroy. In that instant I wanted to grab her, grab Bird and Frog and flee this city. The idiocy of this notion crashed down: a man and a bird and frog and a woman with the intellect of a child—flee where, exactly? We'd all be dead before the first snowfall.

Mom knitted her fingers together and went, "Here's the church . . ."—tenting her forefingers—". . . here's the steeple . . ."—thumbs lowering like a drawbridge—". . . open up the doors . . ."—curling her wrists, upturned fingers waggling—". . . and there's all the people."

She smiled as if she'd shown me a new trick. In truth, she'd first shown me this trick when I was three years old and now showed it to me each time I visited.

"That's great, Mom."

"Now you do it."

When I returned to the prowl car its passenger side window was smashed. I flicked pebbles of Saf-T-Glas off the seat, not caring, and drove home. I opened the apartment door in time to see Frog—who'd somehow managed to worm under the aquarium screen—performing an awkward Fosbury Flop out of the aquarium.

"You little turd!"

The frog nearly made it under the refrigerator before I nabbed it. I plucked dust bunnies off its tacky skin and dropped it back in the tank. The phone rang.

"It's Hollis, my son." He sounded like a kicked dog. "You're to come in tomorrow morning. The unit's reassembling."

"Someone got a lead?"

"Leads, no. More a shifting of command."

"Exeter's been sacked?"

"Of a manner, yes. Temporarily relieved of his duties."

"By who?"

"The Quints, lad. They've been harkened."

The line crackled. Hollis breathed deeply, as though the simple act of voicing their name had robbed him of breath.

The Quints. Heaven's own bagmen.

24 AMIRA AND THE QUINTS

The next morning I found a girl asleep in my prowl car.

She lay across the back seat on a cushion of flattened cardboard boxes. Barely teenaged: thirteen, fourteen. Greasy hair, face streaked with grime, a parka that should be burned in the interest of public health.

She was a heathen. An Arab. And she was awake, watching me.

I sat in the front seat and craned my neck so I could look at her. "What are you doing?"

She said nothing, curling her knees into her chest and peeking at me over the tops of her kneecaps.

"What's your name?"

Still nothing. Had her parents died in the Soul Glow plant

bombing? If so, she must have been on the street for a while.

"If you're not going to give me your name I'll make one up for you. You want that?" No reply. "Fine. Your name is . . . Gertrude. Do you know what I am, Gertrude? A police officer. If you stay back there I'll drive to my work and put you in a cell."

She spoke her first word. "Amira."

"Is that your name?"

She cocked her head, a gesture that said maybe it was and maybe it wasn't.

"Amira," I said. "Arabic for princess, isn't it? Your highness, may I be so bold to say you need a bath?"

She nuzzled her head into her armpit, sniffed, and offered me a quizzical look. I thought about it a good minute or more. Why not? What did it really *matter* now?

I got out and opened the back door. "Come on."

I took her upstairs to my apartment. I gave her the discount tour: the shower, kettle, cupboard with the bag of instant oatmeal. Was I really going to leave a heathen waif alone in my apartment?

"You can shower and eat," I told her. "The door'll lock behind itself. Steal or wreck anything and I'll find you. And don't touch my bird or frog. They're delicate."

Wind roared through the prowl car's busted window as I lead-footed it to the stationhouse. In the precinct lot sat a quartet of menacing cars. Buick Roadmasters. Detroit rolling iron, they used to call such cars, back when there was a Detroit. Their battleship-grey panelling was scored with bullet scars. Sharpened metal spikes jutted from their grilles to increase their predatorial aspect.

The Muster room was sparsely occupied. I didn't see Doe. My late arrival went unnoticed. All attention was riveted on the four identical men sitting next to Exeter, who looked visibly nervous behind the lectern.

The Quints existed in the same category as The One Child and New Nazareth's beatified Seraphim Sisters: true miracles. Their genealogy was an abiding myth: separate trains of conjecture had it they were born under a blessed or cursed star; their parents had been occultists or atheists or the most devout Followers ever to tread God's creation; their father either spent five years in a garret communing with the Lord or five years in prison on a pedophile beef; their mother was either a living saint or a filthy whore who'd earned the street name of Smooth Bones. Some conspiracy-minded Followers believed their parentage to be a melding of science and the Divine: DNA scraped off the spear lodged in Christ's side cultivated in a petri dish and married to the egg of a virgin to create perfect clones. The Savior split into five equal portions and returned to earth in a test tube.

The Quints' formative years were not so much different than The One Child's: they were paraded about during New Jericho's Stadium SuperChurch services, symbols of the Lord's sacred machinations. But aspects of their personalities soon presented themselves. Some accounts claimed they'd bound their nanny to the cellar door and urged their pet cats to chew off little bits of her face. The generally held and far less gruesome assumption was that the Republic recognized their practical value: less as emblems of God's love and more as enforcers of it.

The Quints had vanished shortly after their tenth birthday. A full decade passed before they had re-emerged into the public eye. The only remaining "before" photo of the Quints had been taken prior to their disappearance: ten years old, dressed in choirboy outfits, sandy hair buttonhooked with a cowlick, all smiling the same toothy, carnivorous smile. The single "after" photo had run in every Republic newspaper: the Quints standing before the grey facade of a nameless Republican complex, still identical but nothing childlike remaining in them—you got the sense you were looking at the result of a human tempering process, five children heated in a forge, rolled out, heated again and taken out glowing, hammered and honed and sheathed for future use. They had been rendered elemental of purpose. *Tools*. Sharp and glittering.

Not quite human. This was the how the Quints were described by those forced to interact with them. Some critical facet of their humanity, judged injurious to future endeavors, had been burned out of them.

And indeed, lounging next to Exeter with long limbs dangling, the Quints did look somewhat less than human. Lean of body—whippet-like, the word that sprang to mind—with limbs that tapered, thick where they met their torsos but turning leaner, bonier, toward the extremities: arms and legs like honeycomb candles. They wore woolen stovepipe trousers, Kevlar vests over black tees, albino calfskin dusters so white you could see the tracery of blue veins shadowing the uncured leather. The shade suited the Quints, whose skin was so shockingly pale nobody could be blamed for the assumption they'd spent the last decade denied access to sunlight. Hair delicate as spider threads spilled over their duster collars. Prematurely balding at the same pace: four widow's peaks sliced back from their foreheads in equilateral *V*s.

There were only two ways to tell them apart. The first was the pattern of scars hacked into their flesh. Each bore traces of brutal wounds on their necks and faces and hands and, I suspected, parts of their bodies hidden under clothes. The plainer identifiers were the three-inch numbers tattooed on their necks: 1, 2, 4, 5 respectively.

So far as I knew, the Quints were nameless—or not quite, as their names were numbers: Quints One through Five.

What was most remarkable this morning was their number: only four. Number Three was missing. AWOL? Unlikely. Dead? Considering their reputation, this seemed equally unlikely.

I slid into a chair as Exeter went on:

". . . Operation of the precinct will be remanded into the care of these gentlemen here." Exeter nodded at the Quints. "We plan to throw our full support behind their designs to stem the issues currently disrupting the long-held serenity of our city."

Hollis sat on the opposite side of the lectern. He looked utterly exhausted: skin drooping on his neck like a tube sock round a skinny shank. Every man in the muster room looked much the same. A lot of sleepless nights were carved into their faces.

"Now, these gentlemen have just arrived, so I haven't had an opportunity to speak to them about coordinating efforts—"

"You'll be granted no such opportunity," said Quint Two. "Coordination bespeaks parity, of which there will be none."

"We put ourselves in the hands of these capable men," Exeter went on anxiously. "The Lord shall guide us. Should they require intelligence in the way of known heathens, ghetto hotspots, etcetera, we are duty-bound to provide it."

Quint Four rose. His movements were chillingly brachial—a spider with half as many limbs. He crossed behind his brothers to hover directly behind Exeter.

The Chief flipped a glance over his shoulder, gripped the lectern, swallowed, went on: "In the interests of public tranquility, I expect we'll continue to search out and punish the culprits, as our Prophet has requested—"

Quint One, legs crossed and fingers knitted over his kneecap, tilted his chin and said, "Is that what your Prophet requested?"

When Exeter affirmed this, the Quint removed one hand from his knee and ran a finger down a scar curving under his jaw.

"Requests made by your Prophet will forthwith be afforded as much attention as the howling of a dog."

Quint Five, sitting closest to the lectern, stood, crossed in front of his seated brothers and stopped behind the seat vacated by the Quint who currently stood behind Exeter. That Quint, Four, guided Exeter from the lectern and bid him sit in the unoccupied seat.

"Gentlemen," said Four, "my brothers and I extend our thanks for welcoming us into your bosoms. Evidently you are unable to keep the devil off your doorstep."

The Quint standing behind Exeter produced a small bundle from his duster pocket and unfolded it on his flattened palm: a black satin sack.

When he slipped the sack over Exeter's head, one plainclothesmen laughed: actually more of a hysterical, confused yip. The sack was pulled sheer across Exeter's face so we could all see his nose and the jut of his chin.

Exeter spoke the first few words of a prayer before the Quint to his right pulled a thin bone-handled knife from his boot and stuck it through the black cloth and into Exeter's neck.

Exeter made a sound like he'd been doused with icy water. The blade passed through his throat, through his windpipe, the tip winking out the far side. His arms dipped then went up again, fists clenched, thumbs stuck out: giving us an involuntary thumbs-up. Gurgling, drowning on his own blood. Loafers beating a rat-a-tat-tat on the tiles. Blood from his carotid artery jetted round the knife handle.

The Quint who'd done it, Two, leaned in close to Exeter's ear. I watched his lips move.

What do you see? he asked.

Exeter's legs slowed and stopped. Gravity pulled his neck from the knife blade; he fell sideways into the Quint on his left, who raised a knee to casually deflect Exeter's bagged head from his lap. The body thumped on the floor.

Four cleared his throat. "It is difficult to find the right words at times like this."

Hollis jerked up, teeth bared like some feral animal, backing through the throng and out the door. The Quints let him go.

"Should your services be required," One addressed the rest of us, fingers re-knitted over his knee, "we'll reach out and touch you."

Two: "Questions?"

Five: "No?"

Four: "Dismissed then, gentlemen."

Out in the parking lot I had to force myself not to break into a run. I needed to put space between myself and the sight of Exeter laid out on the piss-yellow tiles, a pool of blood shaping itself around his head. The motor pool cage was unmanned. I grabbed a set of keys and scribbled my name on the sign-out sheet . . . then crossed it out. It was stealing, technically—but when a man takes property that isn't his and uses it as a tool of survival, does it count as stealing?

I ran into Garvey in the garage. A rumpled combat jacket draped over his shoulders, paper-bagged bottle of Hallelujah

Energy Boost sticking from one pocket.

"What the hell happened?" His canines were stippled with pinholes of decay. "I never had much use for Exeter, but hog-sticking him like that . . ."

He pulled the bottle from his pocket, tore the bag in thin strips around the mouth and took a desperate chug. "Where are you going?"

"Haven't thought that far ahead," I told him.

"Can I come with?"

The prospect of sharing a car with an antsy, drug-addled Garvey was not one I relished.

"We should work separately. Cover more ground."

He gripped my shoulder. His fingers—blackened tips, as if he'd burned them on a hot plate or something—twined with my hair at the back of my neck and twisted through it. Slowly, deliberately. *Lovingly*.

"We're buddies, aren't we?" he asked. "Been through a lot. Still pals, right?"

"We're whatever you want us to be, Garvey."

"We're close." Twisting, twining. A rash of gooseflesh broke out over my upper arms. "We go *waaaaay* back. . . ."

I removed his fingers, gave his hand back to him. He tucked it to his chest as a cripple might.

In the prowl car, I scanned the CB dial: nothing but static. On a channel way down the dial I swore I heard someone sobbing softly into the open frequency. Chalked it up to some atmospheric anomaly.

62 GOAT AND RABBIT

The heathen girl was still there when I got home.

She'd showered and eaten and now sat in the farthest corner of the room, balled up where the walls met, as if her being there might be tolerable so long as she took up as little space as possible. She looked much nicer having reacquainted herself with soap. Kitchen countertops gleaming, the air hung with a hint of pine. She'd tidied up.

I plodded into the living room, kicked off my brogans and slumped on the sofa. Amira's gaze was latched on me.

"Okay?" she said.

Okay her still being here, or was I okay? In either case, "Okay."

She uncoiled herself and traipsed delicately across the room like a schoolgirl attempting to sneak out of class unbeknownst to her headmaster. She poked a finger through the birdcage's lattice, wiggling it. Bird twittered, pleased with the attention.

"She'll bite you."

Amira yanked her finger back.

I said, "Can you blame her? What if a giant came along and stuck its big fat finger through your window?"

She said, "It's a pretty bird," in a way that suggested such a creature wasn't capable of anything so mean-spirited as biting her.

"Her name is Bird."

She asked, "Do you play with it?"

"You can't play with a bird. They don't fetch sticks."

She gestured to the aquarium. Her top lip curled to touch the tip of her nose.

"He looks slimy."

"Plenty of animals are slimy or ugly or smelly," I said. "So are lots of people. You stunk this morning. Frog can't help being slimy. That's the way God made him."

"I like furry animals," she offered.

"He's really more sticky than slimy. Touch him. You'll see."

Amira was disinclined to accept my offer.

"What are you, afraid to touch him?"

Her eyes held mine. A calm dauntless shade of grey. "I'm not afraid."

"Well, he needs to be fed."

I cracked the freezer door and shoved aside butcher-wrapped goat flanks until I located the package of beef heart. I hacked off a half-ounce and popped it in the microwave.

I said: "How old are you?"

"Eleven."

I rubbed my jaw, considering her. This was a shrewd eleven-year-old. The microwave dinged. I cut the meat into tiny cubes and slid them off the cutting board onto a saucer.

"Grab some toothpicks," I said to Amira, pointing to the drawer they were in.

The frog swam circles round the flat rock in the centre of the tank.

"He's blind," I told Amira. "But he's got a great sense of smell."

I pinned a shred of meat on the point of a toothpick. Frog clambered onto the rock and nosed along in his ungainly way, zeroing in on the beef heart and, with a graceless little lunge, snatched it off the toothpick.

Amira was fascinated. "Can I try?"

She laughed excitedly when Frog made his move and snatched the meat. Amira stuck a cube to her finger and waved it before the frog's mouth. She did not draw back at his lunge. The cube disappeared, leaving a spot of wetness on her fingertip.

Now I was fascinated. "Did it hurt? Does he have teeth?"

"No teeth. It felt . . ."—a considerable pause—". . . slimy."

"You like furry animals, do you?"

She said, "Furry's nice."

"Alright, then. Come with me."

The shop front was tall and narrow, wedged between a soup kitchen and a blood bank, both of which were closed. A wooden ram's head dangled on a single chain above the door, the other having snapped. The neon sign was busted.

The shop was locked. I knocked. The funereal-looking proprietor shuffled to the door and unsnapped the deadbolts.

"Officer Murtag, do come in."

When I stepped aside he got a glimpse of Amira. He set a hand on my shoulder and in an apologetic tone said, "I'm afraid there are still limits to the sacrifices we can arrange."

I shouldered past him. The goods were picked over ruthlessly. A scrawny molting dove lay asleep in its cage. A goat with ribs poking out like staves.

"Look around," I said to Amira. "Pick whatever you'd like."

The owner gripped my elbow. "You realize it won't matter

if they're sacrificed on her behalf. Her soul is permanently stained."

"Are you saying we can't conduct business?"

I'd known this man on an informal basis for years; he wasn't the type to let moral qualms intrude on a sale.

"You'd be throwing your money away but—"

"—so long as it's thrown into your pockets, right?" I said.

After a thorough scouting of the goods, Amira settled on a small brown-eared rabbit, the only one left.

I said: "How much for the cage?"

The owner frowned. "What use is its—?"

"How . . . *much*?"

His quote for the rabbit and cage was outlandish. Amira was over with the goat now. She scratched the bristly hair between its amputated horns; it bleated and chewed the sleeve of her parka. She looked at me.

"Who wants a goat?" I said to her.

"Me," she said.

I sighed. "How much for the goat?" I asked the owner.

Another outrageous price. I agreed so long as he'd throw in a bag of barley pellets. I tossed the sack of pellets over my shoulder and grabbed the goat's lead. Amira carried the rabbit.

"You can't leave with live animals, officer," said the owner. "It's against the law."

I booted the door open. "Feel free to make a citizen's arrest."

"We need to give them names," I said, walking home. "Pets need names."

Amira said, "Can't we call them Goat and Rabbit?"

"No. They need real names. They're yours now. Name them."

The goat gnawed at a patch of scraggly weeds sprouting round a telephone pole.

"Any names I want?"

"Whatever names you want, yeah."

"Okay. The goat will be . . . Dighet."

"Dig it? Dig what?"

Amira pronounced it slowly: "Deeg-hat."

"What's it mean?"

"Goat."

"So, wait," I said, "you're naming the goat *Goat*—only in Arabic?"

"You said whatever I wanted. And the rabbit . . . Hoppsy."

26 VISIT FROM A QUINT

Afternoon into early evening was spent getting the animals settled in.

Hoppsy was an easy matter; his cage rested by the window. Dighet the goat was trickier. He could not be given free rein on account of a destructive appetite: his first order of business upon entering the apartment had been to eat the laces out of my sneakers.

The apartment next door lay vacant. I clambered onto the fire escape and cracked the window with a screwdriver. We lined one of the empty bedrooms with newspapers. Amira positioned a sheet from the society section—a full-page photo of The

Prophet—face-up where Dighet might be inclined to piss on it. We filled a bucket with pellets and another with water.

"You should check on him twice a day," I told Amira, who nodded solemnly.

We were eating canned stew I'd scavenged from the next door apartment when someone knocked on the door. I put a finger over my lips and nodded to the bedroom closet. Amira slipped into the closet while I slipped into my shoulder rig and unsnapped the trigger guard.

Another knock. I went to the door. The bedroom closet made the softest click.

"Who is it?"

"Mary Kay calling."

Fear stole over the crown of my skull and shrink-wrapped the skin down my throat. I knew that voice.

I opened the door. I had to.

The Quint—Number Two; the one who'd stabbed Exeter—stood squared in the frame. He had a good head and a half on me, though there couldn't be more than a hundred and fifty pounds cladding those bones. He was dressed the same as earlier with the addition of a wide-brimmed felt hat; he had the look of travelling preacher.

He pressed a finger to my heart. "You've been touched."

✠

His car shone like an alligator skull under the streetlamp. Its interior was coffin-dark. Its roof was strapped with shotguns, pistols, what looked to be a sniper rifle. A pine-scented crucifix was garrotted from the rearview mirror. The backseat was full of children's toys. Teddy bears and ragdolls. All the eyes had been inked out with a black marker.

"You're looking at my tattoo," he said once we'd gotten on the road.

I hadn't but it struck me as unwise to contradict his assumption.

"Nobody does tattoos anymore," Two went on, "bodily adornment being a sin. An old Navy man did ours. He'd never learned to draw much more than anchors and hearts and skulls, those being the sum of the shipmen's requests."

The car hit a pothole. The Quint cracked a window; wind hissed through the slit, ruffling the hair of the black-eyed toys in the backseat.

"Your city stinks of rotten meat."

He wrenched the wheel, whipsawing across the opposite lane. The Buick's tires skipped up over the curb and back to the macadam. Reaching out, Two brushed his fingers across my cheek: like being brushed with the bone-stubs of something long dead.

"Tell me, Acolyte Murtag . . . does the name Victor Appleton tickle your brainstem?"

"No. That's a blank."

The Quint offered the most animal smile ever to grace a human countenance. Every square inch of his face was scarified: wire-thin scars crisscrossed his cheeks and lips and even eyelids, horizontal intersecting with vertical, overlapping like the cured reeds of a wicker basket.

Why not just tell him? Tom Swift, Porter Rockwell, Damascus Towers, Jeremiah. It would be no different than siccing two packs of rabid dogs on each other. But I didn't.

We pulled up beside the gutted remains of The Manger. The club's back end was blown apart, blackened rafters poking at the sky. The sidewalk was littered with wilted bouquets and candles melted to pools of colourful wax on the concrete.

The Quint kicked his way through the flowers and crunched a framed photo of Eve under his boot. He knocked around inside for a few minutes and came out with streaks of char on his face.

"Come, Acolyte. We've the Lord's work to do."

The joint standing catty-corner to the Manger was nameless: only a buzzing neon martini glass marked it an establishment currently accepting clientele. A bleary porthole window was inset in its swinging door; the Quint shouldered it open and I trailed him inside.

The bar was dark, the only light shed by the cathode rays of an ancient TV bolted over the scarred bar. Even the air tasted scummy. High-backed booths ran up the left side; all save the last were unoccupied. A gilt-edged portrait of The Prophet—his more censorious expression, as required by law in such establishments—hung over a rack of dusty RC bottles behind the bar. A jukebox played "Missionary Man."

The bartender possessed the plastic face of a used car salesman. Brilliantined hair, plaid shirt with rolled-up sleeves, flyspecked apron. His was a face best served by mood lighting.

"What can I get you fine Followers?" he said a little queasily.

"Soda water," said the Quint. I nodded the same.

The Quint sipped his soda and, finding it to his liking, downed the glass. The bartender refilled it swiftly. A cockroach scuttled down the bar ledge. Big as a communion wafer. I slipped my coaster over top of it. The coaster scuttled forward a few inches. I set my glass atop it, pressed down until it went crunch.

"Sorry for the state of the place," said the bartender, wiping a grotty rag down the bar.

The Quint said, "There was an explosion across the road."

"That was a while back."

The Quint's arm snaked out, corralling the bartender's rag-hand. "I trust your memory goes back that far?"

The bartender squirmed. "It does."

"Tell me what you saw."

"Saw? Nothing. It's a different breed of clientele: they had all the young ones, the spangly nightclub crowd; we . . ."—he cast a desperate eye around the place, urging us to draw our own conclusions—". . . appeal to earthier tastes."

"So you didn't see anything?"

The bartender's hand turned white in the Quint's grip.

"Heard the explosion alright. We all rushed outside to look."

"So you saw . . . not a thing?"

"That place over there was none of our concern," the bartender said. "No reason to spare it a glance."

"No*thing*? Not a single thing?"

The Quint's nails punched into the bartender's hand.

"Please," the guy blubbered, "I'm a loyal Follower. . . ."

"If you saw nothing," The Quint said equitably, "tell me—what good are you?"

Withdrawn from the folds of his albino duster, the Quint's gun didn't quite resemble one: only a black effigy in the rough shape of a gun, dark traceries wafting from the barrel like raw diesel smoke. Speaking, it made hardly a sound: the *whuph* of a propane barbecue igniting.

The bartender's head split open. One half vapourized into a fine red mist while the other hung like a waxing gibbous moon, the remaining eye staring out with horrible awareness.

The Quint walked to the last booth with cool momentum, duster flapping like the wings of a crippled moth. He surveyed the two old men who occupied it and shot the pair. Their heads ricocheted off the wall, bodies tossed out of the booth. One of them wasn't quite dead; his liver-spotted hand reached out to the Quint.

"What do you see?" the Quint whispered to him. "Please, tell me what you see."

But the man was past answering. Two shot him in the face. Next he shot the jukebox and walked out the swinging batwing door.

By the time I staggered out to the street the Quint was walking back from his car with a jerry can in each hand. We bumped shoulders—his body was cold steel—and the collision sent me sprawling to the wet flagstones.

"You butchered them," I choked.

He faced me down. "The Lord butchered them. I was only His blade."

I lay dumbfounded out on the street until the Quint emerged from the bar trailing a line of gasoline. He hooked his fingers into my collar and yanked me backwards with him. I let myself be dragged a few feet before pushing off with my heels to get myself partway to standing, at which point he shoved me in the direction of the Buick.

I crumpled into the passenger seat. Another *whuph.* A vein of fire wound across the street under the bar door. The porthole window lit up orange. The Quint watched awhile, and when the door blew off its hinges, felt his work was done.

We drove. Steam fumed from manholes to form curtains of vapour. The Quint drove casually, three fingers guiding the wheel. Face flecked with blood. We came upon an oil-drum fire. Indigent men clad in rags were warming themselves by its light. The Quint slowed down.

"Hand me one of those," he said, indicating the toys.

I gave him a teddy bear. Heavier than a stuffed animal ought to be—then I saw the pin looping from the fur of its belly, a pin the Quint pulled before tossing it out the window where it landed with a soft thump.

"Christmas comes early," he called chummily.

We pulled away as the men peered with bafflement at the bear. They had receded a quarter-block into the rearview when an explosion rattled the windows.

We came upon two Followers trundling a shopping cart. A man and a woman, both quite young. A black-eared dog was yoked to a lead tied round the cart's handle.

"Hand me another."

In the cart, dozing atop the couple's possessions with a pom-pommed toque snugged over his head: a young boy.

I said: "No."

"They're agitators."

"They're a homeless family."

We cruised on past. Two's eyes were riveted on me. I sent a prayer up: *Please Lord, a few days to set my house in order. Make amends. Save whatever I can.*

What is the velocity of a prayer?

We pulled over. The Quint's revolver butted my chest.

"Open the door."

The pressure of the barrel intensified. I jerked the door open and went down on my ass on the curb, my feet still in the Buick's foot well.

"When you're needed, you'll be summoned."

I'd been cast out a few blocks from the apartment. I limped home. Amira was still up. I walked into the bathroom and stripped for a shower. Water too icy to work up a lather so I just stood in the spray with my teeth chattering.

I dressed and retrieved the spare key from the cupboard above the fridge. Amira was sitting on the floor cross-legged—Hopi Indian style, my mother would've remarked. I sat the same. The key rested on the bare wood between us.

"It's yours," I told her. "Put it somewhere safe. Come and go, fine by me."

I slid the key toward her. She put it in her pocket.

"The day may come I don't walk back in that door," I said. "If that ever happens, think to save yourself. Let the animals go. A pond for Frog. Bird can fly away. Rabbit and Goat . . . don't worry, they'll figure it out. Worry about *you*, okay?"

"Okay."

"Go to bed, Amira. You can sleep in my bed. I'll sleep on the sofa."

Once she was asleep I cracked the window. Cool currents swept over the Badlands, air infused with the scent of Cherokee rose. Out of that silence the explosions rolled back to me.

Judges 15:4: *Samson caught ten jackals and tied them tail to tail in pairs. He fastened a torch to every pair of tails and set them lose in a field of Philistine corn.*

The phone rang. I nearly jumped out of my skin.

"Hello?"

Distant, frail: weeping.

"Hello? Who is this?"

"Sometimes . . ." Angela's voice. ". . . Jonah, sometimes it's better not knowing."

"Angela? What's that matter? What are you talking about?"

Click.

I sat by the window until sunlight broke over the cathedral spires. The power had yet to be restored.

Article IV:
He Falls for the Second Time

27 New Bethlehem Makes a Choice

They picked me up in a van not long after six o'clock.

Brewster drove. Henchel sat in the passenger seat. Filling the bench seats: Applewhite, Garvey, most of the Acolyte crew. No Hollis. No Doe.

I wedged in beside Garvey. The van had the desperate stench I associated with the uptown men's shelter. We wound through block after deserted block. Not a soul to be seen. A wasteland, except for the most part, things were structurally intact. The odd blackened patch where a bomb—one of the Quints' teddy bears?—had gone off, but in the main, the shops and buildings still stood.

"What about Hollis?" Applewhite asked.

"AWOL," Henchel said. "Nobody's seen him since Exeter."

"Chickenshit." This from Garvey, who was fussing with the tattered end of his sleeve, teasing the threads obsessively.

We drove to The Prophet's estate. The old guard shack had been blown to bits. Brewster badged past the whey-faced plainclothesman who occupied the hastily rebuilt shack. In the driveway: the Quints' Buicks, a TV truck with a satellite dish jacked up on a pole, and Doc Newbarr's car.

Tonight, for the first time in the city's history, The Prophet would deliver his weekly sermon via satellite feed. The Stadium SuperChurch had been vandalized—spray painted banners reading MAY YOUR SINS GO UNPUNISHED—and besides, Followers were too terrified to attend. We had been called in as props: by flanking The Prophet while he delivered his sermon, we'd stand as proof that law and order still reigned.

The wardrobe assistant had a conniption at the sight of our stubble and our gravy-stained tunics. We were dispatched to the mansion's many bathrooms with safety razors and motel soap and a stern order to return as human beings.

A makeshift studio had been set up in The Prophet's sitting room. Klieg lights shone upon the wide walnut desk. A cameraman hovered off to the right: The Prophet's left profile was widely acknowledged as his most appealing. We fanned out behind him. We looked a bit more professional having shaved and soaped. The Quints stood directly behind The Prophet's chair.

The Prophet entered stage left. It was the first time anyone had seen him in weeks. He hadn't thinned out like the majority of the citizenry—rather, he had ballooned up. His bulk strained against that vanilla suit. He walked—*waddled*—into the camera frame. The boom mike picked up his tortured breathing.

"Come unto me and fear not!" he barked. "Have I not sighed for thee—wept for thee? Do I not live for thee? Fear not! Do I not watch o'er thee? Dost thou not cling to me—cry to me—need me? Fear not!" His voice went ragged. "My eyes are upon thee, my arms around thee, to keep thee and guard thee. Trust in me. Call to me. Fear not!"

He collapsed into the chair behind the desk. He blotted the beads of sweat on his brow with a linen hankie.

"Trying times in New Bethlehem," he said. "All have suffered, none more so than me as I witness my good works going for naught. Angered with us, the Lord sent a rain of frogs and still His worshipers fail to honor His wishes—persisting with your blasphemies! As Deuteronomy 16 counsels: *You must circumcise the foreskins of your hearts* to admit the healing love of the Lord and yet, like stubborn heathens, your bosoms remain walled off!"

One of the Quints cut his harangue short. "You're off the air."

"What's the matter?" the camera operator asked his techie.

The tech fiddled with a nest of cables snaked into some kind of control box. "We lost the feed."

"Well, get it back!" The Prophet said, his face red as a boiled ham. "I can't be cut off in the midst of a citywide benediction!"

"Something's disrupted the signal from the trunk line," the tech said.

The monitor went from static to a still shot. A cement-walled room. Two figures wearing cherubim masks stood behind another figure who knelt with hands lashed. This figure was naked with her head lowered.

"Pardon the interruption, gentle Followers."

Swift's voice.

"Please stand by for the Immaculate Mother's address to her devotees."

One of the masked figures was huge. It had to be Porter Rockwell, the Golem. Which meant the other one was Swift. Rockwell nudged the naked woman with his book. She looked up dazedly. The Immaculate Mother. She tilted her face to the left: the profile widely acknowledged to be her strongest. The vanity of the gesture sent nausea crashing through my gut.

"It was a lie," she began. "All of it. The structure was a tool. A tool to maintain equilibrium. Why? People lie and steal and kill, so you have to scare, shame, threaten them into being good Followers. So we lie."

"She's been drugged," The Prophet said.

"Who's to blame?" she went on. "Big fish eat little fish. Sheep and shepherds. Not everyone can be a shepherd. Most are happy enough sheep. Whose fault? Me?" A violent head-shake. "The rules existed before I came along; I only played by them."

Porter Rockwell knelt behind the Immaculate Mother, shoulder gripped so she would not fall over. His free hand held a knife—no, not a knife: a wheat sickle.

"All your gods are dead," she prattled. "All your gods . . . all your . . . dead . . ."

"It's your choice," Swift said. "If I hear from you, then it will be done. If only silence, she lives." A carefree shrug. "So what say you, good flock of New Bethlehem?"

I turned and left the makeshift TV studio. Nobody cared or tried to stop me. I walked out to the sprawling mansion grounds. I stood outside waiting and listening.

What say you, New Bethlehem?

The first came from a long way off. The honk of a car horn. A few short bursts, timid in its way, then loud and ongoing. It was joined by others: air horns, sirens, pots bashing pans and so much more. The whole city was answering. It rose to a discordant crescendo and, as a child who hollers himself hoarse, ebbed to a satisfied silence.

I caught movement along a hedgerow and spotted the peacock from my previous visit. Most of its luminous blue feathers had fallen out. It lay on its side, breathing heavily. I removed my duster and settled it over the bird. Something was the matter with its leg. Its neck hung like boiled spaghetti. I cradled its head along the crook of my arm.

"Look who's here."

I turned to see Doc Newbarr.

I said, "What are you doing here?"

"Coincidence," he told me. "The Prophet's regular sawbones is indisposed. The Prophet's been experiencing gastric distress. Bleeding ulcer."

"You do anything for him?"

A shrug. "Used to be medicines. Now? Told him to drink lots of milk."

"I'm leaving," I told him.

"Your crew's not going to be upset you skipped on them?"

"They may be."

"Well, I'll give you a lift."

"I'm bringing this bird."

"Okay," he said simply.

"Did you watch it?" I asked once we'd driven past the gates. "The Immaculate Mother?"

"I watched," Newbarr acknowledged. "Shouldn't have, but there are things . . . can't live seeing it, can't live not seeing it. When they took her head off there was hardly any blood. Nothing but a trickle out her neck, like comes out of an old water fountain."

When we pulled up at my place, he said, "I've got a cabin out of town. Built for my wife and me, although she never got the chance to enjoy it."

Newbarr's wife had died of cancer, though I didn't recall what kind.

I said, "You're leaving?"

"Soon enough. Getting my ducks in a row. It's a ways south; plenty of forest. Well back off the road. Canned food. A cistern. Lake nearby's swimming with fish."

The peacock made congestive popping noises in the back seat, the sound of acorns bursting in a fire.

"What I'm offering is I'll draw you a map. Would you let me do that?"

I said: "I'd appreciate it, yeah."

"Okay, then. We're settled."

"Thanks. And Doc . . . just one more thing."

When I told him what I wanted he said, "That's strong stuff. What do you want it for?"

"A contingency, is what I'm thinking."

Newbarr frowned. "Very odd contingency. I've got a quarter-bottle of it in my medical kit. Enough to do the trick one time. I'll get it to you next we meet."

28 The Little Astronaut

The next morning I found myself standing over the toilet, trying to urinate as the peacock stared at me from the bathtub.

Its leg was broken. Amira had noticed that right off. She immobilized it using a popsicle stick and trash bag twist ties. Next she hunted through the dumpster behind the building and returned with a moulded brick of styrofoam. She gashed two holes in it with a steak knife and managed to thread the bird's legs through the holes. The peacock had flapped its wings, clearly distressed. Amira found a Tensor bandage I'd had lying around after an old ankle sprain and wrapped it round the bird's wings down under around its body. She filled the bathtub and set it inside. It had been there all night.

"Same as with horses," she'd told me. "Float them in water to help their broken legs heal."

When I came out of the bathroom, I saw Amira had fixed us bowls of oatmeal. We sat in silence but the apartment was full of noise: budgie twittering, peacock splashing, goat bleating through the wall.

"I have to go out," I said. "You stay, take care of the critters."

My man was easy to locate. I found him right there in the white pages.

He lived in a scabby brownstone overlooking Saint Matthew's Square. I mounted the crumbling stone steps and knocked. Soon as the door opened, I knew why Swift had wanted me to meet this man.

"Caleb Murphy?"

"Yeah?" He stared up at me from behind the security screen. Evidently I'd caught him during breakfast: a can of chili with a fork stuck out of it.

I flashed my badge. "May I come in?"

This made him smile. "I got plenty of worthless tin, too." Tapping the chili can with one squared-off finger. "See? Actually, mine's not so useless: holds my vittles."

Gapping my duster, I showed him the butt of my revolver. "How 'bout this lump of pig iron—got your attention?"

His smile widened. "Sure, boss."

Murphy let me in. He swept an arm round the room.

"See anything you fancy? We're having a fire sale. Every little thing must go. Every little thing 'cept me, that is."

I saw a cabinet full of tchotchkes and freak show arcana, including what looked to be a pickled fetus. The windows were smeared with dubbin or lard gone dark and cakey in the heat; sun leaked in through cracks thin as spider legs.

I couldn't keep my eyes off Murphy. My guess was that he'd be accustomed to it, having made his living as an object of grisly attention. He stood three feet tall, if that. Proportionally his body was the same as anyone's—all except his head. His skull was no bigger than a grapefruit. His features were crowded together on that tiny canvas: his face was an expressionist painting by an artist with a skewed grasp of symmetry.

He said, "Used to be you'd have paid two bits for the eyeful you're getting."

He pointed to a coffee tin sitting on a TV tray. An ink drawing of an eyeball was taped to it. I deposited all the change in my pockets and said, "Why do you figure I woke up with your name written on my chest?"

"You did?"

"Yep."

"I suppose you should start by asking yourself what manner of people you shut your eyes in the company of." Upon inspecting the tin, he offered a bemused snort. "There are worse ways of waking. This one time I woke up drenched in chicken blood. I was bending elbows with Otto the Geek and ol' Otto, he bit the head of a peahen; I was too drunk to notice it'd sprayed all over me. Next morning I'm covered—let me tell you, chicken blood's thick. Like waking up in syrup. So a name on your chest ain't so rough. Unless they carved it with a penknife. They do that?"

"No," I admitted. "Lipstick. Do you know a Tom Swift?"

"Should I?"

"He's the man who wrote your name on me."

"Then your beef's with him, ain't it?"

"Ever worked in a travelling show, Mr. Murphy?"

Murphy grinned. "After they told me I was too pretty for Broadway."

"Tell me: was your stage name Pliny the Pinhead?"

"Not sure."

He cut his eyes at the coffee tin. I contributed a shekel.

He barked laughter. "You need me to tell you my stage name? Whatever they're paying you, Kojak, it's too much. *Pinhead*. Awful descriptor. People only use ten percent of their brain, anyway. Einstein used eleven and was a genius. So I use all what I got."

"What's with your windows?"

"Neighbourhood kids kept mashing their noses to the glass for a free eyeful. My only rule: looky-loo all you want, but pay for all you see. Kids don't have two coins to rub together. I smeared lard over the windows so they couldn't gawp."

"You know, they've made some real advances in the curtain sciences," I said. "They cover whole windows now."

"You a home decorator?" Murphy sneered. "Here I am thinking you're a flatfoot with a fairy streak."

"I dabble in home decor consultation. Buy some curtains." I took a shekel out of his tin. "My consultation fee. You get the friend rate."

His expression curdled. "Ain't you a peach. Taking advantage of a handicapped fellow. Then again I s'ppose you got your own cross to bear, conceived lacking a sense of decency and all."

"Let's start over." I dropped the shekel back in, then opened my wallet to show Murphy all its brothers. "I have questions. I'll pay for the privilege of your information."

He scuttled to the sofa; his gait reminded me of a fiddler crab. He wore grubby stevedore pants with thick rainbow suspenders slung over his bare shoulders. Torso white and fleshy, with an undeveloped baby chest.

"Shoot."

"While you were part of this travelling show—"

"Freak show," he corrected. "Spade a spade."

"Freak show. Did you ever come into contact with The Prophet's old tent revival?"

Murphy snorted. "You could say I did. Their show, our show, we were rolling through the same scratch-ass one-donkey towns. We hooked up. Easier to draw in the rubes when you had a bigger spectacle on offer."

I dropped a shekel in the tin. "You ever have much reason or opportunity to traffic with them?"

"Interesting choice of word. *Traffic.*" Rolling it in his mouth, tasting it. "I used to do this trick, blow a soap bubble and slip my head inside—the Astronaut Helmet, we called it. The Immaculate Mother loved that bit. She'd stop by my caravan so

I could give her a private showing."

"Do they know you're in town—The Prophet and his wife?"

"Know?" Murphy circled one finger like a propeller. "Who you figure pays for this abundance? I'm a kept man."

"How so?"

Another snort. "Listen, Perry Mason, why don't you drop your whole nut in the kitty and I'll tell you straight, no more drips and drabs. Truth is, the only time I've ever let it slip was this one time I was drunk. It'd be nice to tell it with a clear head."

Everything in my wallet went in the can. Murphy gave me my money's worth.

"She looked much better in those days," he said. "Not the shrunken parody we saw on television. Young and attractive and really believing in what she was doing. Converting the masses. Saving souls. Something about a purpose makes a person beautiful; something comes shining straight out of them. I'm sure she pitied me." Murphy shrugged. "I've made a lot of hay on pity. But she wanted me, too. Oh, yes. She wanted it real bad."

I remembered what she'd said that night: *I fucked the little astronaut. Fucked the tiny bastard and loved it*.

"Not sure The Prophet knew at the time, or if he would've even cared," Murphy said. "Our Mother didn't fancy birth control, seeing it was a sin."

He forked chili into his mouth and smiled. His teeth looked like shoepeg corn.

"Soon as it became clear she was in the motherly way, their show and ours quit company. Now you may wonder why, when that monstrosity sluiced out of her, it wasn't offed straightaway? That's because some people, like The Prophet, see value in what the rest of us find valueless. I'm guessing when it came out and he heard the sounds it made, he said to himself, this—*this* is worth something."

The sounds it made. "The One Child . . ."

Murphy touched his nose. "The Virgin Birth. The Miracle. Your Immaculate Mother and I conceived it in a caravan mired in slop in the middle of bumfuck noplace. Funny," he said expansively, "how this world worships freaks. My son isn't one of God's miracles—he's one of His darkest mistakes. And you *bow* to him. Sometimes I wonder if the stars aligned differently maybe it could have be me or Otto or Henrietta the Mule-Faced Woman carted about in biers, fussed over and adored. But The Prophet's got his grift down pat: he's got the biggest damn coffee tin in Creation and you rubes kept it filled to the brim."

How had Tom Swift known about this?

"Why are The Prophet and Immaculate Mother paying for you to live here—is it in repayment for your silence?" I asked.

Murphy said: "Partially, sure. But my son's a little mush-head—he really never grew much bigger from when he was born. All he does is make noises, and even those not without prompting. But he's a willful creature. When he gets aggrieved he's this habit of shutting his blowhole till he passes out. The Prophet got to worrying . . . what if he kills off the few brain cells he's got? He's forty pounds of useless, then. The Prophet got to thinking maybe a father's touch could calm the kid down."

I was amazed. "What do you do?"

"Say he's colicky—surprising that a grown man can get the colic, but when that man's got an infant's brain less so—anyway, in that case they call me over. I dandle him on my knee, coo and cajole. Over twenty years I been doing it."

"His mother . . . The Immaculate Mother couldn't?"

"The boy's genetics are more mine than hers. He responds to me."

"And that's all?"

"Every week on Prophet's Day they pick me up in a shiny black car and bring me to the SuperChurch." Murphy drew himself up with odd pride. "There's a trapdoor leading under the stage cut just my size. I crawl under to a tiny chair, positioned under a hole drilled in the stage. Leaning on the chair is a pole with a needle taped to the tip. I wait until my son's bier is set over the hole. And when The Prophet gives the cue I stab through the hole and prick my kid with the needle."

He lazed on the sofa, body quivering like an overstuffed maggot. "Don't think much of it, either," he said, sensing my disgust. "Could be I'm stabbing a turnip."

He waited for me to ask it.

"Why? Why prick your soft-brained son with a needle?"

"You see," he went on, "what all you gormless rubes mistake for singing ain't singing at all. Those sounds are my son *crying*. The harder he's bawling, the more melodious his tune."

If I sat another minute I'd commit homicide on this man. I made it halfway to the door before retracing my steps to grab the coffee can.

"You high-toned sonofabitch!" Murphy hopped off the sofa, fists balled into impotent little knobs. "Hand it back! I earned it!"

I took one final glance round this dusty ghoul yard and its vicious little landlord—set in a boxing stance as if to fight me for the contents of the can—and said to myself, yeah, you earned it. Earned it all and more.

62 Taking Mom

I drove east on a deserted Falwell Memorial Boulevard. Raphael's Roost was unscarred by the bombings. I hurried inside, where I found my mother facing the cherub-festooned portrait.

"Mom. Hey, Mom."

She said, "You've cut your hair."

"Want to go someplace, Mom? Will you let me take you?"

"Oh." She touched her hair, bobby pinned into a bone-white nest atop her head. "Oh. I don't imagine they'd allow that. Rules, you know. All sorts."

"Don't worry about the rules." I took her carefully by the hand. "Let's gather some stuff."

The discharge orderly was my burly nemesis. His nametag,

pinned high on his muscled chest, now read: REMO PALLADINI, HEAD ORDERLY.

"And where are we headed this afternoon?"

"Taking my mother for a walk."

An indulgent smile from Palladini. "This is a holding facility, Mr. Murtag. Your mother is an inmate of the Republic. Criminals don't go for walks."

I pulled my revolver. "Open the door, Remo."

Mom said, "Oh, no. Jonah . . . you can't behave this way. . . ."

Palladini sprung the electric gate. "I'm calling the cops as soon as you step out of here."

"You do that, Palladini."

We drove home in silence. Mom hadn't been out of the Roost in quite some time. Hardly anyone was out. Sidewalks empty, shop fronts all dark.

"Is everything okay?" Mom asked.

"Okay how, Mom?"

She tapped the window with one finger. "The city seems different." She glanced at me with panic in her eyes. "Was it always this way?"

"No, Mom. Everything is different now."

This settled her some. She eased back in the seat as the empty sidewalks fled past. Where *had* everyone gone? There was no place to go. The wide-open spaces past the city limits were lawless and brutal. You had to be a special kind of crazy to live out there, and anyone who had grown up in New Bethlehem wouldn't last more than a few months. City dwellers were domesticated. Tame. Easy meat for the buzzards roaming the wastelands.

But the fact remained. The city felt like . . . like a corpse or something. Something that had just recently died and perhaps didn't quite comprehend its own death yet—its synapses were still firing fitfully, its eyes still imprinted with the last sight they had witnessed just before its heart stopped beating. But it was still dead, even if it didn't know it. Maybe that was how it happened. How cities became ghost towns. I'd always thought it would be a slow process, a town gradually suffocated by bad luck and bad circumstances, holding on for years before the last few residents packed up and abandoned it. After that the buildings would fall down and rot into the earth until all that remained was the foundations.

But maybe it could happen fast, too. A city dies overnight. And that was somehow eerier. Like a pristine diorama—everything still in place, clean and tidy, the electricity still running but nobody around. As if the entire citizenry had been vaporized in the midst of their day-to-day tasks, leaving a perfect emptiness.

"The lights are on but nobody's home," Mom said. She smiled. "One of the orderlies always said that to me. I guess he thought it was funny."

"I guess he did, Mom."

Amira was there when I opened the apartment door. I drew the girl aside while Mom fawned over the budgie in its cage.

"It's my mother," I told her. "She's been given the Cure. You know the Cure?" When Amira shook her head, I explained: "If you said or did anything that made people think you were dangerous, they"—drawing a line down the centre of my head with a finger—"and then they"—fingers clawed, I removed an invisible chunk—"and you weren't a threat anymore."

Amira said, "Is she sick?"

"No, no. She's very nice. I want to keep everyone under one roof. Does that make sense?"

"I like her hair. A cloud of snow."

When the time for introductions arrived I was amused by their postures: hands clasped behind backs, eyes cast down at their shoes—or bunny slippers, as was the case. Like a pair of young girls on a playdate organized by their parents.

"Mom, this is Amira. Amira, Mom."

Amira said: "Pleased to meet you."

Mom said: "Oh yes, and you."

Mom's body vibrated: so much time had passed since she'd been in a child's company.

"I like your hair, missus . . ."

"Murtag," I said.

". . . Murtag," said Amira. "A big puffy snowcloud."

"Oh." Mom touched her hair. "Thank you so much. I like your teeth. So white and straight. Must take good care of them. They look like . . ."

She trailed off, unable to finish her thought. The awkward moment was interrupted by the peacock making its popping-acorn noises. As we went to the bathroom to check on it, Mom touched Amira's shoulder gingerly.

"Like beautiful little seashells, yes? Your teeth."

Amira had emptied the tub and filled it with fresh water. A tin of kidney beans sat on the toilet tank. Amira doled a spoonful onto the bird's styrofoam raft.

"You made this?" Mom asked Amira.

The girl nodded. "Its leg is broken," she said. "It can float until it gets better."

"How very clever."

The phone rang. I left them in the bathroom to answer it.

Dead silence on the line. No, not quite: faraway breathing, snuffling almost, kind of like the other end was within the proximity of a sleeping baby.

"Murtag?"

It was Garvey. He sobbed softly, as an infant might.

"Come over, Murtag, would you?" A hitching breath. "Only a little while."

30 The Land of Milk and Honey

A van was parked outside Garvey's apartment. Powder blue paintjob, windows blocked out with masking tape. Painted on the side was a mural of the Immaculate Mother cradling a newborn babe. Garvey lived in a three-storey walk-up above a Levite Ave bakery: Golden Rays of Sun. He enjoyed waking to the smell of baking bread. The bakery was shut down; a vandal had spray painted the sign to read Golden Rays of *Sin*, a defacement deeply lacking in wit.

I let myself in. The door was unlocked. Garvey sat on a sofa littered with Hallelujah Energy Boost bottles. The coffee table was spread with electronics: a calculator and a stopwatch and a digital cooking thermometer. Junk now, Garvey having disassembled them to their component wires and diodes. He was presently dismantling his wristwatch with a screwdriver.

Garvey glanced at the TV, tuned to static—that being all any TV could pick up anymore.

"You know," he said vacantly, "I'm pretty sure there's something to all that."

"To what, Garvey?"

"A pattern to the static. Watch long enough, you see shapes moving in there."

Soon he'd be glimpsing Jesus' face in the TV snow, same as loons claimed to see it in their grilled cheese sandwiches or the oil stain on their garage floor. He took a swallow from the nearest HEB bottle, arranged a few stray wires into a runic pattern on the table and said, "You and Doe weren't around. So it fell to us."

"What fell?"

"Duty."

He fussed with his wristwatch but the screwdriver head didn't match the screw slots so he stabbed the tool into the soft wood of the coffee table, left it quivering and went to the window. It overlooked the city's southern rim. The view stretched to the southernmost limits and the Damascus Towers.

"That's where they're holed up," said Garvey. "The heathens who've made a mess of our lives. That's their . . . nest."

"How do you figure?"

"The Quints sussed it out."

"So you're going to . . ."

He didn't answer. It smashed together in my head. The van I'd noticed down on the street. How much explosive was packed inside of it? Garvey had martyrdom on his mind.

"We're Followers, Garvey. We . . . we don't do those sorts of things."

He shrugged. "Sometimes the tactics of your enemies are the only ones that work against them."

"It's suicide, man. A sin."

"I considered that," he admitted. "And this morning, when the Quints showed up with the van and opened the doors, those sacks of fertilizer stacked to the roof . . . it went through my head. But somebody's got to. Us or them."

I followed him into the bedroom. A kid's room: evangelical singers were tacked on the walls. The southern wall was plastered with half-naked men; I recognized them as being ripped from the Summer Fling issue of those Sears and Roebuck catalogues he'd been tasked with bagging up as evidence—evidence that never did find its way to the lockup, I suddenly recalled.

A tuxedo was laid out on the bedspread.

"I was supposed to be married in it," Garvey said of the monkey suit. "Cost a pretty penny."

He drew a beach towel off a box on the dresser. An aquarium. Something was coiled round the rock. I drew closer. It was a rattlesnake.

Garvey said, "It's a hognose. My papa's before he died. Almost as old as me, this tough old pig."

"Poisonous, yeah?"

"His venom sacks were cut out years ago. Not to say he won't bite you—just won't kill you if he does."

"He got a name?"

"Duke."

"You don't still . . . ?"

"Handle him? That's not part of my beliefs anymore." He pocketed his hands to hide the puncture scars. "Besides, without the poison it's not a true test of faith."

Duke uncoiled from the rock, tail making a sound like a baby's rattle. Its face was accordioned in as though someone had used a tiny hammer to render it snub-nosed.

"What does he eat?"

Garvey said: "Used to be mice, but the pet shop's gone. He'll happily enough eat eggs. Quail if I can find them, but he'll put away a chicken egg."

The phone rang. I trailed him into the kitchen and heard his side of a short conversation with someone—one of the Quints, maybe.

Garvey said: "Yes . . . half an hour, okay . . . all glory to God."

He hung up and vanished into the bedroom. The door shut.

Ten minutes later he came out in the tuxedo.

He said: "How do I look?"

"Your bowtie's on crooked."

He allowed me to unkink his tie and centre it below his chin.

Garvey holstered his revolver. "You'll take good care of Duke?"

"I will."

I trailed him down the stairwell. "Don't do this, Garvey. Don't be such a fucking . . . Follower."

He turned. His face was clouded with dull rage. He opened the apartment door and stomped out, down the stairs to the street. I watched him. He got in the van, which accelerated down the block, hit the corner and slued round the bend.

Sometime later the air went as shimmery as a clean stretch of tarmac on a summer's day. Hot wind buffeted my face. When the second Damascus Tower began to fall I turned away.

31 Big Decisions

I drove home. Duke the rattlesnake lay curled in its aquarium on the passenger seat.

I entered the apartment foyer. Doc Newbarr must have stopped by; a brown bottle had been left in my mailbox. I opened the apartment door to find my mother and Amira on the floor playing Scrabble. They sat cross-legged, hunched over their tile racks. I set Duke's aquarium beside Frog's tank. We peered at the snake with a mixture of disgust and perplexity.

"Gross," said Amira.

"Maybe he thinks you're gross," I said. "Not everything can be cute and cuddly. But it's true. Finding something to love in a snake is an uphill slog."

The phone rang. I picked up on the tenth ring and just listened.

"Jonah."

I said: "Swift."

"Surprised?"

"Not really. They say when all's said and done the cockroaches will be the last things left," I told him. "How did you know they were going to bomb the Towers?"

"A gypsy peered into her crystal ball and forewarned of a big bang in my future."

"The Quints won't quit til you're all pushing daisies."

"Let me worry about those hombres," he said. "The gypsy also said you visited Murphy. She foretold Murphy would cough up his secret."

"I paid for it, same as you, I'm sure."

"Did it shock you?"

"Time was it would've. Now, not so much."

"Do you really think the Quints are after me, Jonah? What *am* I, in end tally? An irritant. A thorn in the Republic's side. The Quints—Quads?—wish me dead and I've no doubt they'll have my head before long but tell me: who is the most valuable commodity in this city?"

It took a while to twig.

"Murphy and the Immaculate Mother's bastard kid."

"Correct."

"So . . . the Quints are blowing the city apart just to steal The One Child?"

Swift said: "A man may blow up an entire mountain under the belief there's a diamond inside."

"But The One Child is a . . ." What had Murphy called him? Forty pounds of useless. "Not the miracle we thought he was."

"So long as only a few know that, the illusion is maintained."

"So why not just take him?" I said. "Take him and leave."

"I suspect your Prophet saw his son as a bargaining chip so stashed him away. A day will come where the Quints rip the location out of him by force—but they've got me to deal with first."

"And you—what do you want out of this?"

Swift said, "Only an audience with your Prophet."

"Why?"

A click, followed by the dial tone.

"Who was that?" Mom asked me.

"Telephone solicitor selling pocket devotionals."

Night fell. Amira and my mother bundled away to the bedroom. I sat by the window. When those first blue waves of dawn began to wash over the horizon I took up pen and paper and fired off a note to them.

I have to go. Will not be gone long—today, back tomorrow night. If I am not back by then, call my friend, Mr. Newbarr; his number is below. He will wait with you until I return. I will be back. I promise.

I taped it to Frog's aquarium where they would find it when they awoke.

KIDNAPPING

At street level you could hardly see the dawn. What I first mistook for early morning mist yet to burn off was dust. A grey sheen of it hung in the air like overlapping silk curtains.

The prowl car was coated in dust, too. I emptied the washer reservoir to clear the windshield. When I pulled away dust blew off the hood and roof and trunk, a gauzy rooster tail fanning out my wake.

I stopped at a Puritan's Pantry. Deserted, everything covered in ash. I arced a flashlight over aisles littered with junk food, sticky with soda pop. Corn chips crunched under my boots and the sound made me think of that tractor trailer, all those tiny avian bones. I stuffed a grocery sack full of beef jerky and Angel Cloud powdered donuts and bottled water.

I walked behind the coolers and cut a length of refrigeration tubing with my utility knife, coiled it, headed back through the store, grabbing a buffing shammy hanging beside pine-tree-shaped car air fresheners on the way out.

I drove east until I found myself behind Doe's apartment. I pocketed the bottle Newbarr had left in my mailbox, popped the trunk, grabbed the crowbar, and made for the fire escape. I socked the crowbar into a window and set my shoulder to it. The latch popped. I walked through a vacant apartment to the hallway. Doe was the next floor up. I headed up the stairwell and knocked on her door with the well-soaked shammy tucked behind my back.

"Doe. It's Murtag."

The whisper of feet. The door creaked with her weight set against it.

"Whatever you're selling, we're not buying."

"For God's sakes, Angela. I got a question for you; that's it."

"Ask away."

"We really have to do it this way?"

The deadbolt snapped. The door eased open.

"You could've chosen a more hospitable hour to—"

I jammed my foot into the doorway and hammered the door back. Doe stood there in a fleece nightgown patterned with red umbrellas, eyes crusty with sleep. I caught a whiff of her place—the stench of a hermit's shack—as I pushed the chloroform-sodden shammy into her face.

She lashed out with her leg, foot catching me between the slats but I held fast. "I'm sorry, Angela," I said, gagging on my own pain. "I'm not going to hurt you, I promise. I just need—"

She ripped at my face with her fingers, nasty catlike scratches that went for my eyes. I couldn't blame her. Who's to say I hadn't gone round the bend like everyone else in this blighted city?

I said, "It's okay, I swear it's okay," as her eyes clouded over, lids drooping, and she went limp.

✠

By the time she awoke we were well outside the zone of guaranteed public safety. The chloroform left a red stain round her nostrils and lips. She looked like a girl who'd gorged herself in a gooseberry patch. She kept silent. She wasn't scared, just wary.

I'd taken Doe's car, thinking it'd go easier on gas. No stations between here and our terminus; I'd have to siphon from abandoned vehicles, of which there was no shortage.

The land was flat, spare, quiet. Wind hummed against the car frame. Creosote bushes rose roadside; flat windswept rocks dotted the earth like cobblestones. A sharp-shinned hawk rode an updraft in the cloud-scudded southern sky.

Doe rattled her handcuffs. "Necessary?"

"For now."

"I need to pee. Happy to do it right here if we're on a tight schedule."

I pulled into the rough shale of the breakdown lane. I unlocked her door and released the cuffs from her left wrist then closed it round my own.

She said, "You're coming with?"

"I'm not keen on chasing you."

I led her to a redberry bush over the roadside berm. She picked a path across the shale in her slippered feet. Hiking up her gown, she hunkered down like a baseball catcher.

"You staying for the show?"

"I'll look away."

A dark trickle cut down the berm. She wiped and stood and we went back to the car. I didn't bother cuffing her this time. I was going to need her help.

"So where are we headed on this field trip?"

I didn't say. She already knew. She said, "Fine way to get us killed, dearie."

We were down to a half a tank of gas when I started scavenging. The first car was a late-model Chevy two-door; it lay nose-down in a spillway falling away from the road. I grabbed the jerry can and length of refrigerator tube from the trunk. A ripe stench—please God let it be spoiled food—hit my nostrils as I searched for the gas cap release inside the car. When I sunk the tube into the tank and sucked, it came up dry. Evaporated or harvested by highwaymen.

I drove on. I caught sight of a vehicle behind me—a dark speck in the rearview growing larger as it gained, taking on make and colour: a hunter green Ford Explorer. The paintwork was scarred to bare metal. A sticker on its front bumper read: MY KID IS AN HONOUR ROLL STUDENT! I kept the needle steady and drew my revolver, cocked it, laid it cross my lap.

The Explorer nosed into the passing lane and inched up until we ran even. Its windows rolled down—the highwayman didn't quite look like a highwayman. More a stockbroker who'd slogged through a rough day on the trading floor. He wore a white pinstriped shirt gone yellow under the arms.

I flipped my badge over the window frame, let it hang. He turned to inspect it. The left half of his face was all but torn off. The flesh under his eye and down his cheek was missing; a thin web work of scar tissue had tightened over the bare muscle. He saw the badge. His hands lifted from the wheel in mock-fear: *Ooooh, scary mistah policeman!* He hammered the brakes and trailed us for a while before cutting down a corduroy road leading into the flood plains.

The sky was darkening toward dusk when we came upon an Oldsmobile. A well-appointed model, the sort a Minister might've been ferried about in by a liveried chauffeur.

It was parked in a gravelled crescent cut away from the road. In the backseat was a child's backpack bearing the image of Saint Ignatius O'Reilly, the popular Saturday morning cartoon character.

"Door's locked," I called to Doe. "Grab the tire iron."

She'd changed into the spare clothes I'd brought: a pair of jeans torn at the knees, drab wool sweater draped over a white t-shirt, steel-toed boots. When I smashed the window, new-car smell hit me. Glossy leather and the odometer reading under 2,000. A Republic registration sticker on the dash. I clawed under the driver's seat for the gas cap release; the first lever my fingers closed on popped the trunk. I kept hunting about until Doe's voice stopped me.

"Jonah."

Doe's stricken face swam in a pool of light cast by the dome light.

"Oh, God, God, God . . ."

There were two of them. A woman and a girl. A Minister's wife and child, maybe. Perhaps she'd stolen her husband's car, taken her daughter, set off for in hopes of escape.

They lay, daughter curled into the mother's chest, inside the trunk. The industrial fabric on the trunk lid hung in rags, bare metal underneath blood streaked strands. Their bodies shrivelled, flesh shrunk round the bones and faces heat-wizened. Apple dolls were what they looked like. Life-sized apple dolls. That they appeared to be smiling was a trick of bodily corruption, skin curling from their teeth, which were straight and white and emphasized the probability they had been mothers and daughters of privilege.

"How do you figure they ended up in here?" I said, looking away. "Highwayman?"

"That, or whoever was driving."

"What—husband? Father? *Why?*"

"Why any of it?" Doe said simply.

When I went to close the trunk Doe asked what the hell was I doing. "We can't leave them there," she said.

"We don't have much choice. Moving them's going to be . . . messy."

Doe set a hand on the woman's shoulder and gave an experimental tug. Some part of the woman's anatomy gave way; a substance too thin and black to be blood, some noxious serum, soiled the carpet round her head.

She only said, "You're right. But we're not taking the gas."

"I don't see's we got a whole lot of option in the matter."

"It's ghoulish. We may as well crack into a coffin to steal the coins off a stiff's eyes."

"Well," I said evenly, "you don't have to help."

In the end she helped.

The dashboard clock read 10:32 when our hi-beams illuminated a sign reading NEW BEERSHEBA CITY LIMITS. Below that: POPULATION . . . but someone had spray painted over the number and left a black devouring mouth, a zero, in its place.

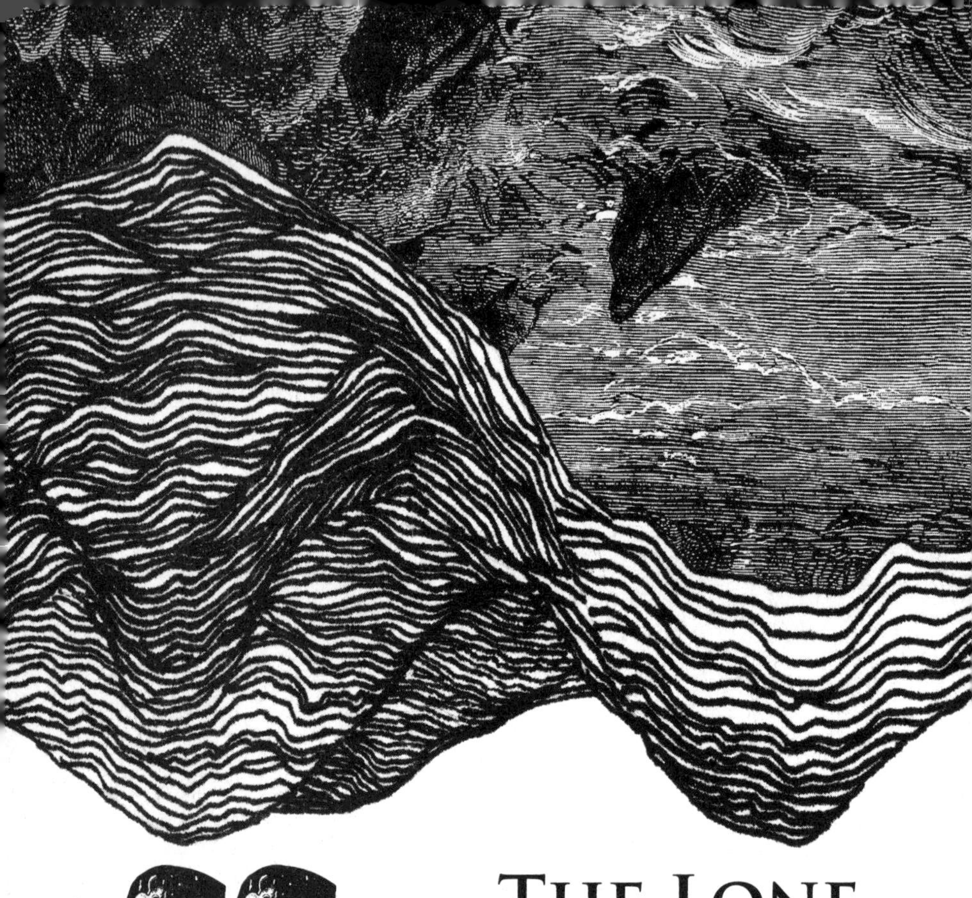

33

The Lone Lookout

The watchtower stood on wooden posts thirty feet above the grasslands overlooking the eastern outskirts of New Beersheba. A fire-spotter's tower of a sort you'd find in the forest. A spotlight made a slow strafe of the city perimeter. A Bronco was parked beneath it.

I eased up a quarter-furlong from the tower and cut the headlights.

"What do you think?"

"Ought to announce our intentions," she said.

I stood outside the car and laid on the horn. The spotlight pinned us; I squinted into the glare with arms raised. "We're Acolytes! New Bethlehem!"

The spotlight made a circuit round the car. A bullhorn-amplified voice said, "Come on if you're coming."

We picked our way across the salt flats. Tips of salt-crusted weeds sparkled like diamond dust. A rope ladder had been lowered; I followed Doe up it to a trapdoor cut out of the watchtower's floor.

The tower was the size of those panic rooms well-to-do families used to have installed way back when. A pane of plexiglass running each of the four walls gave the place a fishbowl feel. A military-style cot hugged the far wall. Hotplate, a few sacks of rice. Two radios, CB, and a transistor hanging from a nail not far from the spotlight, which was set up beside a pair of binoculars on a swivelling tripod. Leaning on the wall next to the specs: a long-bore sniper rifle fitted with a starlight scope. I clocked the photos of a woman and a young girl beside the cot.

The watchman appeared too old for active duty, though one might argue there wasn't much active about this duty. He wore an out-of-date plainclothes uniform with the insignia of the New Beersheba PD. His face had the mournful aspect of a basset hound, and the skin under his dark brown eyes was thin as onionskin in the lamplight.

A folding card table was spread with wires and soldering gun and a green fibreglass circuit board; the sight brought to mind Garvey's coffee table spread with disassembled crap.

"I'm building a crystal radio," the man said. "Gets so god-awful lonely out here you want nothing more than to hear a voice not your own, even if you gotta pull it outta thin air."

He gave his name as Jeremy. He didn't ask our business, but he did asked if we wanted to take a gander at the city and when I nodded, he unscrewed the starlight scope from the rifle.

"Range of fifty furlongs," he said. "See clear to downtown. What used to be, anyway."

Images formed out of the green phosphorous. Buildings staggered over what was left of the downtown core, black obelisks and razed apartments stabbing up like canine teeth. No movement; a city still and static as mausoleum shadows, coldly austere as a moonscape.

"My granddaddy fought in a war they used napalm," said Jeremy. "Brutal stuff. Said when the flyboys dropped it, looked like a fat tongue of fire lickin' over the jungle. Left a jet-black scar. Seems like the same thing happened to that city there."

"And your job is to what," Doe wanted to know, "keep everyone inside?"

"Keep the *information* inside," Jeremy said. "It's not the people who're dangerous, not after everything that's happened—it's what they *know*. Can't leak what happened, who did this 'n' that, how it all fell apart. That's gotta stay in the city."

I said, "So what do you do to make them stay put?"

"I don't do much." Jeremy shrugged. "Me? I'm old."

He walked to the plexiglass that looked out over the city.

"That in there, that's Hell. You're thinking I overstate myself; I can tell. But you go on in. You'll see. A little piece of the world fell away and a little piece a Hell pushed itself up in its place. Every day I stare into it; every night I struggle to sleep at the foot of it. Sometimes I think of the people still inside and figure it's only what they deserve—broke the Lord's Commandments, fell away from the path. They earned their ails. So what'm I gonna do? Shoot some poor bastard who found themselves a way out of Hell?"

I said, "We're going in tonight."

"Day or night, it's all the same," said Jeremy. "Night may be better. Less scavengers."

"What neighbourhood's closest?"

"Two furlongs straight on you hit the Minister's district. Million-shekel homes crumbling away. Why do you have to go inside? You don't need to stick your head in an old tiger's mouth to know it's fulla rot."

When it became clear we were not to be dissuaded, Jeremy sent us off with an Inova T5 tactical flashlight—good, he assured us, to a furlong—and a Coleman Krypton lantern.

"You gotta consider the people inside as forest animals—more afraid of you than you of them," he said, his last words to us before we left. "But there is this *one* fella. I've heard he's blind as a bat now, but still. Chances of you bumping into him are near zero, but if there's only one shark in the whole ocean . . . well, there's still that one."

I knew who he must've been talking about.

We trudged toward the city limits in silence. Jeremy laid out a path until the spotlight beam turned coarse, particles of darkness overtaking those of light.

When full dark fell again neither of us made a move: simply stood in that vast emptiness, me tight to Doe's side—no moon, no stars, both of us perched on the verge of an ineffable blackness that began the very next step and possessed no limits or end.

"You don't have to," I told her. "But I need to know."

She snorted. "You knock me out and handcuff me and drag me all this way and *now* you tell me I don't have to go? Little late, don't you think?" She stared over the black city and said, "Besides, you think you're the only human being born curious?"

The Lost Quint

"What do you know already?"

We weren't far from the Ministers' estates. Their dilapidated flame-scorched contours stood out against puffy night clouds.

Doe checked up. "What do you mean?"

I said, "I'm asking if you were aware of this state of affairs before we arrived. If a *swift* little birdie told you."

She turned to me, her face white as a harlequin mask in the flashlight beam.

"If you dragged me all the way out here to force some kind of apology, you won't get it. I didn't know about any state of affairs. That was never discussed between him and me."

"What *was* discussed? How did you find him?"

"Swift found *me*, Jonah. He has that way of finding people. Reclamation projects. He . . . he *knew* things. I didn't credit him at first but in time I did."

"Aren't you afraid of him?"

"Are you?"

"I am."

Doe said, "Is that because he stands to ruin the way of life you've known?"

"Partly, yes."

"Well, the Romans were scared of Jesus Christ."

We walked down the block to a four-way crossing. The street sign read LUCIAN COURT.

"There," said Doe. "See them?"

She pointed to the corner lot. All around it were bombed-out houses falling in upon themselves. Twinkle of smashed glass. Burnt-out husks of luxury SUVs. All of it blackened except the tiny spark she gestured at.

"What are they?"

"Flowers," she said. "Roses, it looks like."

The house was unremarkable in every detail except that it was largely unmarked; the homes on each side had been reduced to soot-grimed skeletons. A three-storey redbrick with attached three-car garage. A modest balcony projected off the second floor over the garage, its rail still strung with Christmas lights.

The flowers—healthy white roses in bloom—were planted in a patch of well-tended earth the size of a manhole cover. A hand-trowel and a box of plant food nearby. The flowers looked to have been well-cared for, even though nothing else in sight was so lucky.

Doe said: "Creepy."

The front door was unlocked. We entered wordlessly. A narrow hallway. Mud-spattered galoshes on a doormat embroidered with cherubs and BLESS THIS MESS.

The front room was wide and starkly furnished. A dusty glass-topped coffee table spread with copies of *God's Word Today* and *Ignite Your Faith*. A ceramic rabbit in the shape of a chocolate Easter bunny sat in the centre of the table; its ears had been snapped off and the hollow cavity stuffed with the same roses we'd seen outside, wilted now. I shone the flashlight over the walls. A display case filled with trophies—for figure skating, mainly. Two plaques mounted on embossed wooden backings. One featured a pair of crossed scimitars: The Kingdom of Heaven Award. An ornate cut-glass cross occupied a second case: The Crystal Cross of Spirituality, awarded several years ago to Follower Lucas Hogan.

It was the photograph that I lingered on, mainly as it seemed so out of place. A young girl leaning against a concrete pillar in a wash of sunlight. Blonde hair tucked up under a hat that looked like a Confederate soldier's, only white. She wore a dress, also white, of some diaphanous material that picked up the sun and sparkled like insect wings.

Somewhere in the house a voice rung out, "Hello? Hello?"

"Acolytes," Doe called back.

The voice: reedy and fearful and male. "Take whatever you can use and go away."

"We're not thieves," I assured him. "We've come from New Bethlehem."

"I see . . . I've never heard of a female Acolyte. Little more encompassing in New Bethlehem, are they? Come, come in. I'm in the kitchen."

The kitchen was tricked out nouveau style: stainless steel fridge, stove with gas burners, one of those whisper-quiet dishwashers. There was a smell here: sweet and awful, like the syrup at the bottom of a bus terminal garbage can.

The room was dominated by a chopping block table. A man sat in the light of a guttering candle.

"Enter of your own free will," he said, "and leave some of the joy you bring with you."

"Lucas Hogan?"

"The Lord his grace and mercy upon us, yes, that's me."

Hogan wore an official Minister's robe. Frayed at the sleeves and torn down the front; the swath of sparsely haired chest led me to believe he was naked underneath.

"You've come to collect me?" he said eagerly. "Take me back to New Bethlehem?"

Doe said: "We saw the roses."

"A beacon, aren't they? Someone civilized, god-fearing, still lives here."

Hogan may once have been handsome but hunger and sleeplessness had done a number on him—it was as though a sinkhole in the centre of his face, localized to his nose, was drawing his features ever-inwards. He wore massive Blueblocker sunglasses.

"We have a few questions," I said. "Do you know of a man named Tom Swift?"

"Is that the name he's going by now? I'm not surprised. He has many names."

"What did you know him by?"

"Here he was Victor Appleton," Hogan said.

"How did you meet him?"

"At a Candles for Christ fundraiser. I was with my wife and daughter. We were all quite taken with him. If you've met him, you'll understand that Victor is a man with a captivating quality."

A mild thumping arose behind the pantry door. The wind?

I said: "The photo in the front room . . ."

"Celeste, my daughter," Hogan said quickly. "A figure skater. A ballerina on blades."

"She looks graceful," Doe offered. "And obviously very accomplished, judging by the display case."

"She was graceful, yes, thank you for saying so. My daughter's skating instructor said she had the strongest, the most agile legs she'd ever seen. I never thought much of it until . . ."

"Tell me, Mr. Hogan." I said. "What happened here?"

"Victor Appleton," said Hogan simply. "Victor happened."

"Where did he come from?" I pressed. "How did he ingratiate himself?"

"Oh, he was very smooth. Charismatic—oh so charismatic. He was . . . even back then, with the world so ordered and everyone known, sometimes—very rarely in life, but *sometimes*—a person can appear in your midst and nobody has a clue *where* he comes from. We were all so pleased he was there. He was special. Even now, hate him though I do, I cannot deny that he is a special man. And so you see, officer, he didn't have to ingratiate himself. We prostrated ourselves before him."

"What did he do?" asked Doe.

"It happened during SuperChurch services," said Hogan. "Seventy thousand Followers packed like sardines. The explosions—seven, eight, nine, I don't know; they went off all around the same time—blew right through the congregation. Our Prophet was vapourized in the middle of an acoustic guitar singalong. I would've been killed myself had I not been using the facilities. My wife wasn't so lucky."

Doe and I exchanged a quick look. "Our condolences on your lo—"

More scuttling from behind the pantry door.

"Drafts," Hogan said, waving the sounds off. "House falling apart."

I noticed a screwdriver wedged in the pantry door jamb to keep it shut.

"It was mayhem," he went on, "There simply wasn't the infrastructure to deal with the death and injury toll. The hospitals were packed. And even as we tried to cope with that, the bombings continued. Firehouses, parliament, police headquarters. At first we thought it was heathen suicide squads doing it . . . but word began to filter out that it was *us*. Followers doing it to each other. And the Divine Council didn't send any aid. We were damned—this was the word coming back. A damned people. A damned city."

"And then?" I prompted.

"And then the Quints were sent in. Just craziness. Looting. Rioting. Dead bodies in the streets. Block upon block of bombed-out husks." Logan paused, lost in recollection. "We got together—some Ministers, district officials, whoever was still around. We wanted to hammer out an exit strategy. I was with my daughter Celeste. Victor attended with an associate, some mountain of a man. Nobody had any idea *he* was behind all the destruction at that point. He'd brought a case of Republic Claret. . . . I don't know what he dosed it with, or how. We all went out like lights. And then he must've dosed us with something more potent; no other way we would've slept through what was done."

The walls . . . I could hear something inside them, scrabbling noises not unlike the clawing of trapped animals. Did Doe hear that?

Doe said: "What happened, Follower Hogan?"

Hogan removed his sunglasses. His *eyes*. In the mutable light of the candle they were blobs of pewter. No cornea, no iris.

"I don't know how it was done. Maybe they dipped Q-Tips in acid and smeared it over. Maybe they injected it behind my eyeballs, burned them out at the root. Hardly felt a thing when I came to—just an icy-hot burning in back of my eyes. Then I heard the screaming. He'd done the same to all of us. Thirty pieces of silver; we'd all taken it, Appleton said, and this was our comeuppance. He left us where we lay and took our children. He took my daughter. My Celeste."

"So Victor kidnapped her," I said.

Hogan laughed. "You said you knew him. You think he had to kidnap her? She didn't even say goodbye. Just gone, gone away."

I thought back to Jack Olen Hanratty's description of the Matthew's Square bomber. A beautiful blonde-haired girl in a funny white hat.

The pantry door went thunka-thunk-*thunk*.

Hogan said: "After being blinded I dragged myself back here. Took three days."

"How do you fend for yourself?" I asked.

"Why don't we get going?" he said. "I can answer all this later."

Doe said: "We don't know our way around. We'll wait until morning."

"It's better to move at night. Safer, believe me."

"We'll wait."

After a moment: "I eat what I can," Hogan said, his teeth clenching. "Scavenge the houses around here. Most have well-stocked cupboards. I get by. My wife didn't get the idea of conservation. I didn't know how long we'd have to scrape by until God's grace intervened; quit eating so much, I kept telling her. But she'd never had to suffer a day in her charmed life—"

Doe said: "Minister, you told us your wife died in an explosion."

I glanced at the pantry, then at a skillet on the stove: something had been burned to the density of charcoal. The knives fastidiously, *anally*, arranged on the counter.

"Very clean kitchen you've got here," I said as Doe moved to the pantry door.

"Cleanliness is next to Godliness," Hogan said in a trilling singsong.

Doe gripped the screwdriver in the doorjamb. The wood squealed when she pulled it out. Hogan swivelled, his face exhibiting some feral species of alarm. I shoved his chair into the table, pinning him there.

When Doe wrenched the door open and I saw what I saw—how long did I gaze? A second? Half that? That was all it took to burn it in—my body, every cell of it, inside and out.

"We were both blinded," Hogan sobbed. "I pleaded with her to conserve rations. She didn't get it. She was born a Minister's daughter, raised a Minister's daughter, married a future Minister—she never knew true want."

The pantry shelves had been stripped. The walls were taped with black Hefty bags. The *thing* was spread across a glossy tarp of trash bags. The thing thrashed and shook. The thing had bloody duct tape lashed over its stumps.

"You're wondering why I couldn't just kill her," Hogan went on. "The power was out; I couldn't freeze the bits," Hogan said. "It's the only way to keep it . . . fresh. I gave her a good life. She owed somebody something, didn't she? Surely you'll understand."

I felt Doe's hand on my waist. Trembling as it climbed my ribcage but steady as it unsnapped the holster and like stone as it pulled out my revolver.

She said: "Wait for me in the yard."

Outside I heard the shots. Two, with a short lag between.

Doe met me in the yard. Dry-eyed, blood speckled on her cheeks. She gave the gun back to me.

She said: "I don't want this happening to us."

"To us?"

"New Bethlehem. Our city."

My eyes snagged on movement over her shoulder, down the end of the street. My jaw fell open in shock.

It *couldn't* be. This city was too vast, the chances next to nil. I squinted down the dew-wetted tarmac into the clearness of the floodplains beyond. I whispered, "Shhhhh."

She turned, looked. We waited.

There. A glint of white. An albino-white duster—but torn now, grimed with blood.

If there's only one shark in the whole sea . . . well, there's still that one.

It was the Quint. Number Three. The lost one.

She grabbed my arm. "*Run*."

We dashed through Hogan's backyard at a dead sprint, Doe matching me stride for stride. I cut through Hogan's gazebo, crashed awkwardly through the warped wooden latticework, sprinting a few steps to vault the chain link fence into Hogan's neighbours' backyard. We pelted across the lawn, blood hammering in my eardrums, so wired I swore I saw fine blue electricity snapping off the tips of my fingers. I trailed Doe across the lawn over the fence into the next yard, bear-walking behind a hedgerow, wondering why, the Quint was blind according to the lookout—but it wasn't a matter of being seen but rather sensed, *smelled*. As if we were being hunted by a giant mole rat or an albino earthworm.

We broke past the hedgerow into the yard, running through a child's sandbox with high-kneed, churning steps; I trod on a rusted Tonka truck half-buried in sand, twisted my ankle and hissed in pain. I limped past a dog run housing a canine skeleton with its teeth clamped to the chain link and its sleek skull shining with dew. Doe cut sharply through a darkened breech between houses and we were on another street running in what I felt to be the right direction but not entirely sure.

Mailboxes in the shape of cathedrals. Burnt houses leaned predatorily, hungrily over the road. I hazarded a glance over my shoulder and caught the knife-flash no more than a block off, skirting the flank of a fire-gutted garden shed. How many shots were left in my revolver? Four, Doe having used two; I spun awkwardly, pistol out, trying to draw a bead but there was nothing to orient on—only block upon block of nerve-chafing dark. We followed the blind curve of the road into the barrens, fleeing across sand overlaid with a layer of fog so thick we couldn't see our feet.

I barely heard the shot; the only way I knew we'd been fired at was the puff that bloomed in the fog two feet ahead to our left. I grabbed Doe's shoulder, cutting hard right and in doing so nearly ran into the watchtower we'd have otherwise fled right past.

The car was just where we'd left it—for a panicky instant it looked to have sunk into the earth but this was only the effect created by sand drifting round the tires. I moved toward the driver's side but Doe darted in front and I was forced to do an end-around, flanking the trunk and sliding into the passenger's seat. Doe keyed the ignition, set the tranny in reverse and goosed the gas; the tires spun, yowled, spat sand.

I said: "Ease it, ease up; you're gonna mire us!"

"I got it, shut up I got it."

She dropped into drive and gave it gas. The chassis groaned, rocking forward. The hood squatted so low I feared the crankcase would eat sand. She flicked the headlamps, flooding the barrens and the ice-cold sky beyond . . .

. . . and there he stood, no more than fifty paces away. Colourless duster flapping in a desert wind to make his body look huger, more menacing. The number '3' tattooed on his neck and his cheeks cratered with acidic scars, eyes blazing red in the glow of the headlights.

The Quint's pistol-arm went up. The sideview mirror exploded in a spray of plastic and glass, remnants hanging off the doorframe by coloured wires; Doe wrenched the wheel full left, tires gritting in their sandy grooves; the windshield spidered as a hole punched through six inches wide of her skull to burrow into the backseat upholstery; she stood on the gas as if weighing herself, tires spinning, smoking; I scrabbled for my revolver as another slug whanged off the moulding somewhere above my head.

Doe hauled the wheel right, slammed the gearshift into reverse and stamped the gas; my gun was ready when the car caught traction, sluing assways in a drunken arc, wind lashing through the shattered windshield as the undercarriage scraped a half-buried rock to send blue sparks fanning up before the grille. My finger jarred the trigger and a bullet punched into the roof. The interior reeked of cordite as Doe reversed in a long sweeping bend then dropped the transmission without taking her foot off the gas; the engine screamed like a scalded cat and before the gearbox bit, she cut side-to-side and sent up a rooster tail made red by the brake lights.

I got a leg up and kicked the busted windshield, popping it from the frame and watching it crumple onto the hood. I thumbed the dome light and found three fresh cartridges in the grooves of the rubberized floor mat, snapped the revolver chamber, teased out the spent shells, filled the empty cylinders and calmly said, "Turn back around."

"What?"

"Turn around. I am going to kill that thing."

Doe actually smiled. "I like a man with a death wish."

We charged across the flatlands in a shaky little car, creosote bushes and salt-plants crushed under the piebald tires as the night pushed in at us, wind rippling the skin of our faces like boat sails. The car took a bad hop off a hillock, wheels accelerating as the hood reared up and nosed down into the sand to send what seemed a dune's worth up over the hood, blanking out the high beams. Sand blew clear of the lights and there, pinned in the glare like a moth to a velvet sheet, was the Quint.

I squeezed off a shot, two, three as we pounded in on him like the hammers of Hell but they missed and the Quint squared to the onrushing car, leering as he returned fire. A headlight deadheaded in a shower of electric sparks; a crisp metallic *ka-*

ting! as another slug drilled the radiator.

The Quint juked deftly and we might have only clipped him with the fender had Doe not calmly juked the same way, centring him back on the hood to slam into him broadside.

The Quint broke over the grille, engine squeal and buckled metal as the airbag deployed, a ghostly bubble pinning Doe back in her seat but she kept the pedal floored with the Quint's body now lodged in the windshield gap, his rancid duster flapping inside the car and a maddening cockroach hiss coming from—from where, his body?

The flappings and hissings and mere proximity revolted me so much I reared back and kicked, my ankle howling, but I ignored the pain as I hoofed at the Quint's spine until the body tumbled free of the windshield, bumping over the hood down off the trunk.

Doe finally slammed the brakes, bringing the car to a lurching halt.

When we got out, the Quint lay face down in the glow of the brake lights. Saf-T-Glas winked in the sand. The duster torn up the centre, wadded round the shoulders and spread out on either side like a pair of diseased angel's wings. He wasn't moving and was in all likelihood dead, though with a thing such as that you had to wonder.

The watchtower spotlight shaped a bright halo round the Quint's body. We took a step back, shielding our eyes.

"That's it," Jeremy's bullhorn-amplified voice advised. "Stand back."

His first shot missed its mark, catching the Quint's shoulder. The hydrostatic pressure was still enough to send blood jetting out his ears. The second tore off the crown of his skull.

The spotlight snapped off. Jeremy said: "God watch over you both."

Confessions

I awoke in the car. We were parked somewhere in the Badlands.

Doe was awake, sitting next to me. She said, "There's something you should know."

She sat up in the driver's seat. I was reclined in the passenger's seat. I lifted my eyebrows, waiting for it.

"I'm pregnant."

I almost laughed. "No, you're not."

She said, "I know my own body."

"Pregnant?" My head was swimming. "Me? I mean, *us*?"

"You think I get around that much?"

"Okay," I said. "Okay, okay. That's . . . so great. You're pregnant. We're sinners, but that's okay, too. I mean, it is, right? Isn't it fine?"

She drew away. "I can't, Jonah . . . I won't be keeping it."

"Please don't say that. You haven't—"

"Thought it through? Don't insult me, Jonah."

I said, "You didn't even give me a chance to say whether I wanted it."

"Do you?"

"Yes, of course, for God's sake, *yes,* I want our child."

Months ago I could've placed a call to the Parenthood Ministry and they would have dispatched agents to enforce the pregnancy. Not to say I would have done so, but the option existed. Now what the hell could I do?

"You have to look at it rationally," she said. "It's so small right now—not even a person. A bundle of cells. It won't know it ever existed."

"We'll know, won't we?"

"Just some cells," she said. "Grey cells. No face, no hands, nothing human about it."

"We could get out," I said. "Of the city. Calvin Newbarr, he's got a cottage someplace. He'd know a thing or two about delivering a baby—"

She cut me off. "Listen to me, Jonah: the decision has been made."

"So why tell me?" I said angrily. "Seeing as every conclusion was foregone."

"Because it seemed fair that you know. And because I could use your help. I need . . . what's his name? Jewish, runs a record shop? We busted him a few years back for—"

"Goldberg."

"Tibor Goldberg, right. He knew a guy, didn't he?"

I hung my head. "That's supposing either Tibor or the guy he used to know are still in the city."

Doe said: "Can you help set it up?"

"I don't know," I said honestly. "You're asking me to seek out a hit man and make arrangements for a murder."

"You do understand I'll find a way regardless."

"You'd make a good mother, Angela."

"Please. Just stop it."

She keyed the engine. The car rumbled to life. She set it in gear and we drove back to the city in silence.

Arrangements

We ran out of gas two blocks from Doe's place. I left her without saying goodbye.

The prowl car was where I'd left it. When I got back to the apartment there was a note in the mailbox from Doc Newbarr. A pencil-drawn map to his cabin. There were a pair of messages on the answering machine. One from Hollis, saying to visit him at home. Another from Swift, saying simply: *Whenever you're ready.*

My mother and Amira were sleeping in the same bed. I left them and went to find Tibor.

The checkpoint shack leading into Kiketown was destroyed. A strange calm overhung the ghetto. Street signs had all been repainted: Pilate Court read as Yahweh Court; Iscariot Gardens was now Abraham Gardens. Divine Discs was closed. Goldberg's apartment was above the shop. I laid on the horn.

"Goldberg! Tibor Goldberg!"

The upper-storey window rattled up. Goldberg leaned out.

"The fuck you want?"

"Just a question."

"I don't converse with heathens." Tibor was wearing a yarmulke. *Proudly*.

"What's written back on the checkpoint? My Yiddish is rusty."

"*Kristlekh Sotn Avekgeyn*," he said, spitting the words at me. "Christian Devils Go Home."

"One question," I said. "I come in peace."

"Try anything and you'll be leaving in pieces," Tibor warned.

I waited patiently as he snapped the lights on and unlocked the shop doors.

"Thanks," I said.

Tibor said: "*Geh cocken offen yom*."

"Translation?"

"Go shit in the ocean."

I followed him in. He took a seat, heels kicked up on the counter.

"Of course you realize you've run a good chance of getting shot coming here, you dumb schlemiel."

"Calculated risk," I said. "You guys are holding it together well."

"Always someone was oppressing us. We're still here—and will be, when you and your people are just bones."

"I'm looking for someone to perform an abortion."

"Right to the point, huh? And you thought who better to consult than Tibor Goldberg, the unscrupulous Jew, uh?"

I showed him my palms. "You could sit there all day ragging me and what? It's gonna change anything? Wish it were so."

"Do you?" He seemed genuinely curious. "Thing is, you weren't one of the really bad ones. In that way, you're nearly human. The bitch of it is, I'm left to wonder if it's laudable—you could've been a bastard, same as your partner—or worse, because you knew how bad it was but didn't lift a finger to change a thing."

"Can you help or not? Because if insults are all you've got, I've got plenty of those in escrow all over what's left of this city."

"Give me your badge."

I dug into my trousers and handed him the badge. It meant nothing to me now. He buffed it on his vest, clipped it askew to his pocket.

"I'll be back," he said, and disappeared up to his room. He returned ten minutes later.

"Tonight," he told me. "No payment. He just wants a favour."

"What sort of favour?"

"He'll discuss that beforehand. You agree, it's done. If not . . ." He shrugged. "509 Makht Avenue. Eleven o'clock."

I said: "There is no such place."

"There is now. Used to be Zundel Avenue."

37 Secrets and Lies

Deacon Hollis's house was the smallest on his court. A split-level California rambler, redbrick covered with adobe that, in the moonlight, resembled undercooked meatloaf. Frail light burned in the window. I knocked. The curtains parted. A shape moved in the direction of the door, which opened a crack. "That you, Murtag?"

"It is, sir."

Hollis's house was rathskeller dim. This proved fortunate, as it prevented Hollis from catching the dread that flickered across my face at the sight of him.

"Didn't know it was you, lad. Must be going blind." He launched into song: "Mi-iii-y eyes a-a-har dim, I can-*not* see; I have not got my specs with me . . ."

"If I may say so, sir, it's not your eyes. You're shitfaced."

"Always said you were a top rank investigator." He chortled. "Very little gets by you."

I trailed him into the front room. His home stunk: the shuttered stink of unstinting habitation. A pair of loungers sat before the window; Hollis took one but when I went to sit in the other he uttered a grunt of objection.

"Where my wife used to sit. Take the sofa, wouldn't you please? Glad you've come, lad. You and I could use a little chinwag in these, the last days before doomsday."

I sat on the sofa. "I can't help notice what you're wearing."

"You've seen one before?"

"A scapular, isn't it?"

"Green, for Saint Mary."

He fingered the simple Catholic charm: illustrated cards affixed to felt backing and strung round his neck on a loop of string. One card: Virgin Mary holding a dove. The other: a dagger-pierced heart encircled by the words, *Immaculate Heart of Mary Pray for Us Now and at the Hour of Our Deaths*. I also spotted his Republican rosary wrapped round the neck of a bottle beside his feet.

"I've kept them hidden under a floorboard all these years," he said. "A bottle of good Irish whiskey and my Catholic school scapular. My wife, God rest her, she never understood—why risk your safety for cardboard, string, and a dusty bottle of booze? I told her I'm the head of the Acolytes"—thumping his chest with his fist—"who in blazes would dare check my floorboards?"

"You're not Irish Catholic. You're a Follower of the Republican faith."

He took off the scapular and handed it to me. "Made it myself, in the basement of Our Lady of Lourdes. Couldn't have been older than five. I've been to many a masquerade, son, but the face under the mask has never changed."

I handed it back. He poured me a respectable measure of whiskey, the rosary clinking against my glass. It tasted like peat moss and burned its way down.

"Do you dream, laddie?"

"I've had them."

"Taciturn! Admirable trait. Lately I've been dreaming. I say dreaming but I mean daydreaming, musing," he said, "about souls. I've come to wonder if everyone is born with one. I don't mean down religious lines—no, merely the idea that some people aren't given souls. What is it that animates us if not the soul? But sometimes you come across a person and in him sense a lack of human capacity. The standard measures of tenderness or mercy."

He took a long pull from the bottle and shook like a wet dog.

"Isn't it possible the angels are overtaxed? Possible a soul here or there gets waylaid? So a child is born inhuman—an oversight of Heaven. Say that child was a boy and that boy is now a man. Say that man has come to believe himself soulless." He ran a finger round the rim of the bottle, trailed it down his throat as if dabbing aftershave. "Tell me, then—what fear need such a man have of any place called Hell?"

"What made you call me, sir?"

"Taciturn. Beautiful." He tottered up. "Come in the kitchen."

On the table: a bullet reloader and six standard issue centre-fire bullets lined up next to Hollis's service revolver. A picture frame with the glass removed. The shape of a star there in the sun-faded velveteen.

"I moulded it into slugs," he told me. "My Star of Gilead. Made of pewter, turns out. The cheapest, softest metal on earth! There were fake gemstones on the five points, too; when I melted it down, they melted, too. They weren't even glass."

"Can I ask why?"

"They're coming for me," he said, then after pausing: "The Quints. They're not exactly human, are they?"

"That's a fair assessment."

He chuckled mordantly. "A werewolf, silver. Vampires, a stake." He turned a bullet over in the candlelight. "Every monster can die. Just need the right tool. What do you think?"

I said nothing.

"Exeter," he went on, "was Episcopalian—sad bastards are born useless. A lot of times I wanted to stick a knife in him myself. But the way they did it: head sacked like a common heathen, blade poked through his neck like a Christmas goose . . . we had a deal. That business with Exeter was a deal breaker."

"Who had a deal—you and Exeter?"

He shook his head. "We were complicit in it, but the deal was brokered outside. Head office. Dispatches came from Kingdom City. Right from the tippy-top."

"What dispatches?" I said, confused. "What did they say?"

"The bombings, lad." He took another pull, his eyes charting me. "We knew they were coming."

"You mean . . ." I couldn't grasp what he was saying. "The Divine Council orchestrated them?"

He shrugged. "Knew about them, at bare minimum."

"Who else knew?"

"All I can say for sure is Exeter. Our task was to provide the illusion of an investigation. Exeter did a good job—canvassing all home and garden centres for fertilizer purchases?" A stiff laugh. "What wasted effort!"

"Did you know who was behind it?"

"I only knew who wasn't and made sure our focus stayed on them."

"What about the targets and times? Did you know Eve was going to be . . . did you send Doe and I to The Manger knowing what would happen?"

"I didn't know," he said. "But if you're asking had I have known, would I have sent you anyway—yes, I may have. I won't apologize. You're told what you need to be told, you don't go seeking answers above your station. That goes for me, too."

"How was this smokescreen supposed to benefit you?"

"Exeter and I discussed that—in fact, it marked our sole civil conversation. After the rubble cleared, we felt a reward should be in order. It's too late now. Lad, you asked me who knew the bombings were coming. That's only half the question you need to ask.

"Okay, so who didn't know?"

Hollis said nothing, just watched me.

I said: "The Prophet."

"And Bingo was his name-*o*."

I'd heard enough. I left him then, walked out to the car. Hollis followed me out. Thunderheads gathered in the western sky.

"Have you ever had the feeling of a rope around your neck, lad?" He checked each cartridge in his revolver, snapped the chamber shut. "I'm going to tell you—when that rope starts to pull tight, you can feel the devil bite your arse."

He leaned on the hood of my car, not quite ready to let me leave.

"I killed that farm girl."

I knew who he was talking about immediately. The girl in the Mormon farmhouse off RR #7. Young patrolman Hollis responding to a 533: *Failure to Conform*. For which he'd been awarded the Star of Gilead for conspicuous gallantry.

"Cut that wee girl's throat. Found her tangled there in the razor wire . . . I damn near cut her head off. Entirely too much adrenaline. You get into a killing like that, this haze, this reddish curtain, it falls over your vision; all you've got in your nostrils is the smell of blood."

"Why are you telling me this?"

Hollis's tongue protruded a half-inch between his teeth. He bit and chewed at it restlessly.

"What I'm saying is that if I'm evil—and yes, I am—I should not have to bear the brunt of that evil, its kindling in me, all by myself. Do we not live in a world that allows it, at times rewards it? So I'm a touch inhuman. Maybe I was born so. But the monsters coming for me, they're inhuman, too. That's why I can kill them. Like parries like. What do you think? Can I kill them?"

"I don't really care."

He heaved up off the hood. "Go on, hero, save who you can. May God save the rest."

"And you? Who'll save you?"

He touched his lips to his scapular.

"I'm a bog-trotting black Irish bastard. I'll save my own damned self."

Point of No Return

Rain began to bucket down as I drove away from Hollis's house. A few fat drops splashing the windshield became a steady drum. The feel of lightning inside of me, electrifying my bones, yet not one bolt cracked the sky.

I ticked over Hollis's revelations. They had *known*. Couldn't have found two more willing pawns than Exeter and Hollis: one a bureaucrat, the other a brute. Both soulless. The two of them had run the old end-around on The Prophet, compromised the safety of the city.

Headlights came up in the rearview mirror: dazzling brights that had me shielding my eyes. The car ran up tight on my bumper and slingshotted past; in the driving rain I couldn't catch sight of the driver or even the make. Slashing in front of me, now only a pair of taillights rounding the bend not far from the Kiketown checkpoint.

I motored into the ghetto at a crawl, my nerves stretched tight as fiddle strings.

I parked down an alley and cut the engine. Rain poured off shop awnings and out of downspouts. I slogged up a narrow stairwell to a locked door. My knock went unanswered. I felt along the top of the doorframe and found a key.

To say the apartment was sparely furnished was an overstatement. Halogens gave it the ambience of a lizard's terrarium. All the light touched was a military-style bed wrapped in thin plastic in the centre of the main room. Beside it was a filing cabinet stocked with gauze packets and medical tape. Beside that was the machine.

The kitchen. Drawers and cupboards empty. A pump-bottle of Medina antiseptic soap beside the sink. I walked into the bathroom. A plastic stool at the far end of the tub. A reddish tinge to the enamel.

Main room again. The machine . . . Powder-coated steel frame, squat and boxy like some primitive robot. Dials, knobs, pressure gauges. Set on rusted casters. A big red "on" switch. Manufactured by ASCO Apothecaries Co. Electric-Manual Suction Unit. Two clear jars, vacuum caps screwed on top. A trio of tubes: one linking the jars, one screwed to the unit, the last dangling free.

She wasn't going to do this. I couldn't let her, could I? We'd have to talk. I couldn't stand the thought of her strapped to this terrible thing, tubes snaking into her, the life inside of her taken away in such a cold, clinical fashion.

Footsteps on the stairwell. A knock.

"It's me."

"Come in."

Doe entered wet and shivering. Teeth chattering. I jerked a towel off the bathroom rack. She sat on the crinkly plastic-covered bed. I slapped the security chain on the door; I wanted to take a good look at this sawbones before he got inside.

I sat beside Angela. "Not trying to start anything, but . . . you're sure?"

She glanced at the machine, the suction unit, at me, then down at her feet.

"Goldberg said the doctor would have something for the pain," she said. "So that's good."

"When this is over I'd like you to come with me," I said. "A quiet place where you can recuperate. I'm not asking you marry me—not trying to sweep you off your feet. Okay?"

"Okay."

"Promise me."

"Until I'm recovered. Promise."

Footsteps mounted the stairwell. A timid knock. I eased the door open a crack.

I caught the briefest flash of ghostly, heart-stopping white as the door smashed back into my face, flimsy security chain snapping. A blood-spattered medical bag flew at my face and though I got my elbow up to block it, I couldn't block the boot that followed directly behind, catching me under the chin. The room tilted, spun on some hidden axis, first the ceiling rushing at my face, then the floor, dark whorls of wood grain and my face meeting it. . . .

Nightmare

Blood.

Soaked into the fibres of my shirt. Taste on my tongue. Coagulated in my sinus cavities. My eyes were gummed shut with it. My left arm hung above my head, encircled by cold steel, shackled to something—the radiator, to judge by the steel ribs pressing my back.

A huge hand, more of a talon, steadied my skull. A wet cloth wiped my mouth and eyes.

"Wakey, wakey."

Soon as I opened them, it was all I could do not to close them again.

Angela, naked, laid out like a Maltese cross: wrists and ankles cuffed to the posts of the bed in the centre of the room. Her body laid bare. That tiny, unmistakable belly-bump. A catheter tube trailed between her legs. A pouch of clear medication hung on a pole, feeding to a needle inserted into Angela's arm.

"Epidural. Never administered one before."

The Quint—Number Two, the same one who'd stabbed Exeter, same one who'd killed those rummies at the bar—sat nearby, on the bathtub stool.

"I may've stuck the needle in too high," he said without concern. "Only things moving are her lungs."

"Please. What . . ." I spat a red sac onto the floor. ". . . what do you want?"

"To get rid of it."

". . . Get . . . get rid?"

"That's what you and Acolyte Doe planned on, wasn't it?"

Something composed entirely of bear claws and piranha teeth and fishhooks spun relentlessly inside of me, puncturing things, shredding the lining out of my stomach.

"We broke the law," I said. "Arrest us."

"I've never arrested anyone in my life." He scooched toward me on the stool, little bum-jumps until his face was inches from mine. "I'll give you two choices. You can erase the life in her belly. Or *I* can. But it'll hurt more if I do it."

"What you're asking . . . it's . . . I can't."

"Think of me as the father who caught his son smoking." He waggled a finger. "You're going to smoke every last one of those cigarettes, young man."

"Tom Swift," I said. "Victor Appleton. I can help you find him."

I would tell this creature anything, throw everyone under the bus and swear to it all on a stack of satanic bibles if only he'd not do what he was planning.

"What makes you think," he said, lips parted to reveal a slit of tombstone-coloured teeth, "we need your help? That we don't know where Swift is—and haven't all along?"

The storm clashed and cycled, throwing rain at the windows.

The Quint considered me with eyes grey as arctic ice.

I said: "You're going to kill us, anyway."

"You don't really believe that."

"I do. Absolutely I do."

"Then tell me, Acolyte Murtag: why can I still see the hope in your eyes?"

He unlocked the cuffs. I went to the bed. Angela lay naked—ragged scar across her right breast, thatch of untrimmed hair between her legs—not so much different than a corpse laid out on a mortuary slab. Drool leaked out of her mouth. The only moving part was her eyes: they darted wildly in their sockets.

"I don't know what else to do, Angela. He'll kill us."

I hunted through the medical bag and found a flexible cannula scope that fit over the suction unit's tubing. Also a pliers-looking device—a speculum?—and a tube of silicone cream.

"How does it work?" I asked the Quint. "Do I switch the machine on first, or do I . . . does the tube go inside her, then I switch it on?"

He chuckled. "You may as well ask me the best way to burn a Bible, Acolyte Murtag."

I knelt between Angela's legs, careful not to disturb the IV drip. I tested the speculum's operation, spread its lips and thumbed the trigger to lock it in position with a rusty-hinged squeak. I smeared its blades with cream and sat dumbfounded, wondering which way to insert it. The instrument looked vicious in my hands: this shiny metal duck's bill.

The speculum slid into Angela's body a few inches before meeting resistance. No idea of the topography in there, the twists and bends; I withdrew it, more lube, eased it in vertically. This way it followed some natural curvature and I was able to lock the blades in position.

A rivulet of blood came. Not much, but it still sent icy sparrows fluttering behind my ribcage. I dabbed it with a surgical napkin with badly shaking hands. I left the machine's dials at their pre-set calibrations. I mapped Angela's insides, the location of her uterus—somewhere round her navel?—and bent the cannula hose in an arc that marked my best guess like a blind man drawing a map to a place he'd never been.

Thunder throbbed low across the sky, this shuddering rumble-roll above the rooftops like a freight train passing overhead; the lights dimmed, vapour thinning in the phosphorous tubes to cast a witchy green-blue tint over the room. The Quint looked on with smiling anticipation.

"I'm going to . . . I'll thread this inside, alright?" I told her.

I knuckled sweat out of my eyes, gripped the hose and inched it in. It hit a bony overhang; I pulled it out, reconfigured the angle, slipped it back in. The plastic bedcover squeaked. Again the hose butted that unknown protrusion but I rotated it slightly, allowing the head to clear the obstruction and break into a frictionless pocket. Blood-veined liquor, what I took to be amniotic fluid, drooled down the speculum handle.

"Wait," I said. "Look . . . take a look at that. I'd say that's done it."

The Quint had been observing with an interest that was, at best, clinical. He shook his head.

"But listen," I pleaded, "the egg, the placenta or whatever . . . must have broken. You can see here."

He scratched his temple with the barrel of his revolver. "If you'd prefer I take over . . ."

"No, I, no . . . no, please."

"Carry on, then. When you're composed."

I didn't know that I'd done it the right way, but I didn't know what else to do. There was no instruction booklet and anyway, the Quint wouldn't give me the time to read it.

"I'll turn it on, Angela. If something goes wrong, I'll turn it off right away."

She didn't say anything. *Couldn't.* Too drugged, too numb. I squeezed her hand, though I doubt she felt much. We were going to get through it. She would live. We'd get out of here. Away from all the madness. We could try again, if she wanted. Anything was possible.

I reached over and pushed the red button on the machine. Nothing. I tried again. Could be a blown fuse. Or the diminished power grid couldn't handle the voltage? I got off the bed, went to the wall socket and unplugged the cord. Blew on the prongs and reinserted it. Nope.

The Quint reached over and casually switched the lights off.

Voltage re-routed, the machine hissed to life. So goddamn *loud*.

Oh Jesus good Christ oh God

I stumbled toward Angela in the darkness, fumbling madly, trying to find her and help her. Save her. She was making these horrible gargling noises that rose above the hiss of the vacuum machine.

I grabbed the tube leading into her. I felt this ghostly tension, some sort of resistance but my adrenaline was running so high, it was so dark, my head was ringing so awfully, I failed to make note of any of it.

I just . . . I just pulled.

A sigh. Whether it came from Angela's mouth or another part of her I'll never know.

The tube came out. Soon after, the lights switched on. The machine switched off.

And I began to scream.

MEMORY LAPSE

Where was I? Where was here?

Here was a kitchen. An apartment I'd never been in before . . . had I? It was dawn. A new sun curled over the cityscape. A thin bar of sunlight relaxed on the linoleum near my hand. My bloody hand.

Blood from where? I headed into the bathroom, flicked the light switch. No power. Huh. I turned on the spigot, ran my hands under the cold spray until the blood washed away.

There was a bed and a strange machine and broken glass and tubes and blood on the wall, blood everywhere and a woman on the bed and the woman was dead.

I knew this woman but I couldn't remember how.

Rigor mortis had yanked her shoulder sockets out of joint. She was shackled and there was something the matter between her legs. I leaned against the archway separating kitchen and main room, staring at the woman—not directly at her, a spot on the wall above her. She looked familiar in a way. She looked *tough*. Not quite tough enough to withstand all this but then, who would be?

I glanced out the window. The day clear and pristine. A night rain had left puddles on the road. I'd be fine without my coat so I draped it over the woman, tucking the collar around her neck. I felt poorly for her but there was nothing more to be done. All I knew for sure was that I hadn't been responsible for her dying—though I couldn't say whether I'd tried to prevent it.

I wanted to leave. *Had* to, really.

A white business card was balanced above the doorknob. A telephone number and below it was written: *When you're ready*.

It was the sort of day that, as they say, made a man wish he rose early more often. The air was cool but not cold, unburdened by the gas fumes that would permeate it as the day wore on.

I wandered, backtracked, a route taking me past an alley. A car was parked there. The understanding came: that was *my* car. I rooted through my pocket for keys and unlocked the door and slid into the seat. I circled the ghetto. Glass bottles arced out apartment windows to shatter on the hood. I took the hint and drove out into the city. Shivering but I didn't know why.

Hollis. Garvey. Swift. Newbarr. Amira. Names began to filter back, unattached to faces. My memory gathering old scraps of itself like a bird building a nest.

I stopped across the street from a place that, same as the car, I identified as my own. My name on the callbox: J. Murtag. Silence when I thumbed the button. Power must be out. I tried every key on my keyring. The last one moved the tumblers. I walked up the stairwell and opened the door. My own door, I guess.

Inside was an old man in a silly hat. I felt that I ought to know him, too. Behind him stood two females, old and young. The girl was a heathen. Both of them were bald for some reason.

A rabbit hopped about a cage. A bird twittered somewhere.

I said: "I'd like a shower. May I do that—use your shower?"

The old man bit his lip and said: "It's your shower, son. Do what you like."

Behind the bathroom door I stripped and inspected myself. A belt of dried blood ran round my hips. The water was as cold as a glacial runoff; I stood under it a few seconds before my knees gave out and I crumpled into the basin. Icy spray beaded on my shoulders and ran down my back. The doors began to unlock, images pouring into my mind . . .

A knock at the bathroom door. Someone asked was I alright. Yes . . . no . . . I didn't know—leave me be for Christ's sake. I stared at the wallpaper skirting the tub . . . a pattern of tiny angels blowing trumpets . . .

Angels. Angel.

Angela.

Something cracked. Not any bone, though I would have preferred it. This crack was inside my head and it brought forth a rush of horrible memories. . . .

Next I was drumming my hands and feet on the basin, shrieking, bellowing. I must've screamed myself into a blackout because next thing I knew the door was broken down and they were on me: Newbarr, Amira, my Mom.

They led me dripping and quaking into the bedroom.

"Get some rope, Amira," I heard Newbarr say.

They lay me on the bed, swaddled like an infant. Amira returned with loops of yellow twine scrounged from God-knows-where. They fastened me down.

"Until he settles down," Newbarr said, knotting a second loop round my hips.

How long did I lay there? Things slipped in and out of focus. I wept and sweated through the sheets, leaching the moisture from my body. At some point the ropes were loosened. Someone slipped into bed beside me. A stomach pressed my back through the clammy sheets; Mom's chin nestled at the slope of my shoulder. Another body curled into my chest, young muscles settled tight to me.

None of us said anything. Our exhales aligned: three chests expanding and contracting at the same pace. I wanted to tell them it was useless, that I was beyond the redemption tendered in such gestures, but it felt so good—the warmth, the restful motions of their bodies against mine—that I didn't say a word.

The sky had gone dark behind the shade when I got up. Mom and Amira were still sleeping. I left them in bed and went into the front room. Newbarr sat on the window ledge, smoking a cigarette.

"I quit years ago," he said when he saw me. "Wife couldn't stand it. Kissing an ashtray, she said. But they do calm the nerves."

My trousers were neatly folded over a kitchen chair. I yanked them on.

"I need a few hours," I said to him. "Give me until daybreak."

"What now?"

In my pocket were two different telephone numbers to call when I was ready. I'd rub them together to see if they'd catch a spark.

Two numbers. Two maniacs. Two agendas. Play both ends against the middle. Give them what they were seeking. Everybody got what they wanted. Everybody died.

Article V:
He is Stripped of His Garments

14 Two Trains A-Runnin'

I walked down the street uncradling payphone receivers and hanging them up when only silence met my ear. The sky was greyed over with rolling thunderheads, this upside-down ocean flexing deep to the horizon.

I saw dogs—house pets, as they must have been at one time—roaming in feral packs. I passed through the gates of a cemetery ringed by empty homes, the windows cataracted with dust. The heads were busted off every angel monument.

I tried another payphone, got a dial tone. I fed it and dialled.

"You said whenever I was ready."

"Cutting it close," Tom Swift said. "We were getting set to start without you."

When I told him where I was, he said: "I'll collect you directly."

The day turned cold. A dust devil whipped a cone of litter down the sidewalk. A cobalt blue van banked round the corner. Swift's head popped out the passenger window.

"Hop in. There's work to be done."

Driving was Porter Rockwell. Swift looked pallid and sickly.

"Wait a minute," I told him. "I have to make another call."

Swift stared out the windshield. "To who?"

"The Prophet. I can get him."

Swift's fingers drummed the van's door. "Why now, Jonah? Why the turnabout?"

The answer came to me with ease. "You're no worse than the rest of them. And Angela's dead, so what the hell does it matter anymore?"

Swift's face betrayed a hint of emotion for perhaps the first time. "How?"

"The Quints were involved."

Swift wiped the ichor seeping below the frames of his sunglasses. "I'm sorry to hear that. What's your plan, Jonah?"

"I'll make a call. One call. Then I'll take you to him."

"Just like that?"

"Just like that."

"So make the call, Jonah."

I crossed to the phone and dialled the Acolyte-only dispatch. An automatic router clicked on after two rings, which should patch me through to the highest-ranking Acolyte remaining, which now that Hollis was gone should be—

"Who's this?"

"It's Murtag. Is this Brewster?"

"Ghost from the ether." Brewster sounded dead tired. "What do you want?"

"I got him," I said. "The guy behind it all. Wizard of Oz. I'm bringing him in."

Brewster said: "Great. You're on your own. I got my own detail right now."

I knew what that detail must be—bodyguard detail for The Prophet. In fact, I was betting on it.

"Why don't you just kill him?" Brewster wanted to know.

"Wouldn't The Prophet want to see this guy himself?" I said. "Just so he could know for sure? I'll bring him in. He's harmless as a kitten."

I wish it were Henchel instead of Brewster. Henchel was an idiot. Brewster was at the very least possessed of baseline cunning.

He said, "You sure it's the guy?"

"It's him."

He gave me the address. "Come alone . . . just the two of you."

I hung up and said, "We're all set. Almost."

Swift: "Almost how?"

"They think I've captured you. But you wouldn't have been taken in willingly."

He laughed. "You're saying I ought to look a little worse for wear."

"You can have Rockwell do it, if you'd rather."

"No, I'd rather it was you."

He sat on the bumper as I tugged the laces free of my brogans, knotted them, wound the one long strand round the knuckles of my right hand.

I said, "Take your sunglasses off."

Swift shook his head. "Avoid my eyes. They are, as you know, windows into the soul."

I laid into Swift as hard as I'd ever laid into any man. The ribs and gut and chin, shots that started out clean and tight before the adrenalin burned off and exhaustion turned them into sloppy gas-armed whiffles. The bootlaces unravelled from my knuckles leaving ribbed coils in my flesh but I kept hitting him. I slammed my fist into his ribs until he retched a thin stream of leaden gruel that had slid down his chest like quicksilver.

It felt good. *Really* good. It was all part of the plan, but I would have done it for no reason at all.

The Bunker

Brewster was waiting when I pulled into the vacant Stadium SuperChurch parking lot. He stood with his arms folded while I popped the rear doors, grabbed Swift, and hauled him onto the macadam. Rockwell I'd dropped a half-block away.

I threw Swift down in the parking lot. Brewster drew near. Moonlight plated the brutal planes of his face: a sheer cliff upon which nothing grew, that barren rock still kicking off some feral sense of intellect.

"This the scummer, Murtag?"

"Head termite," I said. "Light his ass on fire, he'll burn you a path right back to the nest."

"Looks like he's been plenty burned already. Let's go inside."

The bubbled dome of the SuperChurch was torn open in a dozen spots. Rain-bloated prayer booklets littered the mildewed carpet: they looked like pale blue toadstools.

"I like what you've done with the place," Swift said. It earned him a backhanded slap from Brewster. Swift just laughed through a mouthful of blood. Brewster led us backstage. Swift was singing in a froggy blood-choked voice:

Plastic Jesus, you've got to go,
Your magnet's burst my radio
Sitting on the dashboard of my car.
But I won't lose faith and I won't lose hope
'Cause now I've got a pope on a rope
Swinging from the dashboard of my car . . .

We arrived at a steel door that fed into a dusty concrete hallway. Brewster shoved Swift through and I followed.

I said, "What is this place?"

Brewster said: "Upscale bomb shelter. Couple a rooms, cots, canned food. Not the Ritz."

I caught the hum of a generator. The lights buzzed at half capacity, staining amber the spider webs spun where wall met ceiling.

"We got a CB radio," Brewster said. "We've been trying to raise the alarm in Kingdom City."

"Any luck?"

"None yet. Could be the signal isn't clearing the bunker. Atmospheric disturbance."

He led us into a room stacked with boxes labelled HALLELUJAH ENERGY BOOST. A wooden chair sat amidst the boxes. Brewster slammed Swift into it—I had to give Swift credit; he was taking the rough treatment like a champ—and cuffed his wrists through the slats.

"What's your plan?" Swift wanted to know. "To teach me the true meaning of Christmas?"

Brewster tagged him in the jaw—never one for trading

verbal barbs, Brewster—and said, "Sit tight, Murtag—I got to check on something."

Once he was gone, Swift said: "Somehow I'd pictured it differently."

He couldn't have meant the bunker, so I suppose he meant the circumstances surrounding his confronting The Prophet. He craned his neck around to nod at Rockwell, who had trailed at a discreet distance and let himself in behind us. Swift greeted casually his arrival, never in doubt. Rockwell took a spot behind the door.

Brewster stepped back inside the room slapping a rubber hose against the meat of his palm. "Okay, Murtag, Let's pluck this loon—"

When Rockwell stepped up behind him, he came without a sound. Amazing just how massive he was—he dwarfed Brewster who was himself well over six feet tall.

Brewster realized the threat too late. Knuckles met jaw, skin met skin. Brewster's jaw broke in about ten places, the U-shaped bone cracking down one side of his face and up the other; with nothing left to moor it, the bottom half of his face collapsed into splintered mash. His soft palate went loose as raw chicken skin, bottom lip folding down as if it was full of lead fishing weights.

Brewster crashed to the floor. Rockwell raised one boot and brought it down on Brewster's face with a sound I'd have given my eyeteeth to have never heard. Rockwell rummaged the keychain out of Brewster's pocket. Brewster's teeth gritted like periwinkle shells under Rockwell's boots. Once his cuffs were unlocked, Swift said: "Let's go."

"Give me a sec," I told him.

I picked through Brewster's pockets until I found his cell phone. I ran through the recently received calls, all of them to the same number and location: REPLCN ARMRY.

The Republican Armoury. Where better to stash The One Child?

I punched the redial button. A voice—Henchel's—went, "Yeah?"

I hung up. The three of us went back into the hallway, which continued down to a steel-plated door at the very end. Swift took Brewster's keyring. The first one he tried slid effortlessly into the lock. Swift's face was grey and greasy with some kind of sickness I could not guess at.

"Moment of truth," he said, and turned the key.

The man sitting alone on the other side of the door was bloodshot-eyed and ragged of fingernail: a beggar in a bunker. Our Prophet. The Heaven-Sent Messenger.

"Father," Swift said to him.

At first I mistook it as nothing more than a show of disdain: Father, Our Father who art in Heaven, hallowed be thy name. But he took off his sunglasses, fixed his gaze, and said:

"But isn't that a touch formal? Dad, is what I should've said. So wonderful to meet you, Dad, after lo these many years."

Daddy Issues

There's a phrase common in police detection that goes: More often than not, the simplest reason *is* the reason. When a wife murders her husband, it's because she has grown to loathe him or seeks his fortune or discovers he's fondling the babysitter. No deep underpinnings or hidden agendas. Humans are, at base level, pretty straightforward. Their motivations are often predicated on raw emotional states: greed, jealousy, rage.

Revenge.

"Dad."

An expression crossed The Prophet's face—wry and resigned: the look of a man who'd been expecting this outcome in one form or another for years—and it was as though a cotter pin had been pulled inside my head: disparate facts and hints and assumptions slotted neatly, obviously, and left me to curse my ignorance.

Again Swift said it: "Dad."

Had the word ever been spoken less lovingly?

The Prophet took the measure of his son—the pigeon chest, the blood—and even in his own doleful state managed to express genuine distaste by way of a flippant shrug. For his part, Swift seemed to be struggling with the image of his father. I suppose he might've expected to find him as he was commonly recalled: the vanilla suit, the copper tan, the high-stepping gospel routine.

Rockwell pushed a second chair in front of The Prophet. Swift sat on it. The two met face-to-face. The same sharpness of jaw. The same widow's peak.

"Lydia Cromwell. My mother." When The Prophet failed to acknowledge this name or the life attached to it, Swift asked: "During your years on the road, just how many women did you fuck, Dad?"

"Stop calling me that," The Prophet said. "You've got no proof."

"Don't get me wrong," Swift went on, "every man has needs. So you fucked your way across the heartland, a horny ten-penny Bible salesman—so what? What I can't quite square is why you'd order every one of your conquests dead after you assumed this office."

I was considering the possibility Swift was mistaken when The Prophet copped to it.

"Those women might have exploited the situation," he said simply. "Tried to impugn me. Unravel all the good works I intended to implement."

Swift nodded as if in understanding to this pragmatic stance. "Were you ever told how they were killed? Did you have the courage to ask exactly how it was carried out?"

The Prophet said: "There was the matter of a new ministry to be founded in New Bethlehem. I needn't concern myself, I was told; I had the Lord's work to attend to. And He has long forgiven me my past trespasses."

Swift said: "My mother and I lived in an isolated farmhouse. It would've been safer if we'd lived closer to a city but my mother, your lover, was stubborn. I don't remember much about her—I was four when she was killed, and at that age you don't recall a lot about people: their voice, the way they smell. Mother always smelled of lilacs. I didn't know then that I was the product of a silver-tongued revivalist preacher in line for The Prophetship of New Bethlehem. But those circumstances isolated her; otherwise she may have moved somewhere safer. Not to say it mattered in the end."

The lights dimmed. The generator coughed, ran smooth. The gas fumes made me dizzy.

"One day a sedan pulled into the drive. Three men in white suits. My mother saw them through the window. She bundled me into the closet and told me *shhhhh*. In the dark with the smell of her wool coat, I peeped through the slats. One man took her elbow, softly, and led her down the hallway. She jerked free, told him she could walk on her own. The back door opened and for a long time, nothing. I stood in the closet, breathing the wool smell of her coat. Footsteps around the house. A voice said, 'In this photo—a boy.' They searched and found me. One man pulled me from the closet. He placed the tip of a knife under my eye and, as delicately as one could do such a thing, slit the skin down my cheek."

Swift removed his sunglasses. The wound looked as raw as it must've been all those years ago.

"A cattle brand. Mark of shame." He glanced at me and said: "But I was never ashamed of my mother. This wound will heal. But every time the flesh knits I take a razorblade and slit it open. It keeps the memories fresh. Yet I do wonder," he said, "why those men didn't kill me."

"I told them not to," said The Prophet. "I said, not the child."

Swift scrutinized his father. "Liar."

The Prophet's eyes ducked to an empty corner of the room.

“The men got back into the sedan. I stood in the hallway, blinking, blood sheeting my face. It was getting dark when I went out to the shack in our backyard. I found her lying over sacks of peat moss. Her skin had gone purple, shiny. Dried foam caked round her mouth.

“I was sent to a Republic orphanage,” Swift continued. “God’s Children, in Kingdom City. I knocked around until I was adopted by a man and his wife. The man’s name was Elwood Chalmers. It was a publicity stunt; he adopted three of us at the same time—Chalmers’ Children, as we were known. He wasn’t seeking an office, not then, but knew such an act of largesse would feather his nest down the road.”

Elwood Chalmers had once been the chief fundraiser and bulldog lobbyist for the Christian Family Coalition. After the dawn of the Republic he continued to work on behalf of state-selected candidates and was later confirmed one of the five Fathers of the Divine Council.

“Chalmers knew how I’d gotten this”—trailing a finger along his eye-wound—“and realized I might be an asset. He taught me statesmanship, the use of faith as a tool: a mallet, a placebo, a balm . . . a bomb. I was a quick study.”

So Elwood Chalmers had taken young Tom Swift—Tom Cromwell?—under his wing. Groomed him for a future contingency. That contingency was now almost fully realized. But why?

“Do you think they didn’t know, Dad?” Tom said. “The graft, the money-hoarding? You’ve been keeping tithes to yourself, sending only a trickle to the Kingdom City coffers. You made the mistake of bilking the boss. The boss was not impressed.”

“But why eradicate us all?” I had to ask. “Make a laughingstock of our Prophet, okay; kill *him*. This . . . you’re talking tens of thousands of innocent people.”

Swift said: “Have you ever heard the phrase ‘Controlled burn,’ Jonah? Forestry term. The best way to rehabilitate a parcel of land is to burn it. Dig a trench round the perimeter, soak it in flammables, and light it. You could trim all the scrub, weed the valuable trees from the junk, but it’s not economical. When things are that overgrown and unruly, it's expedient to get rid of it. Start over. That's what happened in New Beersheba."

"Why destroy New Beersheba? They did nothing to you."

"That was the Divine Council's choice," said Swift. "I had to do that in order to do this. It was a deal we struck."

"So you went into New Beersheba," I said, "backed by the Divine Council. They outfitted you with the explosives. You co-opted people like Lucas Hogan, his wife and daughter, deceiving them while ingratiating yourself. The higher ups in the police force were in the bag. You knew everyone's secrets, their histories—everything the Divine Fathers knew. The local Prophet was clueless."

Swift was nodding, nodding to everything I said.

"Then the Quints were sent in, ostensibly to stop you but really you were both working in cahoots to destroy the city."

"They *do* want to kill me," Swift said of the Quints, "and I'm sure they've been promised the opportunity by someone—maybe even Chalmers. But before that, we each had our jobs to carry out. Destabilize the populace, tear the social fabric apart, then send in the wrecking balls."

"The morning the Damascus Towers were bombed . . ."

"A Quint warned me to get out beforehand. I did. Rockwell did. Others didn't."

"Why didn't you warn them?"

"He had no need of them anymore," said The Prophet.

I said: "I've seen New Beersheba. There's nothing left."

"Soon this city will be carpet bombed, too," Swift told me. "Planes will lift off from Kingdom City to deliver their payload. They'll leave a black scar behind."

"But they'll take The One Child first."

"Of course," Swift said.

I imagined it right from the beginning. Lydia Cromwell meeting The Prophet's gaze through the dust-thickened air of a striped tent pitched in a summer field. Lydia fanning her neck with a prayer booklet; The Prophet sharing the stage with a wife who opened her legs to a dwarf who'd poke his shrunken head into a soap bubble to amuse her: a trick called the Astronaut's

Helmet, back when there were such things as astronauts and space shuttles. No more than a casual glance, random chemicals firing in a pair of brainpans. Years later, men in white suits would leave a young boy with wet britches and a knife-opened face to find his mother gone purple in a dusty shack. Now, many more years later: two cities torn apart. Thousands dead. Lives ruined.

Angela . . .

All sparked by two pairs of eyes meeting across the dusty air of a revival tent.

Rockwell removed a curious bundle from his pocket and handed it to Swift.

DET cord. A grey plunger. That red button. Oh, God.

Swift took one end of the DET cord and slipped it down the back of his pants. "I'm afraid," he said, wincing, "there's just no polite way to do this."

Jesus. I saw it now. The bulged, lumpen look of Swift's belly. How many ball bearings had he swallowed; how much plastique was plugging up his innards? He sat gingerly. The DET cord curled round his hips, plunger swaying gently between his legs.

"Before you go," he said to me, "there is one last thing you should know."

"What's that?"

"I'm not the only abandoned child, Jonah."

He didn't have to say the name. It'd been knocking around the corners of my mind a long time now. She was adopted, too. Never knew her real parents. The anonymous letters she received every month—someone trying to expiate their guilt. The first female Acolyte—who had pulled the strings? Always saying she led a charmed life—who sprinkled that fairy dust? Stacks of uncashed checks; *Love you always* written in the memo line.

The Immaculate Mother saying to me, *You're her friend. My daughter's friend . . .*

"Angela was my half-sister," Swift said. "Unlike me, she wasn't a child of adultery. They still gave her away, though."

I said, "Why?"

But before the word cleared my mouth I knew why. She wasn't born a freak. Angela had been born normal, and as such was worthless. So they'd secretly put her up for adoption and hid their parentage . . . almost.

"Her mother did what she could for her," The Prophet said. "From afar."

"She's dead," I said. "Your daughter is dead."

"All my daughters are dead," The Prophet said. "And my dearest wish is that all my sons were dead, too."

Tom bared his teeth. "Oooh, we're getting to that, Dad."

66 Endgame

The wind blew at gale force as Rockwell and I cleared the Stadium SuperChurch. Flags adorned with the Republican insignia snapped at the end of their poles. I tugged Rockwell's sleeve and, when he turned to me, I said, "I have to make a phone call."

He offered me Swift's cell phone—a shiny silver dot in his mammoth bear claw—but I shook my head, thinking the Quints might recognize the number. We got into the van. A crumpling explosion rocked the SuperChurch as we pulled out of the lot. A flaming ball of gas barrelled out of the doors, debris raining out of the torn roof and pinging dully off the van's roof. I looked at Rockwell. He was weeping. He did so for a good ten minutes. He wept silently, like a scared child, holding his elbows and swaying.

I drove streets slicked with night perspiration, zigzagging down a switchback hill. I stopped next to a bank of payphones. I walked over and began picking up receivers: dead, dead, dead, dead . . . live. I rummaged my pockets for the second phone number—and dialled.

No hello: only the hiss of an open connection.

"I'm ready."

The Quint—didn't know which one—said, "Ready for what, Acolyte Murtag?"

"I know where The One Child is."

"*Doooo* you?" the Quint crooned.

"If I tell you where, I want you to leave."

Noncommittal: "We could do that."

"You should do. Victor Appleton is dead."

Silence. Then: "How do you know?"

"Because he is. The Prophet, too. There's nothing keeping you here."

"Where is the Child?"

"Will you leave? Do I have your word?"

"If you're lying about Appleton . . ." the Quint said.

"Fuck you," I said flatly, relishing the tension on the other end of the line.

"Where is The One Child?" Biting each word off.

"The Armoury. Take him and go to Hell."

I hustled back to the van. We were only a block away. We'd have time to prepare.

The Republican Armoury was a series of eroded limestone barracks ringed by U-barns, shacks, and Quonset huts. It had gone unused for over a decade—all military matters were now outsourced from Kingdom City—but remained as a contingency: in case of a ghetto revolt, the barracks could sub as a containment facility.

I nudged the van's grille against the chain-link gate, snapping the lock. We parked amidst a few derelict vehicles in the lot and crept a circuit of the compound. We came upon an outlying U-barn. Weak fingerlings of light edged under the corrugated tin walls. I followed Rockwell to a dark wedge cut between two barracks. Clean sightlines to the U-barn. Rockwell dipped into his pocket, pulled out a grey brick: C-4. He kneaded and rolled. It popped between his fingers, tiny air pockets bursting.

We waited. Wind curled down the limestone and licked the hems of our dusters.

"State of Grace."

As I'd heard very few words come out of Rockwell, his voice momentarily startled me.

"He didn't believe," Rockwell continued. "Swift, I mean. I do." Rockwell's eyes swivelled Heavenward. "When you die, you must die in a State of Grace."

A Catholic term. To exit this world in a state of divine sanctification.

"Do you think that's possible?" I had to ask. "After all that you've done?"

He said, "Once the Quints are dead."

Motor-roar washed over the garrets. A familiar grey Buick Roadmaster prowled past the U-barn, braked, backed up. The edge of light skirting the U-barn broke fitfully: whoever was guarding The One Child—Henchel for certain, possibly more—had heard.

The Buick parked round the front. A single Quint exited. I couldn't make out the number on his neck.

A shotgun boomed inside the barn. Holes peppered the corrugated tin. The Quint drew his revolver and dug off two shots. Canned-ham-sized holes punched through the barn's metal wall. The shotgun barked again. The Quint raced forward and peeped through one of the gaping holes in the metal. Then kicked the door open and blazed on in.

Rockwell started toward the car. I caught his wrist.

"You can't do that. You'll kill the kid."

He shook his head. "Concentrated blast."

He loped out to the car as gunshots sang out inside the barn and slid beneath the undercarriage. He was there less than half a minute. The gunshots died away, replaced with choked screams. Rockwell hauled himself out and hustled back.

A piercing, pain-filled screech from inside the barn. One

more gunshot. The Quint emerged with a bundle clutched to its chest. Rockwell telescoped the antennae on the remote. Thin noises carried across the compound: sweet, musical. The One Child was crying.

After placing The Child securely on the passenger seat, the Quint slammed the door and went round the driver's side. He settled behind the wheel, gunned the engine—

Rockwell hit the button.

The explosion was mild. The car hopped off its front wheels five inches or so. The windows blacked out as ash painted the glass. Smoke bristled through the door seams.

The driver's door swung open. The Quint crawled out. He was all black. His hair smoldered. Exposed to fresh oxygen, flames rekindled atop his head, frizzed-out strands igniting from tip to root. He fell onto his back and stared at the sky. Something was sticking from his gut.

We approached cautiously. He didn't hear us. One of his eyes was burned out but he caught sight of us with the other and reached for his revolver. A baffled expression crossed the wreckage of his face. His gun-hand was gone: he was reaching with a stump. Not that it would've mattered, seeing as his pistol was heat-bonded to the flesh over his ribs.

He smiled at us. I noticed what was sticking out of him: the brake pedal. Shorn off in the explosion and driven into his belly.

Rockwell raised his foot and slowly, deliberately, pressed down on the brake pedal. The shaft sunk deeper into the Quint's stomach.

That Quint's smile persisted. *Widened.*

I peered into the car. Dark smoke billowing. The Quint's severed hand clutching the gearshift.

From the passenger's side: noises between singing and hacking.

I burned my fingers on the door handle. A swaddled bundle sat in the passenger seat, black like everything else. I picked The One Child up—so goddamn light. I hugged him to my chest to feel the rapid palpitations of his heart. Miraculously, he was unhurt. Perhaps he truly was the blessed one.

When I came back around, I saw Rockwell still pushing his foot down on the brake pedal jutting out of the Quint's belly. Blood crawled in the chinks between his teeth but he wouldn't stop smiling. When he was dead I handed The One Child to Rockwell. The Child was crying. The most beautiful sound on earth. We both stared at him in awe.

The One Child was naked. Perhaps he'd been naked the whole of his existence. Rockwell was inspecting his body for injuries; for dignity's sake I folded the blanket over those shrunken banjo legs but not before glimpsing the peppering of scars: places his father, Caleb Murphy, Pliny the Pinhead, had stabbed him with a needle. His chest was soft and babyish. The skin hung in the loose folds of an old man. His face . . . God, his face. No rhyme or reason. One eye was planted halfway down his cheek; the other, cataracted, was swung round to his temple. No nose; a pair of gasping nasal holes. His mouth, where the sounds came from, was set high up his forehead, a toothless vertical slit ringed by downy hair.

Two cities, thousands of lives, had been destroyed for this.

I took the Quint's bloodied duster off his body. Then I took The One Child from Rockwell.

"I'll need your van."

Rockwell said, "You'll need what's in the back, too."

"What's in back?"

"What you'll need," he said again. "For what you will do."

I left him beside the wreck of the Quint's car. The interior had caught fire. Flames lashed the windows. Rockwell knelt beside the Quint's body. Evidently they still had business together.

I could have told Rockwell that the car's backseat was full of teddy bears and Raggedy Anns rigged with grenades. I could have told him they were bound to explode in the intensifying heat.

Yeah, I could have.

Escape

"We're leaving. Now. Right *now*."

I stood in the apartment door, panting from a breakneck sprint up the stairwell. It was just past four in the morning. The van was at street level: I'd jounced it over the curb, flung the rear doors open. The One Child was belted into a baby seat strapped to the passenger seat.

Mom and Amira emerged from the bedroom. The adjacent apartment door opened; I leaned out into the hallway to catch sight of Newbarr. Dighet the goat clip-clopped up to his side.

"We're hitting the road."

Newbarr said: "Nice to see you, too."

I grabbed Bird's cage and carted it downstairs and stashed her in the van. I scoped the street in both directions. Three more Quints were still prowling a city slated to be carpet bombed.

I hotfooted it back up the stairs and almost ran over Amira, who was carrying the peacock on his styrofoam raft. I hustled back to the apartment, past Newbarr and Dighet, past Mom and Hoppsy the rabbit. I hefted the aquarium containing Garvey's rattlesnake, Duke. I carted it down to the van. Newbarr and Amira and Mom were all staring at the passenger seat.

"Is that—?" Newbarr said, awed.

"It is," I said simply. "The One Child."

The One Child burbled and chirped, happy enough sounds. Mom said, "He's beautiful."

Three more trips had the van weighted down with everything it could carry: all the animals, plus their food, plus bedding material and a box of tinned food for us. Newbarr pulled his car around front of the apartment.

"How much gas you got?" he asked.

"Almost a full tank."

"Should do us."

Mom had taken the One Child out of its child seat; she sat on the rear bench seat with the child on her lap. Amira had stowed the child seat in back and was sitting in the passenger's seat. The interior ricocheted with squawks, chirps, hisses and bleats.

The streets were dark, the sky dark. My nerves were wadded into hard-packed bundles beneath my skin; I drove slowly, eyeing the road for spike strips and busted glass. It seemed to take forever to clear the city limits but once we did a huge tension lifted from my chest.

Dawn came as a thin red line over the curve of the earth, a natural red unlike that of Newbarr's guiding taillights; this was the red of desert rocks or autumn leaves at the moment of their shedding, red with traces of night yet clung to it or the red of a vein, our planet's femoral artery pulsing, swelling with daylight, and I drove headlong into that redness with the feeling these marked my last hours on earth.

Newbarr's brake lights flashed. He pulled over, waved me

out. Together we hauled away a brittle deadfall to reveal a rutted corduroy road. The van was awakening by the time I reseated myself. We drove two miles into a willow thicket, which emptied into a sun-dappled clearing.

A cottage. A pond.

Heaven on earth.

Nirvana

"We built it together, my wife and I. God rest her soul."

Newbarr stood in the cottage's kitchen: a wood stove, thrift-store butcher block table, hotel fridge. Two bedrooms, a bookshelf, a stack of board games. The Monopoly game was the Ecclesiastical edition—the only edition they made anymore.

Go straight to Purgatory. Do not pass Redemption. Do not collect 200 shekels.

Amira and Mom carted the animals inside. Newbarr and I pulled layers of burlap sheeting and plastic tarpaulin off the generator. Newbarr unscrewed the cap, poured in gas. A few yanks of the starter cord got it cranking over.

"We'll siphon what's left out of the van," he said. "That should last us a long time."

"I'm sorry, but I need the van."

"For what?"

I waited patiently as the connections knitted together in his head.

"Why do such a thing, son?" he said. "Everything you wanted, everything you worked for, right here. You earned it."

"I didn't earn it," I told him. "Or if so, I earned other things, too."

"It won't change anything, you know," he said. "I know it'd be nice to think so, that whatever you do is going to trigger an upheaval, but it won't happen."

I thought of that mantra I'd heard all the time as a kid:

I am just one man. Just one woman. One man cannot stand in the path of tomorrow.

So tomorrow came. Tomorrow became today. Tomorrow just kind of happened.

And for a moment there—just a flash—I hated Calvin Newbarr.

I said: "I've got what they want. How much farther to Kingdom City?"

"You're going to leave me, an old man, here in the middle of the woods?"

"You've been taking care of people your whole life."

"Dead people!" he reminded me. "What help do they need?"

"Thank you for everything you've done, Calvin. I mean it."

He shook his head. "I know why you're doing it. Same reason I brought you out here, I'd say. That martyring instinct—drilled into all of us. Well, go speak to them first. Look them in the eye; let's see you do that."

I walked behind the cottage, down the bank of the pond. I heeled off my shoes, socks, rolled up my trousers and dipped my feet. Amira came and sat next to me. She'd brought Frog in his aquarium. She kicked off her shoes and dipped her feet.

"You're not staying," she said. So she knew, somehow.

"I'm not. That's true."

Newbarr was right about the whole "look them in the eye" bit. It was rough.

"Where are you going?"

"Oh," I said breezily, "Here, there, everywhere."

We twiddled our toes. Water boatmen skimmed across our ankles. And I thought: *What if I didn't?* Thought: *What if I stayed?*

The notion came to me, insupportable in a thousand ways, that we could plant a garden. Tomatoes, potatoes, peas in the soil feathering the water. The future seemed unshackled in a way it had never been—a new optimism percolated through me.

I nodded at Frog. "You going to let him go?"

"I think he'd rather go with you," she said. "See whatever you're going to see."

"I'll take him, then."

"You don't have to."

"Take him? Or go?"

"Go."

She rested her head on my shoulder. The pressure of that girl's head on my shoulder—satori, was what Hindus called it. Happiness.

"Come on." I gave her my hand. "Let's say goodbye."

We walked to the van. Mom was with Newbarr; she cradled The One Child, who snoozed in her arms.

"I have to take him with me, Mom."

"You're leaving?"

"We have things to do."

"Things." The One Child slipped out of her arms into mine. "What things?"

"I won't be long. I'll be back."

She said, "No, you won't."

I nodded. "You're right, Mom. I won't."

I belted The One Child into the passenger seat, which I'd gotten out of the van. I took Frog's aquarium from Amira.

"I suppose this is what you consider bravery," said Mom.

Was I being brave? Don't know I'd ever been. Struck me that all possible paths had winnowed to a single thread. Bravery had fuck all to do with it now.

Article VI:
He is Nailed to the Cross

Church

The road bent and wound and occasionally it rose up over the hood as we hit uphill grades only to bottom away at the crest. The sun streamed through the windshield. I looked at The One Child: face gone red—how often had his skin met the sun? I pulled over, located the Quint's fire-eaten duster and tucked it around the sun visor as a makeshift curtain.

We hit a stretch that cut through an apple orchard. The road was petalled with a layer of blossoms that the van's tires stirred into a strange blizzard; they blew through the cab, white petals beyond numbering soft against our skin, the smell of fruit and the vague drone of honeybees, The One Child laughing then sputtering on blossoms.

A spire stabbed into the sky off to the east: the spire of a country church. I turned onto the broken laneway leading there. A one-room church. Flaking clapboards, windblown shingles. I set the van's brake and checked the gas gauge: near empty. A car was parked outside the church. Good luck for me. Someone up there was looking out for us.

I got out to inspect the car. Newish but dust-covered. A make I'd never seen: Peugeot. Sleek, sporty. I ran my fingers over the lion insignia on its hood, wondering what sort of self-respecting clergyman would drive a car such as this.

Beyond the church was a stream connecting to a lake; that sheen of water, breathless and unmoving, was indistinguishable from the sky above.

I unbuckled The One Child, collected Frog, and rapped on the church doors.

"Hello? Hello?"

Nobody answered. I toed the door open. A fire had scorched the left half of the interior; the blackness ended at the midpoint of the church in almost a straight line. Above the sacristy, direct centre of the church, hung a crucifix. A wooden Jesus impaled upon it. Half-burnt, half whole. The legs were broken off raggedly at the hip.

The One Child's working eye oriented on that crucifix. He began to cry—or sing, I guess. A Pavlovian response.

The song opened into the vestibule and pealed off the fire-darkened wood. A family of mudlarks darted between the rafters on knife-edged wings and out the belfry. I walked out the vestry into a thicket. Willows and mulberry trees. I continued down a grassy knoll to a sandy strip fringing the river. I arranged The One Child on a sandbar and left Frog to watch over him. Back across the thicket to the van.

There was a red toolbox in the back of the van. It held the items that Rockwell told me I'd need. I guess he knew, too. Seemed everyone knew but me. I hefted the box. Rolling metallic noises. I snapped the catches and lifted the lid.

A grey brick of plastique. A battery pack. A roll of duct tape. A red-buttoned plunger.

Thousands of shiny metal ball bearings.

I refastened the catches and carted the toolbox to the sandbar. The stream flowed softly by the shore and quickened toward its deep blue middle. Sun plated the quiet surface of the lake beyond, so searingly incandescent it was as though the topmost layer of the sun had been peeled off and laid flaming upon it.

I kicked off my shoes and peeled off my socks. I removed my trousers and knelt in the water with the toolbox near at hand. . . .

Water ran through my hands, cold and clean. I pushed a ball bearing between my lips. A sharp metallic sting down to the root of my tongue. I cupped a handful of water, sipped, swallowed.

Don't know how long I knelt there. Time scalloped. I phased in and out. Ball bearings went down four or five at a time. I retched. Rivulets of drool plastered my shirt. Spitting, drinking, swallowing. . .

. . . My gut sloshed. My centre of balance swung off-kilter. I felt an urgent pressure on my bladder. I fished myself out of my underwear and, still kneeling, and urinated downstream.

Particles of sunlight angled and bent in the water. My memories bent with them. A few lonely bearings rolled about the toolbox by the time I stood. Knees popping, legs quaking: I'd gained many pounds.

I picked up Frog's aquarium and waded out until the current pulled at my heels. The river rushed over the lip to fill the glass, picking Frog up and sluicing him out.

The willful creature swam *against* the flow. For a while the current pinned it in place—those delicate legs kicking, kicking, making no progress—then slowly, achingly, Frog began to ford upriver. I watched it peck along, battling a current that knew nothing of this stubborn creature so hell-bent on defying it.

"I love that frog," I heard myself say.

It swam into the deeper currents where the patina of riverbed blended into cool blues, moving sideways but never backward.

I clambered back onshore. The One Child hadn't moved but the sun had; he was once again exposed in its glare. Ants crawled on his face; he huffed but the ants were all over him, his hair, trapped in the fluid leaking out of his eyes. I carried him into shade and brushed the ants off. I retrieved the toolbox. I kneaded plastique and rolled it into a tube. I wadded the explosives around my hips above the hem of my dripping-wet underwear and lashed it in place with strips of duct tape. Slipped into my trousers again. You could hardly see it.

I poked the sharp prongs of the detonation kit through the fabric of my pants pocket and into the greasy explosive. The battery rested easily in the opposite pocket. I tore long strips off the roll of tape and hung them off a willow branch. Then I picked The One Child up and pressed him to my belly. I fastened a strip of duct tape under my armpit and brought it across my chest, across The One Child's chest, securing the loose end over my hip. The One Child made a quizzical noise.

"Shhhhh," I told him. "You're okay."

Another strip ran from my opposite armpit; a grey X across my front. His body tightened to mine; our breathing fell into sync. By the time I stood to test the strength of my handiwork, my torso was encased in grey tape. The One Child was fastened snugly.

I walked us back to the van. I yanked the Quint's charred duster off the sun visor and pulled it on. I rolled up the sleeves and fastened the buttons as high as The One Child's head.

The Peugeot's door was unlocked. The gas gauge read near full. On a whim I flipped the sun visor down. A pair of keys fell onto the tan leather seat.

An abandoned luxury sedan with a full tank of gas.

Hey, someone up there really *did* like us.

I turned the key and the car rumbled to life.

State of Grace

As we neared our destination I opened my jaws and bit The One Child's head. He had fallen asleep. I had to wake him. I had to make him sing. The One Child choked in shock and began to bawl. Tears leaked out of the queer placements of his eyes. The sound was Heavenly.

"I'm sorry," I said. "But I need to hear you. And I need them to hear you, too."

The song rose up, out the windows in a most mellifluous way, hitting organ-thrumming octaves. The notes went out and out, above the clouds, above the shifting canopy of sky.

Hundred-foot-tall crucifixes lined the road. Their points were adorned with brightly coloured sashes, reds and golds and blues whipping the evening air. Past them but within sight: the lights of Kingdom City. I hit the accelerator and we barrelled into the darkening brink between the crosses.

The One Child and I, two tools of the Republic given an opportunity to do what no tools ever had: to hammer back.

If this isn't a State of Grace then that state does not exist.

And let me say it now as this no doubt stands as my last chance:

I take it all back.

Every word, every doubt. All of it I take back.

I *believe.*

ACKNOWLEDGEMENTS

Thanks, first off, to Brett and Sandra and the team at ChiZine for taking on a thorny book like this. They're a boon to writers and I'm grateful to them.

Second, a debt to James Ellroy, the Demon Dog of crime fiction. I must have glutted on his stuff just before writing this, because there is an attempt in some areas to take on his punchy, snappy, inimitable style. Thankfully I realized that it *is* inimitable, and maintained my own style for the most part. But for the stationhouse scenes and a few others, readers might get an Ellroyian flavour. All honour to the man.

Finally—and this is less an acknowledgement than it is an explanation or perhaps even an attempt at exculpation—a great deal of this book was difficult to write. All books have their tricky scenes or moral underpinnings that give their authors some pause, but I have never written a book so full of hate as this one. Hatred from the perspective of some of these characters towards races, creeds, cultures, and faiths. I guess when you are trying to write a dystopian narrative, you take a look at the current state of things and forecast the most dire possible future should some of those worrisome aspects bear fruit. For me, religion has always held a yin-yang aspect. There is nothing essentially wrong with it, and the idea of needing religion is totally understandable on a human level—as it would be for any species with a finite lifespan. But I find there is a tendency to *use* religion as a tool to manipulate masses of people, and those who are using it do not always have the most honourable of intentions.

This fear informed the writing of *The Acolyte*. And in order for that fear to be sharpest in me as a writer, I felt I needed to go down certain roads, using terms and embracing a state of mind that is reprehensible to me. So yes, not the most enjoyable writing experience, but perhaps a necessary one in this case. Absolutely no offence meant to anyone currently dwelling on the planet earth, or interred beneath its soil.

Yours,
Nick Cutter

ABOUT THE AUTHOR

Nick Cutter is the pseudonym for Craig Davidson, who has written four books, including *Rust and Bone*, *The Fighter*, and *Sarah Court*. His work has appeared in *Esquire*, *GQ*, *The Cincinnati Review*, *Salon*, *The Walrus*, and elsewhere. *Rust and Bone* was made into a film in 2012, starring Marion Cotillard and directed by Jacques Audiard. Under the pseudonym Nick Cutter, he has released two other novels, *The Troop* and *The Deep*.

craigdavidson.net